KEELY HUTTON

Afterword by
RICKY RICHARD ANYWAR

# SOLDIER BOY

SQUARE
FISH

Farrar Straus Giroux
New York

**SQUARE
FISH**

An imprint of Macmillan Publishing Group, LLC
175 Fifth Avenue
New York, NY 10010
fiercereads.com

Our books may be purchased in bulk for promotional, educational, or business use.
Please contact your local bookseller or the Macmillan Corporate and Premium
Sales Department at (800) 221-7945 ext. 5442 or by e-mail at
MacmillanSpecialMarkets@macmillan.com.

Library of Congress Cataloging-in-Publication Data
Names: Hutton, Keely, author.
Title: Soldier boy / Keely Hutton.
Description: New York : Farrar Straus Giroux, 2017.
Identifiers: LCCN 2016035897 (print) | LCCN 2017005178 (ebook)
ISBN 978-1-250-15844-4 (paperback)     ISBN 978-0-374-30564-2 (ebook)
Subjects: LCSH: Anywar, Ricky Richard—Childhood and youth—Juvenile fiction.
| Uganda—History—1979—Juvenile fiction. | CYAC: Anywar, Ricky
Richard—Childhood and youth—Fiction. | Soldiers—Fiction. |
Uganda—History—1979—Fiction.
Classification: LCC PZ7.1.H913 Sol 2017 (print) | LCC PZ7.1.H913 (ebook) |
DDC [Fic]—dc23
LC record available at https://lccn.loc.gov/2016035897

Originally published in the United States by Farrar Straus Giroux
First Square Fish edition, 2018
Book designed by Andrew Arnold
Square Fish logo designed by Filomena Tuosto

3   5   7   9   10   8   6   4   2
LEXILE: 860L

A portion of the author's proceeds is donated to Friends of Orphans in Pader, Uganda.

*To my parents, Mick and Sheila Harrington, whose love and support have always guided me home*

# Author's Note

A few names have been changed to protect individuals and some details in this book have been fictionalized, but the major events portrayed are based on Ricky Richard Anywar's experiences as a child soldier in Uganda from 1989 to 1992. While researching this project, I spent hundreds of hours interviewing Ricky over Skype, by e-mail, and in person, in addition to studying numerous books, articles, and news reports about the Ugandan civil war and Joseph Kony's Lord's Resistance Army (LRA).

After surviving his enslavement in the LRA, Ricky eventually went on to found the charity Friends of Orphans, a nonprofit organization dedicated to the recovery, rehabilitation, and reintegration of former child soldiers in northern Uganda and others affected by the war. Samuel's character represents the thousands of children Ricky and Friends of Orphans have helped in northern Uganda for nearly two decades. Samuel's fictional account is based on the real experiences of several former abductees recorded in articles, videos, and interviews with Ricky.

The conflict depicted in this book is known as the Ugandan civil war. In 1986, after years of bloodshed under the dictatorships of Idi Amin and other rulers, the guerrilla leader of the National Resistance Army, Yoweri Museveni, ousted the military regime of General Tito Okello and became president of Uganda. His move to dissolve all political parties sparked angry debate among the many tribes in Uganda, who felt they were not represented in the new government. One discontented faction of the Acholi tribe in northern Uganda was the Holy Spirit Movement, a religious sect led by the self-proclaimed prophetess Alice Lakwena. Lakwena launched an insurgency against Museveni's government in 1987, but it failed.

Following Lakwena's exile, her cousin Joseph Kony took over the Holy Spirit Movement and renamed it the Lord's Resistance Army. Kony proclaimed that he was the Holy Spirit and commanded that President Museveni be overthrown and replaced by a government ruled by the Ten Commandments. His plan, however, did not garner enough support to succeed. Frustrated by what he deemed a betrayal, he accused the Acholi people of treachery and aimed his attacks on innocent villagers throughout northern Uganda.

For twenty years, Kony and his LRA terrorized Uganda, attacking anyone suspected of supporting Museveni's government. They abducted children like Ricky and his brother, Patrick, to swell their ranks. Due to the remote locations of many villages in northern Uganda and its surrounding countries, accurate records of LRA crimes are difficult to find. However, it is estimated that since its inception, the LRA has abducted more than 96,000 children, killed more than 100,000 people, and displaced approximately 2,000,000 in northern Uganda. The LRA's inhuman treatment of its victims and its practice of abducting children to fight in Kony's crusade earned the rebel group notoriety around the world and ranked Joseph Kony among the top persons wanted by the International Criminal Court, for thirty-three counts of war crimes and crimes against humanity.

Driven out of Uganda by military forces in 2006, Kony and his rebels scattered across the neighboring countries of the Democratic Republic of the Congo, Central African Republic, and southern Sudan. Many governments, including that of the United States, have joined the Ugandan military's pursuit of Joseph Kony. But despite mounting military pressure and attempted peace talks, Kony remains at large today and his rebels continue to terrorize remote villages, where attacks take months to report.

Seven years before government troops drove Kony and his rebels from Uganda, Ricky returned to his home in Pader district and founded Friends of Orphans. Despite threats and attacks on his life, Ricky has continued his work to heal the people and rebuild the communities of northern Uganda. Though Uganda has been free from LRA attacks since 2006, the twenty-year war left nearly two million Ugandans struggling to rebuild their lives and communities. Hundreds of thousands still live in abject poverty today.

Since its inception in 1999, Friends of Orphans's mission has been to contribute to the empowerment, rehabilitation, and reintegration of former child soldiers and abductees. The organization and its mission have grown over the years to include assisting child mothers, orphans, the disabled, and the poor and displaced, as well as to combat the spread of HIV/AIDS and other infectious diseases.

Ricky's efforts and methods have been recognized by organizations around the world, and he and Friends of Orphans have been the recipients of several prestigious awards, including the Harriet Tubman Reintegration Award. Donations, like the ones made through the sale of this book, support Friends of Orphans in its mission to rebuild a sense of hope and home for all Ugandans affected by the war. Additional information about Ricky's work and Friends of Orphans may be found at frouganda.org.

Ricky contacted me in March 2012 about writing his story. He traveled to the United States in June that year and spent time with my family. I am grateful for his willingness to share the painful memories of his life, his trust in my ability to find the right words to tell his story, and his patience while I wrote and revised this book.

My family and I are honored not only to consider Ricky a good friend, but also to embrace him as part of our family. It has been a privilege for me to write his story and help give a voice to the thousands of children whose voices were stolen by Kony's LRA.

# SOLDIER BOY

# A Ugandan Lullaby

*Sleep, little warrior, sleep,*
*For the hares in the forest are sleeping,*
*The moon looks down from the skies;*
*Brighter than stars are thine eyes;*
*And thy mother her vigil is keeping.*
*Sleep, little warrior, sleep.*
*Sleep, little chieftain, sleep,*
*For soon the world will be waking*
*And babyhood gone*
*Like the verse of a song;*
*Thy mother's heart may be breaking.*
*Sleep, little chieftain, sleep.*

# SAMUEL

2006

**Samuel lived by three rules.**

Never doubt Kony.

Stay alert.

And trust no one.

He didn't just follow the rules. He lived by them. He lived *because* of them.

Sitting in the shade on the low porch of a sprawling compound, he couldn't recall the traitorous thought that broke his first rule, but proof of the betrayal hid beneath the bloody bandage wrapped around his thigh. His captors promised the medicine was working, but he could feel the angry swelling beneath the stained wrapping covering the bullet wound where the infection had taken hold.

Samuel understood infection. In his eleven years, he had seen it burrow deep into the bodies of other children. Their feet. Their legs. Their chests. Their arms. Spreading like brush fire until it consumed them.

He picked at the frayed edge of his bandage and struggled to keep his thoughts from evaporating in the fog of painkillers dulling his senses. The drugs ate away at his second rule. He'd spent the last week swaying between fitful sleep and blurry consciousness, unable to form a clear understanding of where he was or what his captors wanted.

A peal of laughter nudged Samuel's attention away from his wound. His head lolled to the side as he watched a faded and worn soccer ball arc through the cloudless Ugandan sky before dropping into the midst of a group of excited children. It bounced off the forehead of the tallest, a teenage boy with legs like the gray crested crane, long and knobby-kneed. He sent it soaring across the dirt field to the waiting chest of a teammate. The huddle of children squealed with delight and scrambled after the ball, kicking up clouds of red dust with their bare feet.

Hard as he tried, Samuel couldn't fit together the images of the laughing children and the razor-wire fence trapping them within its boundaries. His eyes drooped closed from the effort as another numbing current of painkiller pulled him under. Splinters of a memory prickled beneath Samuel's muddied thoughts, and the joyful laughter on the field dissolved into terrified screams.

*A sudden attack. Samuel and other panicked rebels grabbing their weapons. Government soldiers charging, guns raised. Explosions ripping into the earth, silencing screams and scattering bodies. A confusion of commands roaring above the smoke.*

*Bullets firing. Rebels falling. A terrible sharp pain in his leg. Blood gushing from the bullet wound. Samuel begging for help. Crying out for his mama.*

*Hands reaching for him. Taking his rifle. Taking his panga. Taking his bullets.*

*Leaving him wounded. Leaving him helpless. Leaving him.*

# RICKY
1987

"A powerful home is a place where people work hard," Ricky's mother said, handing him a basket. "You want us to have a powerful home, don't you?"

Ricky placed his school uniform in the basket and set it by the door. "Yes, but I promised I'd help my friends gather wood for the bonfire tonight."

"And you'll keep your promise," she said, "after you fetch me some cassava."

Ricky groaned. During the wet season, the sweet-potato tubers pushed deep into the earth, making them difficult to dig up in the dry season when the ground hardened. "How many do you need?" he asked.

"Fourteen. The whole village is gathering for the wangoo. I want to make sure I prepare enough."

Ricky groaned louder. "Can't Patrick do it? My friends are waiting."

"It won't kill them to wait a bit. Patrick is helping your father close up the school," she said, slicing a mango into bite-sized chunks. "And then he's promised to fix the radio for tonight, so I need your help preparing dinner."

While she wasn't looking, Ricky grabbed two chunks and popped them into his mouth. "What about the girls?" he asked, reaching for more. "Shouldn't they be helping?"

She swatted his hand away. "They are already outside gathering simsim."

Ricky's mouth watered at the thought of the sesame-and-honey treat he hoped his mother would make from the seeds his sisters were collecting. "Are you making candy?"

She smiled. "I thought it would be a nice treat to celebrate the end of another successful school year. Your father tells me you did well in your studies."

Ricky dug his big toe into the dirt floor. "Not as well as Patrick," he mumbled.

His mother looked up from her cutting. "Your brother has two more years of schooling than you. When you're fifteen, you'll be just as smart."

"When I'm fifteen, Patrick'll still be two years older and smarter than me."

She turned to fetch another mango. "Stop worrying about your brother's grades. Just worry about your own."

Ricky crammed another handful of fruit in his mouth before she returned to the table. He stopped chewing when she looked at him with one eyebrow raised and grabbed his swollen cheeks with her sticky fingers.

"And worry about what I am going to do to you if you don't stop eating my mango, Anywar."

Pulpy bits squished between Ricky's teeth as he smiled at her use of his Acholi name, a name reserved for special occasions or when he was trying her patience. "Sorry, Mama."

"You will be sorry if you don't get me some cassava." She delivered a playful swat to his backside. "Now, go! I have much to prepare before we leave for dinner."

Ricky swiped another chunk of mango and ran out the door.

As he made his way into the fields surrounding the family homestead, he tossed his hand hoe in the air. It somersaulted twice in the crisp blue sky before falling toward his waiting basket, where it bounced off the edge and landed in his father's beloved flower garden. Ricky stepped into the garden, and the familiar scent of night roses filled his lungs. A contented smile parted his lips, allowing a sigh to escape as he closed his eyes and breathed in his home.

The sprawling homestead had been in Ricky's family for generations. Tilled soil rolled in gentle waves with row upon row of maize, cassava, millet, simsim, and cotton, which grew in abundance on either side of the compound. A single-story, tin-roofed farmhouse and two thatch-roofed huts huddled together at the center of the property. Beyond the crops, herds of cattle dotted the fields that stretched out to the wild bush.

"Ricky!" his mother yelled. "Get me another mango to replace the one you've eaten!"

"Yes, Mama!"

Ricky jogged over to the tree he'd planted with his brother when he was nine and plucked two mangoes from its branches. Placing them in his basket, he headed down the rutted paths of the cassava field.

Once Ricky had delivered the mangoes and sweet potatoes, he sprinted to the village. Now that school was out for the holiday, the promise of long days spent fishing and hunting with his brother and friends lightened each step as he raced between huts. Nearing the fire pit, he dodged groups of mothers balancing large bowls of food on their heads and swaddled babies on their backs. The infants cooed and laughed from the security of their colorful obenos as Ricky ran past.

He found Thomas, Andrew, and John gathering small branches and dry twigs for the evening fire.

"We're hunting tomorrow, right?" Thomas asked, pulling on a tree branch.

"I don't know," Ricky said. "I have to ask my mother first."

Thomas yanked the branch free and tossed it to Ricky. "C'mon, boy. We're just hunting rats."

Thomas lived to hunt. At seventeen, he was the oldest of their group and Patrick's best friend. He was fearless, and Ricky loved to listen to him tell tales of his latest adventure in the bush. Unlike the elders of the village, who used only their voices to weave tales at the wangoo each night, Thomas told a story with his whole body. He stalked around the fire, leaping high above the flames and pouncing at children as he reenacted a lioness hunting an impala.

"What's your mama afraid is going to happen?" Thomas asked, breaking off another dead branch. "Does she think a rat will nibble your toes?"

"No. She thinks you take too many chances."

Thomas's mouth fell open in pretend shock. "Me? Put you in danger? When have I ever done that?"

Ricky, Andrew, and John stopped their work and laughed at him.

"What?" Thomas asked.

"Have you forgotten about the python?" Ricky asked. "Because my mother hasn't."

Thomas waved the question away. "You were never in any real danger. I knew what I was doing."

Andrew snorted. "No, you didn't. You were spearing fish. The python just swam in your way."

"I'll spear you if you don't shut up," Thomas said, chucking a branch at Andrew's head.

Andrew ducked away. At thirteen, Ricky's classmate barely passed for eleven, but what Andrew lacked in size, he made up for in nerve and speed. Before Thomas could grab another branch, Andrew retaliated with a clump of dirt. It exploded on Thomas's back, leaving behind a dusty scorch mark.

"Just wait until we get to the well tonight," Thomas said, shooting Ricky a mischievous smile. "We still owe you for yesterday."

"I think there's still a bit of dirt in your hair," Andrew said, throwing another clump at Thomas. "You'll want to wash carefully tonight."

Thomas jumped to the left, and the dirt hit John's backside.

Andrew erupted in another fit of laughter. "Beat you to the well!" he said, breaking into a sprint.

Thomas threw down his kindling. "Oh, I'll beat you, all right!"

"You've got to catch me first," Andrew yelled, darting between two women carrying pots of water and peeled cassava to the fire to be boiled for the communal dinner.

Thomas skidded to a stop before colliding with the women, who scolded him for not being more careful. Mumbling a quick apology, he skirted around them and continued his pursuit of Andrew.

With a shake of his head, John piled an armful of kindling in the fire pit and then dusted off the back of his shorts.

At fourteen, Thomas's younger brother was the peacemaker of their group, a role he played to perfection.

"I'd better get to the well and make sure Thomas doesn't kill Andrew," John said, picking up his brother's dropped kindling. "Are you coming?"

"I have to get Patrick first."

"Where is he, anyway? I thought he was going to help us with the fire."

"He had to do something for my father." Ricky tossed his

last handful of twigs on the wangoo. "I'll get him and meet you at the well."

Ricky found Patrick in the thatch-roofed hut they shared, hunched over their family radio, the village's only receiver and its one connection to the world beyond its borders. He crossed the small room to grab his bathing bucket and a hollow gourd used for fetching water from the well, careful not to step on the pieces of villagers' disassembled tools, watches, and clocks littering the dirt floor. "It's time to get washed up for dinner," he said.

His brother looked up from the radio. "I need to finish this. Baba's counting on me having it fixed by dinner. It's been two weeks without any news from Kampala. People are getting nervous."

Ricky picked up a large block of dry soap from beside his bucket and rubbed it over his head until flakes of soap clung to his hair. "Do you think you can do it?" he asked, replacing the soap, which they weren't allowed to take to the well.

"Yes," Patrick said, turning his attention back to the radio.

"Mama and the girls are making a special meal to celebrate the school year ending. If we're late, we'll miss all the good food." Ricky stared down at the pieces of the radio still lying before Patrick. "How much longer is it going to take?"

"Not long. I think I've finally figured out what's wrong." He pointed to a small pair of tweezers lying near Ricky's feet. "Hand me those."

Ricky tossed him the tweezers. "Do you want me to wait with you?"

14

"No, you go ahead," Patrick said, not looking up from his work. "I'll meet you there soon."

* * *

When Ricky arrived at the well, he found dozens of children from his own and neighboring villages already waiting in line with their bathing buckets and gourds, but Thomas, Andrew, and John were not among them. One at a time, the children knelt down beside the small rectangular hole dug deep into the ground several meters from the watering hole used by local livestock. The children dipped their gourds in the clouded water and then poured the water into their bathing buckets. When the buckets were full, they carried them behind the tall grass or bushes surrounding the well for some privacy as they washed. As Ricky neared the well, he scanned the area to make certain his friends weren't hiding nearby, waiting to ambush him with clumps of dirt. When he was convinced they weren't, he got in line.

While he waited, he spotted Daniel, a young boy from his sister Margaret's class, approaching a group of teenagers chatting about their plans for school break.

"May I use one of your buckets?" Daniel asked in a small voice.

"Don't you have your own?" a girl asked.

Casting his eyes to the ground, Daniel shook his head.

Vincent, the tallest boy in the group, stepped forward. He didn't live in Ricky's village, but every kid in the region knew of his cruelty.

"You can use mine," he said, holding out his bucket, but when Daniel moved to take it, Vincent lifted the bucket higher. "If you can reach it," he added, smirking at his friends.

Daniel glanced around at the boys and girls, who were watching with amused interest, and his head sank in shame.

"Jump for it," Vincent said. "Your baba will have your hide if you go home smelling like you do. What were you harvesting today? Manure?"

Daniel jumped. His fingers grazed the bottom of the bucket, but Vincent lifted it higher. "You're going to have to do better than that."

Ricky's stomach burned with anger as the boy crouched lower, preparing to jump again. He'd witnessed Vincent's bullying before, and when he was younger, he'd been the target of it on more than one occasion. He stepped from the line and held out his bathing bucket. "You can borrow mine, Daniel."

Daniel wiped away his tears and reached for the bucket, but Vincent snatched it from Ricky's hand and pushed Ricky to the ground. A sharp breath burst from Ricky's mouth and gravel tore into his palms as he fell back on the dirt path.

"Wait your turn with the other babies," Vincent said. He then turned again to Daniel. "Now you have two buckets to jump for."

Tears slid down Daniel's round cheeks.

Ignoring the sting of cuts on his hands, Ricky pushed himself up from the ground. "Leave him alone."

Vincent laughed and shoved him again. Ricky stumbled back, but managed to stay on his feet. He drew in a shaky breath.

"Aw, what's the matter?" Vincent taunted. "Did I hurt your feelings, baby?"

Ricky felt children staring at him from all sides. The teens behind Vincent laughed and jeered.

"I think I see a tear!"

"Does the baby need his mama?"

The rest of the kids watched in silence. Humiliation and anger simmered behind Ricky's eyes, and his hands trembled in fear. He balled them into fists, hoping no one noticed.

"I'm not a baby." His voice wasn't as loud or strong as he'd hoped, but it was steady.

Vincent leaned in closer. "What was that, baby?"

"I'm not a baby," Ricky repeated, his voice gaining strength from his anger.

Vincent spread his arms wide and splayed his fingers in invitation. "Then what are you waiting for?"

Lifting his chin, Ricky stepped forward and tensed in anticipation of the first strike. Vincent laughed and moved to shove Ricky again, but Patrick stepped between them.

"I'm not a baby," Ricky's brother said, staring down the bully. "Why don't you try pushing me?"

Vincent stepped back at the threatening tone in Patrick's voice.

"Well," Patrick said, "what are *you* waiting for?"

Vincent glanced back at his friends, but they'd all moved away, so he dropped Ricky's bucket at Patrick's feet. "You're not worth it." Then, turning away, he stalked back toward his village.

With the excitement over, the children returned to the task of bathing.

"Thank you," Daniel sniffed, wiping the back of his hand under his nose.

Ricky gave him his bucket, and Daniel joined the children at the well.

"You all right?" Patrick asked when they were alone.

"Yes," Ricky said, wiping his hands against his thighs to clean the blood and calm the trembling. "Every night it's a new kid. You'd think he'd get bored."

"It makes him feel big."

"He is big. He's almost as tall as Baba."

"He may be big, but he obviously doesn't feel big." Patrick took Ricky's hands in his and flipped them over to inspect the cuts. With the same careful precision he used when fixing the villagers' broken possessions, he picked bits of gravel from the deeper scrapes on Ricky's palms. "He thinks acting like a jerk will make him powerful and earn him respect."

"No one respects Vincent," Ricky mumbled. "No one even likes him."

Patrick extracted the last piece of gravel from his brother's palms. "True, but they fear him."

"Not you. Did you see his face when you told him to try

and push you? I thought he was going to have to take another bath."

The brothers laughed. As they neared the well, a clean and smiling Daniel handed Ricky his bucket before running back to their village.

"Vincent only picks fights when he knows it's a sure win for him," Patrick said, kneeling down to scoop up a gourdful of water from the well.

"Which is why he was picking one with me," Ricky said, holding the bathing bucket for Patrick to fill.

After several scoops, the bucket sloshed with water, and the brothers walked behind a bush to bathe. Standing on a flat rock, Patrick cupped water in his hands and poured it over his body before dousing his head. "I don't know. I think you surprised him. He's not used to kids standing up to him."

"I'm not a kid," Ricky said, rubbing water into his hair until the soap flakes blossomed into suds, tickling his scalp.

Patrick took another handful of water to rinse the soap from his hair and body. "You know what I mean."

Suds still clinging to his hair and face, Ricky stood as straight and tall as possible. With a long inhalation, he pulled back his bony shoulders and pushed out his chest. "I'm almost as big as you."

Patrick laughed as he stepped off the rock and picked up the gourd. "You sure you didn't hit your head when you fell?"

"I am," Ricky argued as his brother started on the path for

home. "Someday I'll be bigger and you'll be my little big brother!"

Dumping the remaining water over his head, he grabbed the empty bucket and hurried to catch up for the twenty-minute walk back to the farm.

# 3

# SAMUEL

**Samuel shuddered from the recollection of his comrades** leaving him to die on the battlefield, and he forced his eyes open. He had to stay alert. He could not afford to break another rule. Not today.

Earlier that morning, he'd overheard his captors talking. They planned to move him. He didn't hear where, but knew he had only hours to escape, so he didn't fight when they carried him to a chair on the porch, claiming the fresh air and sunshine would aid in his recovery. He knew it was his only opportunity to see beyond the putty-gray walls of his hospital room and formulate a plan, but to do so, he needed his senses alert. They were the only weapons he had left.

Biting his lip, he pressed down on his wound with two trembling fingers. A spasm twitched through his bare feet, dangling just above the concrete floor. The pain, sharp and lethal, cut through the drug-induced haze. Pain was good. It meant he could still feel. It meant he was alive.

He clenched his hands into tight fists, fighting back tears that must not flow. Tears meant weakness. Weakness meant death. He squeezed his eyes shut until the inferno of pain receded to its normal slow burn.

He stiffened as four adults neared the porch. Placing his hand over the bloody bandage, he strained to listen to their conversation, but cheers from the field drowned out their words, so he concentrated on their tones, examining every pitch and inflection for the long, hushed whisper of suspicion or the short, sharp punch of anger. But the voices fell silent.

A tremor took hold of Samuel's hands. Silence always preceded the kill. It lived in the held breath of a predator preparing to strike. It seized the still air on a battlefield before the first bullet was fired. And though Samuel hadn't deciphered this threat, instinct told him one thing: like the river croc slipping silently beneath the water's surface, death was closing in.

He sat motionless, pretending to watch the soccer game as his four captors approached. The soldier, who'd found him five or six days ago in the bush after he'd been shot on the battlefield and the rebels had left him to die. The doctor, who'd cut the government bullet from his leg and given him medicine to fight the infection. The small, round woman with all the questions about his family, his injury, his time in Kony's army. Questions he refused to answer. And the silent man with the knowing eyes, who made Samuel's palms sweat and his legs ache to run.

The silent man towered over the others. As the group

continued to talk, the man glanced over at the boy. Samuel shifted in his chair, afraid if he looked at the man, the man would see the truth.

The brief conversation ended, and Samuel was seized with the fear of a trapped animal as the adults made their way across the porch to where he sat. His eyes darted along the length of metal fence enclosing the compound, searching the coils of razor wire for any sign of weakness. He found none.

A faded blue sign hung on the fence next to the one exit leading from the compound. Samuel's eyes scoured it for any military insignia. In the center, the outlines of two large hands cradled the country of Uganda. A young girl and boy stood in the middle of the green country, setting a white bird free. Below the image, a banner framed three words: *Friends of Orphans.*

*Friends*, Samuel thought, glaring at the sign. *Friends don't hold you captive. Friends don't keep you alive, only to hand you over to your enemy.*

He ran a trembling hand over his head. His scalp felt coarse beneath his fingers, where stubble had begun to grow. He felt naked and exposed without his dreadlocks, but the woman had insisted on shaving his head to rid him of the lice infesting his filthy hair.

The adults gathered around his chair, and Samuel's eyes locked on the firearm tucked in a holster on a belt that was slung across the soldier's chest. Samuel's fingers twitched with an aching need to hold the weapon, but the woman was in his way.

He flinched at her touch when she placed a hand on his shoulder. "You're going to go home today, Samuel."

He pulled away from her and her empty promise. Adults lied, and Samuel could not afford to break his last rule. He knew the price for trusting adults.

Withdrawing her hand, she turned and addressed the soldier. "Are you sure you don't mind taking him?"

"We'll be traveling north by Kitgum tonight. It's not a problem."

Samuel's mind raced. It didn't matter if the soldier's words held any truth or not. He could never go back to his family.

He gripped the armrests until his fingers ached. He had to escape. From the corner of his eye, he studied the soldier's gun and the metal snaps holding it in its leather holster. He'd fired a gun just like it many times. It held only six bullets, if the chamber was full. Even if he managed to grab it, he wouldn't have enough ammunition to fight his way out of the compound.

He needed a hostage.

As the soldier spoke about their imminent departure, Samuel weighed his options.

In his injured state, he'd get off only one round before the adults overpowered him. That left the children. He scanned the compound for the easiest target and found him seated on the edge of the playing field. The boy was no more than nine years old, giving Samuel two years of height, weight, strength, and experience over his unsuspecting victim. He just had to wait for his moment to strike. He took a deep breath as his plan took shape.

*I have to strike*, he reminded himself. *They've given me no choice.*

His target bounced to his feet with excitement when a teammate scored, and Samuel looked away from the child.

*There's never a choice.*

"Thank you," the doctor said, extending his hand to the soldier.

The soldier reached over Samuel to shake the doctor's hand, and his sidearm hung centimeters above the boy's head. Samuel's fingers flexed, preparing to snatch the gun from the holster until the silent man's knowing gaze caught his own.

"I'll start preparing for our trip," the soldier said, stepping back. "We'll leave at seven this evening." And then he was gone, taking any chance of escape with him.

Samuel averted his eyes.

"I'll fetch fresh bandages to change your dressing," the doctor said, checking his watch. "Do you need another pill?"

The pain in Samuel's leg and the temptation to cocoon himself in the medicine's numbing spell begged him to say yes, but he had to devise a new plan, so with a resolute shake of his head, he stared out at the elephant grass swaying beyond the compound's fence and listened to the scratchy grind of the doctor's footsteps as they faded back into the building.

The soldier was still the key. Samuel would wait until they drove beyond the fence and deep into the bush that separated

Pader from Kitgum. Only then, when tall grass and dense trees framed the dirt road, would Samuel say he needed to use the bathroom. When the soldier stopped the truck, he would take his time exiting and hobble to the side of the road, careful not to draw the soldier's suspicion, but the moment he set foot in the bush, he'd run. His injury would slow him, he knew this, but Samuel also knew the bush, and how to disappear within its tangled wilds.

"Why don't I get you something to drink while you wait?" the woman said.

Samuel listened for two pairs of retreating footsteps. He heard only one, the hurried steps of the woman. Like the oppressive heat, the giant's gaze pressed down on him. He shifted away from the man.

After a moment, the man pulled up a chair and sat down. Samuel cringed, but kept his eyes fixed on the soccer game. The man cleared his throat, and Samuel said a silent prayer, asking Kony to spare him and begging for the Holy Spirit's forgiveness.

The man didn't wear the uniform of a soldier or the baggy green pants and short-sleeved shirt of a doctor. He wore tan pants and a blue button-front shirt. He was different from the others. Though he'd arrived only that morning, everyone looked to him for approval. The pecking order was clear here, and this man definitely commanded the others' respect or fear. Samuel couldn't tell which.

*Government*, he thought as the man laced his fingers together in his lap.

"I know what you've been through, Samuel," he said, "and I'd like to hear your story."

Samuel began to pick again at his bandage. "I have no story."

The big man's gaze traveled from Samuel to the world beyond the compound's fence. "We all have a story," he said.

# RICKY

**When Ricky and Patrick** arrived at the wangoo, a hundred men, women, and children were already seated around the fire to celebrate the end of another school term and the upcoming Christmas holiday. Whispering a quick apology for their tardiness, they squeezed in beside their neighbors, Okot and his sons. Ricky studied his brother's profile as he waited for Okot to pass the bowl of pigeon peas. The boyish features he and Patrick once shared were gone. Patrick's cheeks had narrowed over the last year, stretching long like his legs and arms. Ricky wondered if he was getting a glimpse of what his own face would look like in two years. Would he, too, become a soft reflection of their father, Michael, whose strong brow and firm jaw inspired respect from the men of the village and admiration from the women, or would he retain the looks of his mother, Mary, whose round cheeks and gentle eyes welcomed smiles from everyone she met?

By the time Okot finished taking his share, there were only

two handfuls left in the bowl. Ricky nudged his brother. "I told you we'd miss all the good stuff if we were late."

Patrick scooped out a small amount and handed Ricky the larger remaining portion. "So someday you can be my big little brother."

While the villagers ate, Ricky's father addressed the children. "What story shall I tell tonight?"

"The Story of Nambi and Kintu, Lapwony," a small boy said, using the Luo word for "teacher," a title given to Ricky's father as headmaster of the Acholi village school.

"Tell the story of the Fairy Bee, Baba," Ricky's sister Margaret said. The oldest of three girls, nine-year-old Margaret functioned as the unofficial spokesperson for the trio, a responsibility she carried out with great pride.

Seven-year-old Betty, who sat next to her big sister, clapped her hands. "Oh yes, the story of the Fairy Bee. Please, Baba."

Christine, nearing her fifth birthday, bounced up and down on her mama's knee. "Fairy Bee. Fairy Bee."

"Lapwony told that one last night," an older girl complained.

"And the night before that," a boy added.

Christine stopped bouncing, and her plump bottom lip pushed out into a pout. Mama leaned down and pressed her lips to her daughter's ear. "I'll tell you that one before bed."

Christine smiled and resumed her bouncing.

"How about the story of the King of the Snakes?" Ricky suggested.

Several children voiced their approval, and the air around the wangoo hummed with excited giggles and whispers as Ricky's father stood.

"Once . . ." His voice, deep and rich as the Ugandan soil, silenced the children. Only the crackle of the fire dared interrupt Lapwony Michael. Ricky sat up straighter, his chest filling with pride that with one simple word his father commanded such respect.

"Once there was a beautiful village, tucked between the hills and the great lake. The people of the village lived in peace, tending to their fields and goats. But one day a big snake called Sesota slithered down from the hillside and into the village."

Ricky smiled as the younger kids giggled nervously and huddled closer.

"Sesota came across a family working in the fields, and despite their pleas for mercy, the evil snake devoured them whole."

A branch teetering on the top of the burning pile broke free and tumbled from the fire pit, kicking sparks into the darkening sky. Margaret and Betty squeaked and scrambled back from the smoking log. Ricky laughed and nudged Patrick with his elbow, but he hurried to help his brother replace the branch on the fire when his father shot him a warning look.

"Every day for years," Father continued when the brothers were seated again, "Sesota came down from the hillside until all the people had either fled or been eaten. When the king heard the news, he challenged his best fighters to go kill Sesota, but not one was brave enough to volunteer."

"Waswa!" Christine squealed, jumping down from her mama's lap. "Waswa was brave enough, Baba!"

A chorus of shushes hissed around the fire. Patrick scooped up his baby sister and placed her on his lap, and Ricky leaned over and whispered in her ear. "If you listen quietly, I'll make you a clay cow tomorrow." Christine nodded and then leaned back against Patrick's chest, tucking her head under his chin.

"Yes," Father said. "A simple peasant named Waswa told the king all he needed to defeat Sesota was some jewelry and a water pot. The king thought Waswa foolish, but gave him the items, and Waswa and his son set off to face the feared snake. As they approached the village, Waswa played his reed pipe and sang a song.

> "Sesota, Sesota, King of the Snakes,
> Beautiful presents I bring.
> The King of Uganda has sent me today
> With bracelets and beads and a ring.

"The great snake heard the song and was curious about the man and boy who dared enter his territory, so he slithered down the hillside, singing.

> "I am Sesota, the King of the Snakes;
> Two bold intruders I see.
> But if they bring me the gifts of a king
> They will be welcomed by me."

Deep shadows and glowing light from the fire danced across Father's face as he snaked his hand in the evening sky. The lean muscles of his arm glided beneath his dark skin like Sesota slithering through the countryside to face the unarmed peasant and his son. The children at the wangoo leaned closer in rapt attention.

"Sesota found Waswa and his son at an abandoned home. As the great snake peered into the water pot to see the king's gifts, Waswa continued playing and singing.

*"Sesota, Sesota, King of the Snakes,*
*Enter this water pot here.*
*The King of Uganda has sent you a bed*
*On which you shall sleep for a year.*

"The King of the Snakes entered the pot, where he coiled around and around. As the snake settled into his new bed, Waswa sang him to sleep.

"And what did he sing?" Father asked.

"Sesota, Sesota, Sesota, Sesota," the children sang as they swayed. Ricky hissed the snake's name and tickled the bottom of Christine's bare feet with a blade of grass. She squealed with laughter and tucked her feet under her legs.

"When the snake was asleep," Father continued, "Waswa and his son put the lid on the pot and carried it back to their king, who commanded his servants to make a huge fire for the wangoo. That night, the people burned the King of the Snakes on the fire and rejoiced in their freedom from the terror Sesota had spread across their land for years."

The fire sizzled and hissed like an angry serpent as another heavy branch crumbled under its flames, and Ricky imagined it purging Uganda of the evil snake.

Father sat down, and Betty climbed onto his lap. "Tell another one, Baba."

"Yes, tell another story, Lapwony!" the children begged, but he held up his hand and the pleas stopped.

"I will tell another tomorrow night, but for now, you children go play before it is time to sleep."

The young ones groaned in protest, but they obeyed their teacher and scurried off to enjoy the waning hours of the day.

"It's time for news from Kampala," Mama told Patrick.

Patrick handed Father the large transistor radio he'd kept tucked at his side during the story, and Father wound the end of a wire around the extended antenna.

"Is it fixed?" Ricky whispered to his brother.

"I had it working earlier," Patrick whispered back.

Father handed the other end of the wire to Patrick, who scrambled up a nearby tree and secured the wire to a high branch. When Patrick was back on the ground, Father switched on the radio. For a moment they heard only silence, but then the radio crackled to life. Ricky smiled at his brother as Father tuned the dial and a distant voice echoed from the radio's speaker.

"Well done, son," Father said to Patrick.

"Thank you," Patrick said, unable to contain the pride-filled smile stretching across his face.

One by one, the adults of the village joined Ricky's parents around the radio. The light of the fire cast flickering shadows across their faces as they listened to reports from the capital of the civil unrest among the country's many conflicting tribes. The shadows carved under their furrowed brows and beneath their downturned mouths, deepening the looks of concern they could no longer mask.

The politics of Uganda held no interest for thirteen-year-old Ricky. He dug his toes into the dirt, waiting for Mama to excuse him, but as the news continued, static eroded the newscaster's voice, and Father motioned him over. "Hold the wire, son."

With a disappointed sigh, Ricky stood next to his brother and placed his hand on the thin metal cable. The volume and clarity of the broadcast improved instantly.

Father patted him on the shoulder. "Good. Stay right there."

Ricky glanced over at a group of children gathered near a tangerine tree. The children huddled around Thomas, hanging on the animated teen's every word. John motioned for Ricky to join them, but Ricky pointed to the wire and shrugged.

"Thomas is probably telling the python story," Ricky whispered to Patrick. "You should go listen."

"I want to stay here," his brother said.

"Why?"

"I've heard Thomas's story a thousand times. Each time the

python gets bigger." He pointed behind them. "This time it will be bigger than that tree."

"It's better than listening to the boring news," Ricky mumbled.

Patrick held a finger to his lips. "Shhh."

With nothing else to distract him, Ricky listened to the voice scratching through the radio speakers. He was always amazed that the voice belonged to a man sitting in front of a microphone in the city four hundred kilometers away, a place he had never visited.

*The National Resistance Army fought back against Acholi rebels today. President Museveni vowed to bring an end to such attacks and reestablish peace in northern Uganda.*

"Why is the government attacking the Acholi?" he whispered to Patrick.

Patrick shushed him again.

"But we're Acholi," Ricky pressed.

*The rebels, part of the Lord's Resistance Army, retreated deep into the forests, but their leader, Joseph Kony, promised swift retribution for the attack and threatened severe consequences for any group providing support to the military, threats he carried out in nearby villages, where the rebels looted homes and attacked resisting civilians with guns and machetes. The LRA slaughtered dozens of villagers in the attack, and left hundreds homeless when they set fire to their huts.*

"Are we at war with the government?" Ricky asked.

"No," Patrick whispered.

"But we're Acholi."

"Shhh."

After several more stories about Ugandan politics and the war, the newscaster bid his Luo-speaking Acholi audience from northern Uganda good night and the station began the news segment for its Lugbara-speaking audience in the West Nile districts. The second Father turned off the radio, Ricky dropped the wire and grabbed Patrick's arm. "Come on."

Patrick pulled his arm away and sat down. "Go ahead. I want to stay and listen to the elders' conversation about the war."

"Why?"

"Because if we are to become men someday, we need to know what's happening in our world."

Ricky glanced at the adults and remaining children gathered around the wangoo. They owned no weapons, only tools for farming and spears for fishing and hunting. They were peaceful people who worked together and supported one another.

"War is not our world," he said. Turning away from his brother, he headed over to listen to the end of Thomas's story.

"You'll have to grow up someday," Patrick called after him.

"Yes," Ricky yelled back. "But not today."

After the last embers of the fire had dimmed, Ricky and Patrick followed the family back to the compound and retired to their small hut. As Ricky drifted off to sleep, he thought of the fun he and Patrick had planned for the following day, when their school break officially began. He dreamed of picking berries and nuts with their sisters, hunting in the bush with the men of the village, swimming in the river with Thomas, and playing cobo lawala with their friends. He smiled, imagining himself throwing his spear through the center of the wooden lawala hoop as Patrick tossed it high into the air.

But as the night deepened, the elders' whispers of war burrowed into his dreams. A wild beast with long, sharp claws, dripping with darkness, stalked his family. The monster's eyes burned blood red as it slithered around the village, setting fire to the huts before turning its evil gaze on Ricky. Ricky woke with a start, his face and body slick with sweat.

"Patrick," he whispered.

His brother did not answer.

"Patrick?" he whispered more loudly, nudging his brother.

"What?" Patrick said with a groan.

"Never mind," Ricky said after a moment. But by then, his brother had already fallen back asleep.

# 5

# SAMUEL

The big man glanced from Samuel's face to the constant twitching of the boy's right index finger, as if he were gathering evidence. The gunshot wound, the scars, every flinch and tremble wove into a thick rope of guilt, tightening around Samuel's neck.

Samuel stilled his twitching finger and focused his attention on the field. The children had finished their game and were lining up for the next match. The captains pointed to players, separating former teammates in the selection process.

Same game.

Same field.

Same players.

As Samuel watched the boys take their new positions, fear led his thoughts back to the soldier waiting to take him from the compound. He had faced too many former rebels on the battlefield to believe the soldier meant to take him back to his village. The military would arm him, just as the rebels had, and he would be positioned once again on the front line.

Same players.

Same field.

Same game.

Different team.

He did not trust the words of the soldier or the man sent to interrogate him. The man could bury him in accusations, but Samuel would not speak. He'd witnessed the consequences of giving voice to one's crimes. He wouldn't make the same mistake.

From the corner of his eye, he studied the man, searching for any sign of danger: the clenching of his jaw, a shift of his weight on the chair, the tightening of muscles along his forearms, a taut stretch of his fingers before they coiled into fists. But the man's round face showed no sign of anger or impatience. His hands, clasped loosely before him, showed no hint of restrained anticipation. Samuel had faced the lash of accusations before, and the man did not hold himself like a man in judgment. He held himself like a man in prayer.

The tremble in Samuel's finger took hold of his entire hand. The harder he fought to control it, the more pronounced it became. He had seen men raise their faces to the heavens before. God saw into the hearts of all and whispered his judgments in the minds of praying men, commanding that they carry out his will. God did not forgive or show mercy.

Nor did his servants.

Samuel concentrated on the field of elephant grass beyond the razor-wire fence. He poured every thought into picturing himself racing through the field of tall blades. Farther and farther from this place. He'd run until he reached the safety of the bush, where the darkness would devour him and no man would find him.

# RICKY

Reports of LRA attacks in northern Uganda monopolized the news reports and fireside conversations in Ricky's village for over a year, but as they faded from shocking events to common occurrences, Joseph Kony and the red-eyed beasts of Ricky's nightmares abandoned his thoughts. Occasionally they returned to gnaw at his stomach during quiet moments at school or as he drifted off to sleep, but as Ricky neared his fifteenth birthday, he quickly dismissed them as childish fears. That all changed one sunny January afternoon.

After an exhausting morning spent preparing the fields for planting, Ricky relaxed in the shade of a young mango tree with his father and brother. Patrick laughed at Ricky's failed attempt to reach the high notes as he sang along to his favorite Lingala song playing on the family radio. The music pulled Ricky up from where he lay, and he danced over to where Patrick worked on a dismantled clock.

"Careful," Patrick said, shielding the small wire coils and

screws. "I promised Okot I'd fix this for Paul before he returns from university."

"When will he be home?" Ricky asked as he sat back against the tree. "He promised before he left he'd take me hunting during break."

Father had plucked a mango from a low-hanging branch and was slicing the fruit with a small knife he kept in his pocket. "Okot said his son will be home on Monday. He told me Paul is doing well in his first year."

"That's not surprising," Patrick said, tightening a tiny screw in the back of the clock. "He had a good teacher."

Father handed them each a large slice of mango. "I cannot take credit for the hard work Paul put into his education."

Mango juice spilled over Ricky's lips and dripped down his chin, quenching the thirst of hours of working in the field. "Okot said his son wouldn't have an education if it wasn't for you, Baba."

"I simply made sure it was available to him. The rest was up to Paul."

Ricky and Patrick smiled at each other, both well aware of the long hours their father had spent with Paul at the wangoo convincing him of the importance of working hard at school, but neither was willing to contradict their father's humble opinion of the influential role he played in the lives and futures of many Acholi children.

As a favorite Afrigo Band song flowed from the radio, Ricky laced his fingers behind his head and closed his eyes. "What do you think Paul will—"

A loud crack cut off his words.

Father held up his hand and, turning off the radio, stared beyond the trees lining their property. Ricky searched for thunderclouds, but found only crisp blue skies stretching far above the horizon. After several seconds of silence, another sharp noise tore through the air. The boys flinched, and Father stood.

"Get up," he said.

They scrambled to their feet.

"What was that?" Ricky asked.

Several more cracks and a deep boom shook the ground. Mama hurried out from the girls' hut, where she and her daughters were preparing dinner.

"It's coming from Lira Palwo," Patrick said, pointing in the direction of the marketplace two kilometers away, where people from the surrounding villages gathered to trade crops and goods.

Ricky sucked in a sharp breath as another series of rapid cracks echoed over the trees. Lira Palwo was only a forty-minute walk from their home, if he took his time. "Are those gunshots?" he asked, but before Father could answer, another loud explosion rocked the ground.

Ricky's sisters drew closer to Mama, who wrapped her arms protectively around them.

"What's happening, Michael?" she asked.

Father picked up the radio. "I don't know."

"Could it be the National Resistance Army?" she asked. "They promised to drive the LRA from Uganda. Perhaps the fighting has pushed east from Gulu."

"Perhaps." Father's jaw muscles strained beneath his skin as he stared off in the direction of the market. As the gunfire and explosions increased in frequency, several neighbors, including Thomas, Andrew, and John, joined Ricky's family in front of their home, the closest homestead in the village to the main road. News from the market would reach them first.

"Lapwony," Andrew asked, "is the fighting moving closer?"

"I don't think so," Father answered, "but it's getting more intense and seems to be centered at the market."

"It's market day," Mama said. "There will be many people there."

Thomas spoke up, his eyes bright with excitement. "I'll go see what's happening, Lapwony."

"No, Thomas," Father said. "It's not safe."

"I can hide in the bush," Thomas said. "They'll never see me."

"I think we should all wait here . . . together."

"But, Lapwony," Thomas protested.

Father put a hand on Thomas's shoulder and looked at Ricky and Patrick. "We'll learn soon enough what's happening."

Before they could argue further, he walked over to speak with the other adults.

Thomas nudged Patrick. "Talk to your father."

Patrick shook his head. "You heard what he said. No one is to go to the market until we know what's happening."

"I'm not saying we go to the market," Thomas said. "I'm saying we go near it."

"I agree with Lapwony," John said. "We should stay here."

Thomas let his head fall back in exasperation. "Nothing exciting ever happens here. Aren't any of you curious to know what's going on?" He looked at Andrew. "Well, aren't you?"

Andrew shrugged. "Yes, but I'm not disobeying Lapwony."

"Neither am I," said John.

Thomas turned his attention to Ricky. "What about you? Don't you want to see what's happening at the market?"

The fear that had crackled across Ricky's skin at the first gunshot had faded as it became clear the fighting was not moving toward the village. In its wake, curiosity prickled and scratched at Ricky's thoughts. "A little," he admitted. "But I agree it's too dangerous to go anywhere near the market until we know what's going on there."

John nodded at Ricky's sensibility.

"How are we supposed to know what's happening there if we don't go see?" Thomas asked.

Ricky glanced at his brother. "Maybe we could wait by the road. In case anyone from the market passes."

Patrick stared off in the direction of the market, his brow furrowed in thought. "We'll go only as far as the road," he said, "and only if Father gives us permission."

A broad smile stretched across Thomas's face as he slapped Ricky on the back.

"If he says no," Patrick added, "no more plans or questions. We wait here with the others."

"Of course," Thomas said, pushing him toward his parents.

Patrick shoved his friend's hands away and stood outside the circle of adults. "Father?" he asked. "I was wondering . . ." He hesitated when Father turned to him. With a quick glance back at Ricky and his friends, he cleared his throat. "*We* were wondering if we could wait by the road in case anyone from the market passes."

Father shook his head. "We're safer here."

"But, Lapwony," Andrew said, "we'll be safe by the road, and you'll be able to keep an eye on us easily from here."

"We'll come back at the first sign of trouble," Ricky added.

Father glanced at Mama, who nodded. "You are to stay right by the road where we can see you at all times."

"And if you see anyone who looks dangerous," Mama added, "you come home right away."

"We will," Ricky and Patrick said as Thomas and Andrew raced down the path leading to the main road.

John lingered behind near the adults, so Ricky grabbed his arm. "Come on! Before we miss everything."

"Patrick, watch after your brother," Mama called after them.

"I will," he said. "I promise."

For the next hour, the five friends sat beside the road listening to sporadic gunfire and watching plumes of smoke rise above the trees to the east. Staring down the dirt road, they speculated about what might be taking place at the market and who might be involved.

Thomas kept them entertained with tales of how he would fight off any invaders with only his hunting spear and cunning.

Andrew countered each boast with a joke about Thomas's spear-throwing ability, which led to several wrestling matches on the side of the road. During their fourth tussle, the crunch of gravel drew the boys' attention.

"Look!" Ricky said, pointing to a man on a bike approaching from the west. "Someone's coming."

The boys watched as the man slowly pedaled toward them.

"Should we go home?" Ricky asked Patrick.

"It's only one man," Thomas said, releasing Andrew from a headlock, "and he's not coming from the market."

"Looks like he's headed there, though," John said. "He's probably from one of the other villages."

Andrew dusted off his shirt and shorts. "I bet he's going to the market to investigate."

"I've never seen him before," John said. "Do you think he's a government soldier?"

"Of course he is," Thomas said. "Look at him."

The thin man's shaved head revealed the shadow of a receding hairline. A short-sleeved moss-green shirt clung to his body, and the cuffs of his matching pants puckered along the rim of a pair of leather military boots that sagged like the hide of an old elephant, creased and dull with age.

"He has a gun," Patrick whispered as the man drew closer.

A chill quivered through Ricky at the sight of a thick black strap cutting diagonally across the man's chest. A rifle pressed down the length of his spine, with the curved magazine of the weapon jutting out from the side of his hunched back.

John shifted next to him. "I think we should go back and tell our parents."

"Tell them what?" Thomas asked. "We don't know anything. Let's see what he says."

"He might have news about the market," Andrew said. "Right, Patrick?"

Ricky's brother continued to study the stranger. "We'll see what he wants," he said. "If he seems dangerous, we'll run home."

"Look how slow he's moving," Andrew added. "We could easily outrun him."

Dust kicked up in a thick fog around the bike's tires as the man braked before the boys. "Young children," he said, smiling down at them, "what are you doing here?"

"Waiting for news." Patrick answered without hesitation, but Ricky heard the forced confidence in the way his brother dropped his voice, trying to sound older.

He glanced back to the homestead. His parents were still huddled together with the other adults, talking. They hadn't noticed the appearance of the stranger.

The man readjusted the strap of his weapon, but remained on his bike. "News of what?" he asked.

"Of the fighting," Thomas said. "We heard guns and a few explosions."

The man glanced toward the market and then back at the boys. "You heard gunfire and explosions and you ran toward the fighting, not away?"

The boys looked down, each waiting for one of the others to

answer. Ricky pulled at a tuft of grass, ripping it up from the roots. He was certain the soldier would lecture them about being so foolish as to put themselves in danger's way, but instead he nodded. "You, young children, are very brave."

The compliment lured the boys' eyes back to the man's face.

Thomas puffed out his chest. "We wanted to get closer to see what was happening, but our parents wouldn't let us."

The man looked toward the homestead, where Ricky's family and neighbors were gathered, and his smile broadened. "That is good."

Instinct gnawed at Ricky's stomach and whispered warnings in his mind. Images from faded nightmares sharpened into focus, and his muscles tensed, preparing to flee, but Ricky remained still, scolding himself for childish fears.

This was no monster standing before him. No beast with deadly claws dripping with death or blood-red eyes burning with evil.

He was just a man.

A smiling man on a bicycle.

The man remained with the boys for several minutes, asking questions and complimenting them on their bravery.

Thomas was eager to answer all the questions. "I could go with you to the market," he offered.

"No," the man said. "I think your parents are right; it's best you wait here."

Ricky glanced back at his hut. The adults were now watching the interaction between the stranger and the boys. Mama waved for him to come home.

Ricky nudged Patrick to tell him, but then a second man stepped from the tall grass onto the road.

Unlike the clean military uniform and shaved head of the man on the bike, this man wore torn, faded pants and nothing else. Dark stains streaked the worn green material that clung to his legs, and sore-covered skin thinly veiled the sinewy muscles and protruding ribs of his chest. A rifle, identical to the one carried by the smiling man, rested at an angle on his back, and the broad, curved blade of a panga hung from his waist.

"They attacked before me," he growled between clenched teeth. His sunken, predatory eyes looked everywhere and nowhere. The whites of them, a cloudy pus yellow, made him look more reptile than human.

Ricky thought of the python in the river; how it flailed and coiled around Thomas's spear, searching for prey to strike. He also remembered Patrick's voice behind him on the riverbank that day.

*"Don't move, Ricky."*

"It was mine," the wild man yelled as he paced before the man on the bike.

Gnarled dreadlocks swayed below his bare shoulders with each angry step. His dark skin, slick with perspiration, glistened in the sun, and his chest heaved with labored breaths. He stopped pacing and glared in the direction of the market, where thick plumes of black smoke billowed above the trees.

As the wild man turned to face the man on the bike, Ricky looked back to his parents. The adults and children had scattered with the wild man's screams. Some had grabbed their children and run for the village. Others ran for the bush. Only Ricky's parents and sisters remained.

Father motioned for Mama to take the girls and run, but she shook her head and gestured again for Ricky to come home. Ricky turned to whisper to Patrick when the wild man screamed again.

"That was my market!"

Ricky sat still, afraid to breathe. He glanced up at the man on the bike. The smiling man adjusted the strap on his shoulder again, but did not reach for his weapon, even when the wild man charged him.

"How many have I killed today?" the wild man demanded.

The smiling man shrugged. "Eleven, maybe twelve."

John gasped, and Thomas moved closer to his brother.

"That's all!" the wild man screamed, his hands trembling at his sides. "They took my market."

"Do we know who it was?" the man on the bike asked.

The wild man kicked at the ground. "Another LRA brigade."

Cold terror washed through Ricky, numbing his senses. The wild man's voice grew dull and distant as he continued to rant about the raid on the market. Paralyzed, Ricky stared at the men. They did not belong to the Ugandan military and they weren't here to help. They belonged to the Lord's Resistance Army. They were the rebels led by Joseph Kony that the radio announcer spoke of every night by the village fire.

The wild man gripped the hilt of his machete. "I will not leave here with nothing!"

The man on the bike smiled and the wild man glared over his shoulder, his yellowed eyes narrowing on the boys.

He kicked Thomas first, hard in the stomach. Thomas let out a pained groan and doubled over. The second kick connected with his head. John cried out as his brother fell limp to the ground, but Thomas did not respond.

Stunned by the rebel's savagery, Ricky, Patrick, and Andrew sat motionless beside their unconscious friend. During the attack, the smiling man remained on his bike, and the smile remained on his face, but it was no longer warm and friendly. It hardened into a cruel sneer as he watched the wild man turn his rage on John.

John curled into a ball as the wild man kicked him repeatedly in the back, legs, and head until he, too, collapsed. As the man kicked John's limp body, Andrew scrambled to his feet and turned to run, but stopped short when he found himself surrounded by twenty LRA rebels, who'd arrived unnoticed during the chaos of the wild man's rant. The rebels laughed as the man grabbed Andrew by the back of his shirt and threw him to the ground.

When the wild man finished beating Andrew, he rounded on Ricky. Patrick threw himself on top of his little brother as the first kick landed. At the wild man's command, the other rebels joined in the attack. Feet and fists rained down on the brothers until they no longer had the strength to cling to each other. A din of cheers and taunts buried their cries and pleas for mercy.

When the beating stopped, Ricky lay broken and bleeding on the roadside. Through swollen eyes, he peered between the forest of legs surrounding him, searching for Patrick. He spotted his brother in a crumpled heap yards away. Ignoring the searing pain in his shoulder, he reached out for Patrick, but as his fingers grazed his brother's bloodied hand, a moving shadow eclipsed his view.

"Patrick!" he cried just before a raised foot came down on his head.

# RICKY

A cry pierced the darkness, but unconsciousness, dense and unyielding, washed over him, drowning all thought.

*Ricky!*

It grew louder, more insistent. Panic burned through the fog clouding his mind. In its absence, he heard a voice.

Mama.

He tried to reach for her, but calloused hands trapped his arms. He fought to free himself, but the hands tightened as they yanked at his limp body, pulling him forward. Toward the sound of her voice.

He stopped fighting and opened his eyes. The earth blurred and swayed beneath him. He squeezed his eyes shut and inhaled deeply. His breath caught with a stab of pain in his side. He kept his breathing shallow and opened his eyes again. Rocks, dirt, and grass took form. So did legs. His own legs, dragging behind him, scraping and bumping across the blood-splattered dirt path to his hut.

*Ricky!*

His name became a plea. A desperate prayer.

He lifted his head to answer just as the hands released him and he fell. Gravel bit into his chin, and a bolt of pain shot through his jaw. A low groan escaped his swollen lips when the rough hands forced him into a seated position. Rebels surrounded his parents and sisters, who stood, huddled together, a few steps away. Patrick sat, slumped beside him. Next to Patrick sat Andrew, John, and Thomas. They stared at the ground, afraid or unable to look up at the man pacing before them.

"Where are the rest?" the wild man screamed.

"They ran when you started in on the tall boy," a rebel answered.

"Go get them!"

Ten armed rebels sprinted into the village. Ricky's eyes never left his parents as screams erupted behind him when the rebels discovered families hidden in their homes. His parents' arms tightened around his sisters with every burst of gunfire from the village. Ricky longed to hide within their protective embrace, but the heat of a rebel's body standing behind him pressed into his back, warning him not to move. Instead, he clung to his mother's fearful gaze and repeated in his mind the silent prayers quivering on her tear-drenched lips.

The wild man pointed to the boys. "Take care of them."

A rebel, clutching a fishing spear, grabbed Ricky.

A terror-filled cry clawed its way from Mama's throat, rendering her voice raw as she rushed forward to protect him, but the wild man drew back his arm and struck her across the face. The force of the blow sent her hurtling to the ground.

Ricky sucked in a sharp breath and held it until he saw her move.

"Make sure she stays with the others," the wild man yelled.

Ricky's relief mutated into rage as a rebel, no older than Thomas, dragged Mama back to where his father and sisters huddled together.

He ground his teeth together, allowing the pain in his jaw to restrain his anger, but fear overwhelmed both emotions the moment the rebel with the spear yanked him to his feet.

"No!" Mama screamed.

Ricky trembled with restrained sobs as the rebel took hold of the waistband of his shorts and pierced the material with the tip of the spear. With a violent shove, the rebel released him and repeated the process on Patrick and the other boys. When he finished, he threaded a sturdy rope through the jagged holes and tied the five friends together. He then pushed them to the ground, and another rebel bound each boy's hands behind his back. The coarse rope dug into Ricky's wrists as the soldier tugged to secure the knot.

When the rebels returned from the village, they brought with them baskets of stolen tools, clothes, and food, as well as a dozen terrified adults and children. Cuts, dripping blood, and abrasions, dark with swelling, mottled their faces. Those who could walk limped along, struggling to carry those who could not.

"That's all you could find?" the wild man asked.

"The rest must be hiding in the bush," a rebel answered. "We checked every home."

"Put them inside!" the wild man ordered, pointing to Ricky and Patrick's hut.

Adults and children screamed and struggled against their captors as the rebels forced them into the hut with their fists and guns. John sobbed when the rebels beat a village elder unconscious because he moved too slowly. As they threw his limp body inside the hut, the wild man charged the boys.

"If you cry," he snarled, hitting John across the face, "I will kill you."

Blood oozed between John's teeth as he bit down on his trembling lip.

With the captives inside, the wild man turned to Ricky's family. In response to a jerk of his head, the rebels grabbed Mama and Father and dragged them toward the hut. Margaret and Betty wept in their father's arms, and Christine buried her face in Mama's embrace. Anger boiled deep in Ricky's stomach and quivered through him at the sight of his baby sister's small hands gripping the folds of Mama's skirt.

Father opened his mouth to speak, but a rebel drew a panga from his belt and pressed the machete to his throat. Margaret cried out, and Patrick stiffened next to Ricky. Lifting his chin, Father tightened his hold on Margaret and Betty and backed away from the blade.

"Move," the rebel ordered, flicking the tip of his panga toward the hut.

When Father refused, the rebel shifted his blade to Betty's neck. She stifled a sob and shook uncontrollably in her father's arms. Ricky ached to call out to his sister and promise her everything would be all right, but the rebel's twitchy fingers held the panga too close to her throat, and his parents had taught him never to lie.

Without looking away from Patrick and Ricky, Father led Margaret and Betty through the door into the hut. Another rebel pushed Mama and little Christine to follow. Tears streamed down Mama's cheeks, and she reached a trembling hand toward her sons.

Ricky strained against the rope binding his wrists. Every muscle fought to reach his mother as a rebel shoved her inside the hut with the barrel of his gun.

Ricky scanned the bush surrounding their compound, his eyes frantically searching for help, but the tall grass and thick trees stood paralyzed in the afternoon sun. No breeze rustled their branches. No government soldiers parted their stalks. If the villagers who'd escaped remained close by, they'd chosen to be silent witnesses to the atrocities about to occur.

He searched the faces of the rebels standing guard around the hut, seeking any twitch of doubt or flicker of compassion. He found neither.

A second rebel entered the hut with a long piece of rope. Ricky leaned against Patrick to keep sight of his family. The trapped mob swallowed Father and his sisters in their panicked retreat from the rebels' machetes, but Mama stood motionless, framed by the open door. Her hands shielded Christine's eyes from the violence, and her gaze reached for her sons, pulling them close. Within the hut, a woman screamed, and the villagers stopped backing away. They stared down at the inky shadow pooling on the dirt floor as the rebels corralled them in the center of the hut and tied them to the wooden support column.

Her arms pinned behind her, Mama still looked out at her sons. Ricky's heart thrashed against his ribs. He tried to push to his knees to run to her, but a slap to the side of his head forced him back to the ground.

"No!" Mama screamed when Ricky was hit. He watched as her bare feet tore at the dirt floor until her knees buckled and she sagged against her restraints, her chest heaving with suffocating grief. She leaned forward as far as the ropes would allow. Ricky shook his head as her eyes darted from him to his brother.

As the rebels exited the hut, the truth of what would happen next tightened around Ricky's throat, releasing his breaths in short, clipped sobs. He studied his mother's face, tracing every line and curve.

It was the face that had greeted him every morning for fourteen years and kissed him to sleep every night. Her delicate nose had nuzzled laughs from his baby belly, her rounded cheeks mirrored his own, and her tender brown eyes had chased away his nightmares and calmed his tears. "Mama," he mouthed over and over. "Mama."

Her trembling lips parted to speak, but the door was pulled closed and she was gone.

They all were. His father. His sisters. His mother. Ricky struggled against the ropes binding him, desperate to get to the door. The rebels should have tied him and Patrick to the post with their parents and sisters. Whatever the wild man had planned, the family needed to be together, all of them. He struggled harder, and Patrick pressed against him.

Tears welled in Ricky's eyes as he looked over at his brother. Patrick's left eye was nearly swollen shut from the wild man's kicks, and blood oozed from a wide gash on his bottom lip. As wailing and cries from inside the hut permeated the air, Patrick's pleading eyes never left his, and the wild man's warning scratched at the back of Ricky's mind.

*If you cry, I will kill you.*

"Guard the windows and door," the wild man yelled.

Patrick looked back to the hut, and Ricky swallowed his tears. With their weapons drawn, a small group of rebels encircled the building. Above the din of terrified voices, Ricky heard Mama. She cried out Patrick's and Ricky's names and begged God to save her babies. Ricky opened his mouth to call to her, but the wild man strode toward him, his yellowed eyes searching for any reason to strike. Ricky pressed his lips together, but refused to look away.

The wild man turned to three rebels. "Watch them! If anyone moves, shoot them!"

He then motioned for two rebels to follow him into

Margaret, Betty, and Christine's hut, which also served as the family kitchen. When they emerged a minute later, the two young rebels held dozens of items and food. The wild man held just one thing.

A bundle of burning grass.

He stalked toward the boys and held the bundle centimeters from Patrick's face. Ricky felt the sting of its heat on his skin, but Patrick did not draw back from the flame. The wild man's eyes narrowed. Withdrawing the fire, he kicked Patrick in the stomach. Patrick gasped for air and collapsed onto Ricky.

Laughter, harsh and cold, rang out around the hut, mocking the screams from inside as the wild man turned the burning grass toward Ricky. The flame blurred before his eyes.

*Fire.* All his life it had brought his family warmth and light. It had cooked their food and evoked tales of long ago. In the dark of night, it had filled Ricky with comfort and security. Now, as it crackled and danced next to his face, it filled him with only dread.

Withdrawing the flame, the wild man spat at Ricky's feet. Then he walked over to the hut and swept the burning bundle, like the bristles of a fiery paintbrush, around the doorframe. When he finished, he moved on to the windows, outlining each with taunting strokes.

Ricky stared at the darkened spots left behind. Scars marring his hut, his home. His past, present, and future were bound to the hut and five of the hearts beating inside its walls.

*Margaret.*

*Betty.*

*Christine.*

*Baba.*

*Mama.*

The wild man returned to the door, and Ricky's breath seized in his chest. For a moment time stopped. He trapped it in his lungs, froze it in his unblinking eyes. It teetered on the edge. Suspended in the heartbeat between past and future.

The wild man looked back at the boys. His hard gaze collided with Ricky's. He smiled, revealing teeth brown with rot, and then raised the fiery bundle of grass to the thatch roof.

# 8

# SAMUEL

The big man regarded Samuel and then unclasped his large hands in his lap. "Have you ever seen a tree that's been struck by lightning?"

Samuel dug his fingers into the armrests of his chair until the worn green paint splintered and burrowed beneath his nails.

The man gave him the wooden crutches leaning against the porch post. The tremor in Samuel's hands calmed under the crutches' weight.

"Can you walk?" the man asked.

Samuel nodded as he continued to inspect the crutches. His calloused fingertips ran down their length, but he found no sharp edges to use against the man. Despite a few cracks, the wood felt solid. If he swung one of the crutches hard enough, he could hurt him. He just needed to keep the man from chasing him. A strike to the knee should do it. Samuel pressed up from his chair and leaned on the crutches. The man had given him weapons and a target. All he needed now was an opportunity.

"Come with me," the man said, leading him off the porch. "I'd like to show you something."

Samuel struggled to find an easy rhythm as he followed the man down the steps and around the building. No children played in the back fields of the compound, and no adults lingered beneath its trees. He and the man were alone.

Gripping the handles tighter, Samuel quickened his pace to catch up with the man, but one of the crutches snagged on a clump of grass and he stumbled forward. The man grabbed Samuel's arm to catch him, but Samuel yanked it away and hopped back on his good leg, righting himself before the man could grab him again.

"I apologize," the man said, bending down to retrieve the dropped crutch.

Sweat loosened Samuel's grip on the other crutch as he stared down at the back of the man's bowed head.

*Strike. Strike now!*

His instincts demanded action, but fear of the man's size—and curiosity about what the man wanted to show him—fractured his resolve.

"I didn't mean to startle you," the man said, handing him the crutch.

Without a word, Samuel tucked it under his armpit and they continued across the field.

In the distance stood a wide, towering tree. Its long, narrow leaves swayed in the breeze in thick bunches. Beneath the umbrella of green hung clumps of mangoes, heavy and ripe. Samuel thought of his mother peeling back the leathery skin to reveal the sunset-yellow flesh. He and his sister, Grace, would bounce on their toes with their cupped hands stretched out before them as their mother sliced the fruit. They'd bicker over who got the largest slice and giggle as the sticky juice ran over their lips, chins, and chests.

Grief halted Samuel's steps. He squeezed his fingers into fists around the handles of his crutches to revive the throbbing pain beneath his fingernails and drive away the memory.

When the pain subsided, Samuel proceeded on their walk, ignoring the man's sideways glances and the concerned set of his brow. He also ignored the ache that burned in his injured leg with every swing forward. He ignored everything but the ground beneath him. His eyes scoured it for smooth patches of earth where he could place his crutches without danger of falling or fear of the man grabbing his arm again.

As they reached the mango tree, the man ducked beneath the branches and stood by the massive trunk. Samuel peered up into the canopy of green and noticed that leaves and fruit did not weigh down all the branches. The man pointed to the barren portions. "When a tree is struck by lightning, some signs are easy to spot. Stripped bark, charred leaves, severed limbs." He glanced over at Samuel's injured leg.

Shame flushed Samuel's cheeks as he placed a hand over his bandage.

"The wounds on the outside, if treated, eventually scab over and heal, but they're always visible," the man said. "Decades after a strike, a person may come across the tree and know by its scars the violence it has suffered. But often those are not the wounds that kill." He pressed his hand against the trunk. "It is the invisible wounds that are fatal. The wounds that run so deep they paralyze the heartwood and deaden the roots."

He took a thin branch between his fingers. With little effort, he snapped the branch. A small puff of dust appeared above the break, revealing a gray, hollow tube. The man placed the broken branch at the base of the mango tree.

"Most trees don't die until years after a lightning strike, Samuel. From the outside they look almost normal, but inside the damage done by the lightning eats away at the tree, leaving it rotted . . . empty . . . lifeless."

# 9

# RICKY

Ricky squeezed his eyes closed. Prayers once spoken as one voice by the villagers at the wangoo trembled on his lips. The words stumbled and tripped over one another in their panicked escape until only one word was left.

*Please.*

It screamed in his desperate mind, begging for release.

*Please.*

It pulsed through his broken heart, crying for mercy.

*Please.*

It had to be a nightmare. Just like before. Ricky clung to the belief, a hope so fragile it could not keep out the reality pressing in from every side.

It was just a nightmare. All he needed to do was wake up. Just open his eyes. And Kony's red-eyed beasts with their long claws dripping blood and their fiery breath would have disappeared. Just like before. He would never have begged to sit by the side of the road. The smiling man on the bicycle would never have found them. He would be in his hut. Patrick would be beside him. His parents and sisters would be safe and asleep in their beds. Just like before.

Hands dragged Ricky to his feet, and he opened his eyes. Flames devoured the hut's roof, and white smoke seeped out from around the door and windows. Ricky stared into the blaze and listened for his family's voices, but only the crackling hiss of the fire remained, and his brittle hope crumbled under the weight of his reality. His breaths came quick and shallow as he fought to draw air into his lungs. The world collapsed in a blur of sound and movement, and his knees buckled.

A rebel grabbed his arm and yanked him upright.

"March!" he screamed, pressing the muzzle of his assault rifle to the back of Patrick's head.

Patrick stepped forward, and the rope tugged at Ricky's waist. Tethered to his brother and friends and surrounded by armed rebels, Ricky stumbled down the path leading away from his home. Thomas, Andrew, and John struggled to keep pace behind him.

When the five boys neared the spot where they'd waited just hours before, a rebel lying on his stomach in the tall grass targeted each boy's head through the sight of his AK-47 and mimicked the assault rifle's rapid fire.

"*Pa-ta-ta-ta! Pa-ta-ta-ta!*"

Ricky kept his head bowed and his gaze on his brother's feet as he neared the rebel. He flinched with every fake shot, petrified the next would come not from the man's lips, but from his weapon.

"Faster!" a rebel at the back of the line yelled.

John slammed into Andrew, and the boys quickened their pace. Grief and fear warred for control as Ricky shuffled along the dirt road. Patrick and he had walked this road to school for almost nine years, and every morning Father rode by on his bike so he could arrive at school first to welcome his students.

"When you walk to school," he'd say, "you walk to your future."

"Yes, Baba!" they'd yell, running to catch up with him.

The thought of never seeing his father ride by and speak those words again made tears well in Ricky's eyes, but the blood-stained panga swinging on the belt of the man walking beside him kept the tears from escaping.

The wild man led the rebels and abductees to the village school, where forty LRA fighters surrounded twenty villagers huddled together on the ground. Ricky recognized some of the captives as families who'd fled to the village when the wild man attacked. The rest were from surrounding villages. Two rebels armed with machine guns stood in the school entrance, where Ricky's father had greeted the village children for over twenty years. The wild man approached a rebel in full uniform and gestured to Ricky and the boys.

The rebel nodded and then turned to his men. "Separate the teens and put the rest inside the hut!"

The rebels tore six young people from the group and pushed the adults and children toward a thatch-roofed hut behind the two main school buildings.

In the chaos, Daniel, the small boy from the well, was

knocked to the ground. A woman helped him up, but a rebel ripped Daniel from her arms and shoved them both inside. Several rebels followed the captives into the hut.

Outside, the rebels pierced holes in the six teenagers' waistbands, threaded a rope through the tears, and lined them up next to Ricky, Patrick, and their friends. Kellen, a girl from Patrick's class, sobbed as the rebels tied her father and three younger brothers to the center post of the hut. Vincent, the bully from the well, swayed in the line beside her. Several gashes marred his face, and blood dripped from his nose and chin.

With the adults and children secured in the school, the wild man closed the door.

Ricky was already braced for what came next. Grabbing a bundle of burning grass from a rebel, the wild man tossed the torch onto the roof. Within seconds, fire engulfed the dried spear grass of the thatch and smoke billowed from the windows. Armed rebels encircled the hut, their weapons aimed at the door and windows. If the fire did not claim the villagers, their bullets would.

Disbelief, a dull and heavy anesthetic, filled Ricky's mind and body as he watched the fire spread.

When the fire and smoke had silenced the villagers' screams, the rebels forced the eleven abductees to their feet. In single file, they trudged down the road leading away from the burning hut. No longer able to think or feel, Ricky concentrated on keeping his steps synchronized with Patrick's ahead of him.

*Left, right, left, right.*

There was no thought. Only rhythm.

*Left, right, left, right.*

Ricky didn't know where the rebels were taking them, but he knew they were headed south. He had never ventured so far from home before and feared each step he took would be his last.

They marched for over an hour before the commander at the front raised his hand, and the line stopped. He held a small radio to his ear and signaled for the rebels to enter the tall grass of the surrounding fields, where they continued their march, single file. On the dirt road, they left only a trail of footprints that ended abruptly, as though their owners had vanished.

As the boys and their captors pressed through elephant grass, the blades sliced across Ricky's shins and calves.

*Left, right, left, right.*

After several kilometers, the commander raised his hand and signaled the rebels to return to the road. They marched in this manner for hours. Their constant turns and treks through the fields made it impossible to know if they were traveling east, south, west, or north of his village. Every time panic seized Ricky, he kept his gaze locked on his brother ahead of him. Patrick became his compass. His only way home.

Along the way, they stopped at other villages, where the rebels took more Acholi sons and daughters and left behind more smoldering remains of Acholi homes and families.

In one village, the rebels untied Ricky's, Patrick's, Thomas's,

Andrew's, and John's wrists. Ricky's fingers prickled as his circulation returned and blood flowed through them again, but before they regained feeling, the rebels forced bundles of stolen sugarcane into the numb hands of each of the boys. Ricky hiked the bundle up in his arms and pressed it against his chest.

By late afternoon, they arrived at a big river, and Ricky's arms and back ached with fatigue. The commander led the group downstream to a narrowing, and the rebels hoisted their weapons high above their heads. Then, one by one, they marched into the water.

His arms weighed down with sugarcane, Ricky followed Patrick into the river. Thomas, Andrew, and John stepped in behind him. The glassy surface of the river masked violent undercurrents that pushed and tugged the boys downstream. Inching forward, they struggled to keep their footing. The rope jerked Ricky forward as Patrick fought to cut across the river in a straight line just as the rebels before them had done, but the currents, sugarcane, and rope thwarted the boys' progress.

The cold water stole Ricky's breath as it reached his chest. Following Patrick's lead, he lifted his bundle of sugarcane above his head. His feet slipped on rocks worn smooth by the swift current, and the sugarcane tipped in his numb hands. He leaned against the flow of the river and strained to right his load as water rushed over his shoulders and into his nose and mouth. Choking, he turned his face downstream and dug his feet into a patch of clay between two rocks. Thomas, Andrew, and John stopped behind him.

"Faster!" a rebel yelled. The crack of a rifle shot over their heads punctuated the command.

Ricky glanced back to see if anybody had been hit, then the rope yanked him forward. He turned again just in time to see his brother slip beneath the dark water.

"Patrick!" he screamed, again digging his feet into the river bottom. The rope pulled taut and chafed at his skin as he strained with his friends to save his brother. The mud shifted under his feet. He dug his heels in deeper and leaned back until he thought the rope would cut him in half. His brother's bundle of sugarcane bobbed to the surface, but Patrick did not.

"Pull harder!" he begged his friends.

With every ounce of their waning strength, they fought to free Patrick from the river's grasp. Invisible tears streamed down Ricky's wet face when his brother finally surfaced, clinging to his bundle.

"Hold the cane!" Patrick wheezed. "It will keep you above the currents!"

"Move!" a rebel behind John yelled.

His eyes never leaving his brother, Ricky inched forward until his toes curled over the edge of a rock shelf. Tightening his grip on his bundle, he waded into the deep water. Swirling undercurrents tugged and pushed at his legs, but he held the sugarcane in front of him and kicked as hard as he could. Thomas, Andrew, and John followed.

When they reached the other side, Ricky threw his bundle onto the bank and dragged himself out of the water. Hoisting the cane back into his arms, he looked across the river. A twelve-year-old boy taken from the last village the rebels had raided stood paralyzed at the edge of the water. A rusty chain encircled his waist and tethered him to the waists of three teenage girls standing behind him. Frayed lengths of coarse rope bound all four prisoners' hands. The tallest girl stood at the back of the line.

"Move!" a rebel yelled, shoving her into her siblings.

"My brother," Ricky heard her say. "He can't swim."

"Move!" the rebel repeated.

"Please," she begged, "at least untie our hands."

The rebel aimed his gun at the young boy. "Move."

His eyes wide with fear, the boy crept forward. As he pressed through the water with his sisters behind him, the tug of the current drove him away from the rebels and closer to the eddy.

"Stay straight!" Ricky yelled. "Don't let it pull you into—"

The chill of metal against his throat cut his warning short.

"If you say one more word," the rebel gripping the machete said, "I'll kill you where you stand."

Ricky swallowed hard, and the rebel lowered the machete. Hearing Ricky's warning, the oldest sister attempted to steer her siblings to safety, but the river pulled them closer to the eddy. Several dozen rebels gathered at the bank to see what was delaying the remaining group. Among them was the wild man.

His dreadlocks swung across his back as he paced along the riverbank. "Faster!" he screamed at the terrified boy. "There are pythons and crocodiles in those waters. Do you want to be eaten?"

The boy's lips trembled. As the river reached his neck, he lifted his chin, but the water lapped at his face.

"Move!" the wild man screamed. "Or I'll shoot your sisters and make you drag their bodies across!"

River water streamed down the boy's face. Taking a deep breath, he stepped forward with his hands tied behind his back and no bundle to buoy him. The chain tethering him to his sisters pulled taut, and he disappeared beneath the river's surface.

Laughter erupted from both banks as the girls fought to save their brother. They screamed for help and leaned away from the chain dragging them to the eddy. Not one rebel moved. In frantic desperation, the sisters stumbled backward, trying to pull their brother to the surface, but the current was too strong and the river swallowed the first two girls.

The chain around the oldest sister's waist jerked in one direction and then the other. The muscles in her neck and arms strained against her skin as the chain and unrelenting current dragged her forward. Choppy waves churned the water, and a girl's face broke the surface. She gasped for air, but the river pulled her under again. Her big sister cried out her name, but it was lost in the rebels' laughter.

Ricky tensed. He started to step forward, but the phantom chill of the machete on his neck stayed his feet. He stared at the turbulent waters, praying the girl's sisters and brother would surface, but the river quieted. Struggling against the chain still tugging at her waist, the girl looked to Ricky on the riverbank and a defeated calm washed over her face. Ricky shook his head, but she never saw. She'd already closed her eyes and surrendered to the river's pull.

When the remaining rebels had crossed the river, the commander held up a hand and the line came to a halt. Twenty minutes later, a large group of rebels emerged from the bush on their side of the river. The commanders, dressed in full military uniform, spoke briefly and then called over the wild man. The wild man barked out a string of commands, and the rebels started cutting abductees from their ropes and yanking them from the line, separating siblings and friends. They cut Kellen free from her best friend and shoved her from the line. She cried out, but the rebels drove her and the other freed boys and girls toward the new LRA group with their pangas.

Ricky's heart raced as a rebel, his panga drawn, paused between him and his brother. He should never have persuaded Patrick to ask Father if they could wait by the road. His decision had cost him his family and now it would cost him his brother. Terrified to meet the rebel's bloodshot eyes, Ricky held his breath and stared at the back of his brother's head, praying the LRA wouldn't separate him from the only family he had left. The wild man yelled for the rebel to hurry up, and the rebel moved past Ricky. There was a jerk at the rope behind him, and Thomas fell forward. His bundle of sugarcane hit Ricky in the back of the head. The impact forced him to his knees.

A rebel with short dreads and skin bubbled with scabies grabbed him by the arm. "On your feet!"

His hands still clutching his bundle of cane, Ricky pushed himself up from the ground in time to see the rebels forcing Andrew and John from the line. Andrew stared at the ground as he marched, but John looked back at his brother.

"No!" Thomas screamed. A sickening thud followed the pained cry as a rebel drove the butt of his gun into Thomas's stomach. Thomas collapsed and Ricky jerked backward, catching himself before tripping over his friend.

"Get up!" the rebel yelled, training his gun on Thomas. Ricky and Patrick pulled forward on the rope to help their friend.

The rebels tied Andrew, John, and Kellen to a new line of abductees and forced them to enter the Ugandan bush. As soon as the last abductee disappeared into the jungle, the commander of the wild man's group raised his hand in the air and the marching continued.

# 10

# RICKY

Stumps of burned cornstalks pressed up from the charred earth where the rebels made camp. The land, intentionally burned to clear the field for the next crop cycle, provided the rebels with a resting place safe from villagers who might stumble upon their location. No farmers would be tending the scorched soil for months. As evening fell, another group of about three hundred rebels joined them. Andrew, John, and Kellen were not among them. The commanders declared that the abductees were now part of the Gilva brigade and claimed the female abductees as their new wives. They then separated the male abductees into groups of five to fifteen and placed them under the control of rebel guards. The guards stripped Ricky, Patrick, Thomas, and four other abductees in their group of their clothes and tied them together for the night. Shivering, hungry, and afraid, the boys huddled close, desperate for any heat.

The wild man—the man who'd torched Ricky's home and family—paced before them. "I am Otim," he announced.

The traditional Acholi name took Ricky by surprise. How could Otim torture and kill his own people? Somewhere in northern Uganda, there had to be a village the wild man once called home. There had to be people who once called him by a common name, like Patrick or Thomas. As Ricky watched the wild man, he wondered what Otim's family called him before he joined the LRA, leaving behind all traces of his past and humanity.

"I am very dangerous," Otim said. "I am here with my friend if you try to run." He aimed his AK-47 at Ricky's brother. His yellowed eyes burrowed into Patrick, trying to root out any sign of defiance. "If you run, I will kill you."

Otim assigned three young rebels to guard the boys during the night. The first, a lanky boy not much older than Thomas, stood before them. He held a machine gun and carried two magazines of ammunition on his belt. Unlike Otim, who continued to stalk around the boys, the young rebel remained still as his blank gaze fell upon the abductees.

"I am Kilama."

The familiar name shook free the image of a shy boy in Ricky's thoughts. Kilama was the name of Kellen's baby brother, but the villagers called him by his common name, Matthew. The image of little Matthew burying his face into the crook of his father's neck as the rebels forced them into the school flashed behind Ricky's eyes.

"If you run," Kilama said, "I will be the one to kill you." With his weapon cradled in his hands and a panga secured beneath his belt, Kilama stalked off to patrol the camp perimeter, and another rebel stepped forward.

The new rebel's dreadlocks hung much shorter than Otim's, suggesting he was younger, but several jagged scars ran from his forehead to his jawline, pulling and twisting his features like ripples on a reflection. Barely contained savagery shone in his bloodshot eyes. Like Kilama, he also cradled a weapon in his arms, but his ended with a bayonet.

"I am Trench," he boasted. "The most feared. If you do not want to see tomorrow, just try to run and you will be finished. I will kill you in the most painful way possible."

As Trench took his guard position three meters in front of them, a third rebel rushed forward, causing the boys to flinch. He stood with his broad shoulders pulled back to camouflage his short build and with his hands resting on the assault rifle slung across his chest. His low, heavy brow cast his eyes in deep shadows, but Ricky felt the chill of his gaze as he strode before them.

"I am Lujimoi. I enjoy killing people." He stopped before each boy and pressed the muzzle of the gun into the boy's forehead. "So I suggest that you do something—anything—so that I get to kill someone tonight."

He ordered the boys to lie down in a line on their backs and then he settled into his post behind them.

As night crept over the land, cloaking the rebel guards in darkness, Ricky curled against his brother and Thomas for warmth. When his shivering became so violent that Ricky's muscles ached, he pressed harder against Patrick, but sleep did not come. After several hours, a terrified scream tore from the shadows.

"They're coming to kill us!" the boy next to Thomas whispered.

A second blood-chilling cry ripped through the night.

"I knew it," another boy said. "They're killing the others and then they'll come for us."

Trench and Lujimoi stood, their weapons trained on the boys. The boy next to Thomas began to whimper.

"No talking!" Lujimoi said.

Trench kicked the whimpering boy's legs. "Are you and your friends planning to escape? Is that what you're talking about?"

The boy shook his head.

"I am a good hunter. If you run, I will hunt you down. No matter how far you run. I will find you and kill you." He pressed the muzzle of his weapon into Ricky's knee.

With a jagged breath, Ricky closed his eyes.

"You will be begging for death before I'm through with you," Trench said.

"We weren't planning to escape," Patrick said. "I swear."

Trench moved his gun to Ricky's brother. "Then what were you talking about?"

Another round of screams began behind them.

"Please," the whimpering boy explained, "we were scared hearing the cries of the person being killed."

Lujimoi paused, then howled with laughter and fell to the ground. He clutched his stomach and laughed louder as the pitch and frequency of the screaming intensified. Soon Trench joined in, creating a din that throbbed in Ricky's ears.

"Enough!" Otim stepped out of the dark.

The laughter stopped and Lujimoi got to his feet.

"What's going on?" the wild man demanded.

"Kilama is having nightmares again," Trench explained.

"Then go wake him!" Otim yelled.

Trench scurried into the dark, and the wild man rounded on Lujimoi. "What were you laughing about?"

Lujimoi pointed to the abductees. "They were scared because they thought someone was being killed."

Otim paced before the boys. "Is this true?"

No one answered.

As abruptly as it began, the screaming stopped, and Otim trained his gun on Ricky. "Is this true?" he repeated.

"Yes," Ricky answered. "We thought someone was being killed because of the screaming."

Otim stared down at him. "Someone was."

Confused, Ricky concentrated on the wild man.

"Kilama's parents were being killed," Otim said. He slowed his pacing, savoring the looks of horror on the boys' faces. "They die every night. Again and again. Every time Kilama closes his eyes, he sees his parents dying by his hand, just like they did on the day I took him."

Ricky trembled uncontrollably.

Otim smiled. "And a man who's killed his own parents will not hesitate to kill worthless boys like you."

His words, as sharp and cold as the panga at his belt, cut through Ricky's fear and stilled his breath.

Trench reappeared from behind the boys. "I had trouble waking him, but Kilama is up now."

"And so are the rest of us," Otim snapped. "I don't want to hear another sound from anyone, or it will be the last sound you ever make." Turning away from the abductees, he stalked back into the night.

As Ricky lay in the dark, images of the day replayed in flashes before his unseeing eyes. Rivers swallowing strings of children. Flames stretching toward the sun. Fire burning in the wild man's eyes. Mama reaching. Her eyes, pleading. Christine's hands clinging. Betty crying. Margaret trembling. A panga pressing against Baba's throat. His arms holding, shielding, protecting. Patrick bleeding. Rebels attacking. Kicking. Hitting. Laughing.

A gun.

A bicycle.

A smile.

A suggestion.

*"Maybe we could wait by the road."*

A damp chill seeped from the ground into Ricky's naked body as another cry tore through the darkness, but this time the boys didn't move or speak. With an annoyed grumble, Lujimoi pushed up from his post and went to investigate. As soon as the rebel guard was gone, Ricky looked at his brother.

Patrick lay on his back, his unblinking eyes turned to the sky. When Ricky had woken from a nightmare as a child, the image of his brother's profile beside him in the dark had filled him with comfort. But lying in the razed cornfield, Patrick's misshapen silhouette brought forth a new surge of emotion.

Guilt.

Guilt for asking to sit by the road. Guilt for being the reason their parents and sisters stayed behind when the others fled. Guilt for Patrick jeopardizing his life to protect Ricky. It pressed on his chest, squeezing the breath from his lungs. Ricky needed to tell his brother he was sorry. He needed Patrick to forgive him. Pushing his shoulder into the ground, he scooted closer to his brother. Blackened dried blood was caked on Patrick's lips and brow, and muted starlight reflected off the path of tears carved down his cheek. The set of his brother's swollen jaw and the trembling of his chin told Ricky that Patrick could never forgive him.

Ricky pulled his legs to his chest and wrapped his arms around his knees. The skin was sticky and stung beneath his fingers. Reaching lower, his right hand brushed across a raised line on his shin, and a memory surfaced.

*"Ouch!" Ricky cried, dropping his hand hoe as a warm trickle of blood ran down his shin.*

*Patrick stepped over the row of cassava separating them. "Don't look," he said, taking Ricky by the elbow. "It makes the pain worse."*

*As they made their way through the cassava patch, Ricky kept* his eyes locked on Patrick's face. "It's bad, isn't it?" he asked, unable to control the tremble in his voice.

"Just hold on. It's going to be fine. I promise."

They found Mama among the simsim plants. Concern creased her brow when she saw Ricky's leg. "What happened?" she asked.

"My hand hoe slipped," Ricky said, fighting back tears.

She knelt down to inspect his wound. "I need some lum alele."

Patrick sprinted to the edge of their fields, where the grasses grew wild and tall, and returned with two handfuls of the long, soft blades of lum alele.

"I'll finish filling Ricky's basket," he said, handing Mama the grass.

Ricky's shoulders slumped as his brother hurried back to the fields to complete their chores.

"It's not too deep," Mama said. "Does it hurt?"

Ricky shook his head.

She tucked the grass into her mouth and then wiped away the blood beneath his wound. "My brave boy. Were you racing your brother again?"

"No."

She glanced up at him as she worked the lum alele between her teeth; her eyebrows raised in disbelief. After a moment, she spat the liquid from the wild grass into her cupped hand and poured it over his wound. "Not even a little?" she asked.

"Maybe a little," he admitted.

Mama removed the chewed-up grass from her mouth and smiled. "Always in such a hurry to grow up."

*She inspected his wound and dabbed away a trickle of wild-grass juice running down his calf. "We need to do this several times a day so it doesn't get infected, and try not to get it dirty."*

*"I'll try."*

*"And do me another favor." She took his face in her hands—hands calloused and cracked from years of working in the fields, yet gentle against his skin. Ricky looked up into her warm brown eyes. "Don't grow up too fast, my baby boy." She leaned forward to kiss his forehead.*

A rustling in the dark snatched Ricky from his thoughts. It grew louder, and Lujimoi stepped from the shadows. Ricky closed his eyes when the rebel walked past, but the image of his mama burned in his mind and chest. Only when the rebel disappeared into the shadows and the night quieted again did Ricky open his eyes. He turned to look at Patrick, but stopped when his memory whispered in the night.

*"Don't look. It makes the pain worse."*

# 11
# SAMUEL

Samuel followed the big man to a shea tree, where a young woman stood leaning on a wooden crutch. She wore a blue jumper dress, but only one bare foot peeked out beneath the hem. Behind her, a brown prosthetic leg rested against the tree. She greeted them with a gentle smile, but continued addressing a group of young children gathered around her.

"There are times," she was saying in a soft voice, "when words fail us."

Samuel moved closer. The man did not.

"No matter how many words we speak," she said, touching her fingertips to the forehead of a girl who looked about eight years old, "they cannot always capture what is in here." She then pressed her hand to her own chest and looked at Samuel. "Or in here."

Embarrassment burned beneath Samuel's skin as the children turned to look at him. He met their curious stares with a fierce scowl, and they quickly turned their attention back to the woman.

"Sometimes when our voices cannot speak about what is hurting us, our bodies can. How many of you will participate in the dance performance this afternoon?"

Several hands rose into the air.

"Wonderful. Music and dance let us express many emotions. Joy. Anger. Love. Pain. And so can art." She removed the crutch from under her arm and bent down to pick up a stack of paper. A small boy hurried forward to help.

"Thank you, Robert," she said. "Would you please pass them out?"

Robert nodded and handed each child a blank piece of paper.

"Today, instead of telling me what happened when you were taken from your homes, I would like you to *show* me." She gestured for them to each take a tin of colored pencils from the base of the tree. "Every picture tells a story, no matter how precise the lines or clean the coloring, so don't worry about what your drawings look like. Let your hands tell the story your words cannot."

Robert stepped before Samuel and held out a piece of paper. Samuel stared over his head, ignoring the small boy's presence.

"Thank you," the big man said, reaching over Samuel's shoulder to take the blank paper.

Robert's brown eyes widened, and his small chin tilted up to take in the full height of the man. He nodded twice and released the paper, scurrying back to rejoin the other children, who'd claimed their places in the shade of the tree.

The woman hobbled between them. "Children from an

earlier group agreed to let me share their pictures. If you're struggling to get started, I have them by the tree." Placing her crutch on the ground, she knelt beside a young girl who seemed to be crying and asked her a question.

Without thinking, Samuel turned away from the woman and girl and bumped into the big man's broad chest. The man reached out to steady him, but stopped when Samuel recoiled. Samuel gripped the handles of his crutches until his hands ached, fighting to regain control.

The man tucked the paper under his arm and motioned to Samuel. "Come with me." They wove through the children and stopped at the trunk of the shea tree, where the man picked up the stack of drawings.

"These are more than pictures," he said. "They are fear and pain. They are nightmares."

He handed Samuel two drawings. Shaky, heavy lines, etched deep in the paper, depicted a child carrying a huge pot on her head. Large teardrops fell from her face onto bodies beneath her bare feet. Her clothes hung in tattered strips, revealing bright red streaks on her back. Across the drawing, the artist's dried tears stained and puckered the paper.

Samuel flipped to the next picture. Its controlled lines and small details hinted of an older artist. A boy with his hands tied behind his back lay facedown on the ground. The rope at his wrists stretched to a tree limb above him. The foot of a uniformed man pressed on the back of the boy's head. The rebel's arm waited in a raised position to deliver the first cut. In his hand, he held a panga. On his lips, a smile.

Samuel bit the insides of his cheeks until he tasted the metallic warmth of blood as he fought to cage the scream threatening to escape. The pictures shivered in his hands. He shoved them back at the man.

The man smoothed out the creases on the drawings. "If you hold anger and pain inside," he said, glancing at Samuel's leg, "they fester, like an infection. They must be lanced and treated, or they will eat you alive."

He handed Samuel the new piece of paper. Samuel stared down at the clean sheet. No tears stained its fibers. No images of death marred its surface. It held no emotions. Just like Samuel.

Lifting the sheet and his eyes to the man, Samuel gripped the edges and tore the paper in half.

# 12

# RICKY

They marched from sunrise to sunset. Thousands of steps. The rebels gave them little water and no food. They marched through fields, rivers, and jungle, pressing through tall grass and dense vegetation. Unlike the rebels, who slathered their legs with animal fat to protect their skin from the razor-sharp edges of elephant grass and the rigid tips of spear grass, the abductees suffered with each step as the leaf blades sliced at their bare legs, leaving a patchwork of thin cuts. Tied together and allowed few opportunities to stop, the abductees were forced to relieve themselves as they walked. Their shorts, soiled with urine and feces, clung to their legs and chafed their thighs. The muscles in Ricky's shoulders, arms, and back burned under the heavy bundles of sugarcane and stolen goods pilfered from villages the rebels had raided on their march. His ankles ached and thorns and rocks bored into the soles of his bare feet. The open cuts oozed with each agonizing step that led Ricky farther from home, but he never stopped marching. Weakness was not tolerated, and execution, swift and merciless, was the punishment for those who fell behind.

They hid from the moon. Stripped naked, with his hands tied behind his back, Ricky huddled close to his brother and Thomas in the damp jungle air. The shivering never stopped, nor did the hunger that gnawed at his stomach. Thirst swelled his tongue and cracked his lips, and beatings came without warning or provocation. Sleep offered no respite from the pain and fear. Flashbacks of his abduction and his family's deaths lurked in the silence and dark of night. Only unconsciousness, delivered by beatings and starvation, gave Ricky any escape from the horror of his first days with the LRA.

As the sun dipped below the horizon on the fourth day, the marching halted in a swampy area beside a dense line of trees. The commanders ordered the guards to take their abductees and spread out to make camp for the night. Lujimoi and Kilama once again stripped the boys and bound their hands. Ricky struggled to remain standing. The noises around him eroded into a low buzz. His vision blurred, and his knees gave. He pitched forward and hit the ground hard, unable to catch himself or lessen the impact of the fall.

Patrick and Thomas squatted on either side of him and forced him to his feet as Trench approached. Blood spilled from Ricky's nose and lips as the rebel drew the panga from his belt and stepped behind him. Ricky closed his eyes, too defeated by hunger and thirst to plead for his life, and too numb with grief and shock to care. Trench seized his bound hands and slid the blade between them, slicing through the rope at his wrists. He then cut through the rope at Ricky's waist while Kilama and Luji-moi freed Patrick, Thomas, and three boys abducted from a village that morning to replace the boys who'd fallen behind on their four-day march.

"Eat!" Trench said, throwing Patrick a small piece of roasted goat meat and a half-filled plastic jerrican of water. He then tossed Thomas a hunk of meat and a nearly empty jerrican before dropping a couple of chunks of raw cassava at the feet of the new abductees.

Without a word or sideways glance, Patrick tore the meat in half and handed Ricky the larger portion. Ricky bit into the meat, but his mouth produced no saliva to help him chew. Patrick shoved the jerrican into his hands as he coughed and choked on the dry, sinewy flesh. Swamp water, swimming with dirt and bits of moss, spilled down Ricky's parched throat and over his cracked lips. The sound of his brother gagging on his small portion of meat stopped Ricky from guzzling what remained of the filthy water. He lowered the can from his lips and handed it back to Patrick.

The swelling around Patrick's left eye had receded, leaving behind deep purple shadows that crept across the bridge of his nose and cheekbone. A crescent-shaped cut on Patrick's bottom lip split open as he ate, but he did not move to wipe away the fresh blood trickling down his chin. A deep gash on his head, punishment for not keeping pace with the rebels the previous day, had crusted with clumps of sticky, blackened blood.

Desperate for a reassuring nod or gesture, Ricky stared at his brother, but Patrick kept his gaze fixed on the ground before him. Worried that if he stared at his brother any longer the rebels would notice, Ricky followed his brother's lead and averted his eyes to the tall blades of grass pressing in on them from all sides.

To the left of the brothers, the hushed voices of Otim and Trench drew Ricky's attention. Otim sat on a decayed log, sharpening his panga. His yellowed eyes stared unblinkingly at the machete as he ran a stone down the length of the blade in slow, reverent strokes.

Trench paced before him. "What are we to do with these babies?"

Otim's only response was the grating sound of stone on metal.

"They are slowing us down," Trench said.

"Yes," Otim agreed. "They are."

"And now we are to feed them, too. We should have killed them with the others."

Ricky held his breath, afraid if he released it, he would not hear Otim's response.

Without looking up from his panga, the wild man answered in a voice bordering on boredom, "Komakech has plans for them."

"For them?" Trench scoffed. "What kind of plans could Komakech possibly have for them? Half of them didn't even survive four days of marching."

"I don't know," Otim replied, finishing one last swipe down the blade. He tested its edge with his calloused thumb. "I don't question my commander."

Trench froze at the chill in Otim's voice. "I wasn't questioning you, Afande," he stammered.

A thin smile slid across Otim's face, showing his rotten teeth, at the young rebel's use of the Kiswahili word for "sir." "No, you were questioning my commander, whose directive came from Kony. So you are questioning Kony."

Trench blinked rapidly, struggling to process the sudden turn in the conversation. "No, Afande. Never."

Otim stood, and Ricky stared at the ground. He struggled to track the wild man's movement over the pulse pounding in his ears. When the footsteps stopped, he glanced up.

The wild man stood before Trench and ran his thumb down the length of the machete. A thin line of blood glistened on the blade. "That's good, because Kony's word is the word of the Holy Spirit." He raised his panga to Trench's face and dragged the tip of the blade lightly along one of Trench's scars, leaving behind a broken smear of blood. "And you know what happens to those who question the Holy Spirit, don't you?"

Careful not to move with the panga nearing his throat, Trench answered that he did indeed know.

"So," Otim said, "if Kony wants us to round up every boy and girl in the country, that is precisely what we are going to do. Do you understand?"

"Yes, Afande."

Otim lowered his panga and motioned to the abductees. "Now go watch them. Make sure they don't get any ideas of trying to escape, especially the tall one." Otim smiled at Thomas.

"He's been waiting for a chance to run." The wild man drew a noisy breath through his flared nostrils. "I can smell it on him."

Trench walked over to Thomas. "Is that what you're planning, boy?" he asked. "You thinking of running?"

Thomas kept his gaze lowered and his lips closed. Trench backhanded him across the face, and Thomas fell to the ground in front of Patrick.

Trench crouched down and leaned in close, so that his distorted face hovered close to Thomas's. With a tilt of his head, the rebel waved his rifle before him. "Wipe any thought of escape from your mind, boy." He jabbed the muzzle of his AK-47 under Thomas's chin. The force slammed Thomas's teeth together. Ricky cringed at the sound.

"There's only one way to escape the LRA."

Thomas squeezed his eyes shut, and Ricky pressed closer to Patrick.

*"Pow!"* Trench yelled, causing all six boys to flinch.

Otim snorted in amusement as he strutted past the rebel guard and his prisoners. A warped smile stretched across Trench's face, and his body sagged with relief at having regained his superior's approval.

"Boys like you have tried to run," Trench said after Otim had disappeared into the jungle. "But there's nowhere to run. There's no one waiting for you. There's no one looking for you. They're all dead." Slinging his weapon across his chest, he stood. "We're your family now."

# 13

# RICKY

*Whop-whop-whop-whop.*

Helicopter blades sliced through the morning sky, jerking Ricky from his sleep and the rebels to their feet. They drew their weapons and aimed them at the abductees. Trench pressed a finger to his warped lips and released the safety on his weapon.

Hope coursed through Ricky's veins as he peered up through the heavy canopy of leaves stretching high above. His heart kept time with the helicopter blades as they grew louder.

No one moved as the helicopter carved a wide arc in the air above the bush.

As he listened to it sweep over the trees, Ricky recalled the day his father returned from the Lira Palwo market with a story about a helicopter and a man.

*"He was taken by the LRA a year ago," Father said as he, Patrick, and Ricky led the cattle from the fields to the river for water.*

"How did he escape?" Patrick asked.

"His family alerted the military as soon as the LRA abducted him, and the soldiers tracked down the rebels and freed the man."

"How did they find them?" Ricky asked.

"They tracked them by air," Father said, "using a helicopter."

Ricky's eyes widened. He nudged Patrick. "Think how far you could see from the sky." He quickened his pace to catch up with Father. "Did the man get to fly in the helicopter?"

"No. When the soldiers in the helicopter spotted the LRA's hidden camp, they sent in ground troops to defeat the rebels and liberate their captives."

"Patrick, what if we had a helicopter for hunting?" Ricky spread his arms out like he was taking flight and swooped between two zebu cows lumbering to the riverbank. "I'd fly over the fields and when I spotted a bush pig, I'd signal you on the ground so you could strike." He grabbed his brother's arm.

Patrick shrugged off Ricky's hand. "How long was the man with the LRA?" he asked.

"Two months."

Patrick's brow furrowed as he processed the answer. "How did he survive that long?"

Father kneeled down on the bank of the Agago and pressed his cupped hands into the river. Leaning back, he poured the water over his head and then wiped his face with his sleeve. "I asked him that as well. He said he survived by never choosing to hurt or kill." He dusted off his pants and ducked under the branches of an orange tree to escape the sun.

*Patrick and Ricky followed. "What do you mean?" Patrick asked.*

*"He explained that when given the choice, he chose life. Because he never willingly took a life, God spared his and sent the helicopter to save him."*

Ricky squinted through the slivers in the jungle canopy, praying to see a flash of silver streak across the blue. Patrick and he had not killed. Surely God would send a helicopter to save them. The helicopter cut back across the bush, and Ricky's heart raced. His ears strained to hear beyond the slap of the blades, and his eyes searched the trees surrounding the LRA camp for any movement.

The jungle held its breath. No footsteps echoed through its darkness. No soldiers stepped from its shadows. And as the pulse of the helicopter faded, so did Ricky's hope. In its absence, a realization crept through him. No one was looking. No one was left. Everyone who ever cared was gone. Except for his brother.

Patrick sat next to him with his feet curled under his legs for warmth. His chin rested on his bare chest, and his eyes remained closed as the rebels started gathering their supplies.

Even Patrick was no longer looking.

"The government troops are trying to track us," Otim announced as Trench threaded the rope through the holes torn in the boys' waistbands. "Today, we stay off the roads."

They marched through the bush for hours. Ricky shuffled along behind his brother on the path carved by the rebels' machetes. His head throbbed from thirst and mosquitoes fed on him, but he didn't have the strength or will to brush them away. He reserved every drop of both to keep the sugarcane firmly in his arms and his legs moving forward.

As the sun fell below the jungle canopy, Otim led them into the fields surrounding a village. The rebels crouched down, and with their weapons drawn, they snuck between the thatch-roofed huts. Otim signaled his fighters to encircle the center of the village, where families gathered at the wangoo for supper.

Like a swarm of killer bees, the LRA attacked. Six armed guards forced Ricky, Patrick, and the other abductees to sit on a patch of grass outside the fire pit as chaos erupted around them. With each scream and strike, memories of Ricky's family and village shuddered through him. With every cry for mercy, his parents' and sisters' voices grew louder, until theirs were the only voices he heard. His voice, muted by the rebels' weapons and threats, joined theirs in his mind, where it screamed for release.

Dozens of rebels corralled the villagers while others looted their homes. They crammed everything they could find into sacks and baskets and piled the stolen food and supplies at the abductees' feet. One of Otim's stolen wives dumped a large burlap sack in front of Ricky. His back and shoulders ached at the sight of the load the rebels would force him to carry.

"Separate them!" Otim yelled.

The rebels grabbed the teens from the huddle of villagers and forced the adults and children to sit before the fire. Twelve boys and girls remained standing. Eleven pairs of frightened eyes scoured the faces of the seated villagers, searching for parents and siblings. One pair did not.

Otim was stalking up and down the line of new abductees, spewing his threats, when suddenly he stopped in front of the captive whose head remained bowed. The boy, who looked about Ricky's age, wore filthy clothes frayed with wear. Shoulder-length ropes of knotted hair hung in clumps around his face. Otim lifted the muzzle of his AK-47 to the boy's head and pushed the dreadlocks aside. His eyes narrowed and a predatory smile spread across his face as he cocked his head to the side and leaned in close. "I knew we'd find you." He grabbed the boy by the shirt and threw him to the ground. "No one escapes the LRA."

The rebels shook their weapons in the air and echoed the wild man's claim. Ricky's fingers dug into the ground under his legs as five days of threats and beatings repeated in his mind. Dread cramped his stomach as Otim's hand hesitated over the gun strapped around his chest.

The wild man's eyes never left the boy cowering before him as he ordered one of his rebel wives to bring him a bag of stolen supplies. The girl ran over to where Ricky sat and grabbed the burlap sack, which she set at Otim's feet.

Otim rummaged through the dust-colored bag, throwing farming tools and cooking utensils aside until his hands paused over the item he sought. He smiled as he pulled a rusty chain from the pillaged supplies. A heavy iron lock hung below the loop of metal links. Ricky looked away, but the wild man's voice forced his eyes back to the center of the circle.

"I warned you what would happen if you ran. Didn't I?"

The flames of the village fire receded into the blackened pit as Otim weighed the chain in his hands.

"I warned all of you!"

The rebels forced Ricky and the other abductees to their feet.

"You will learn that my threats are not empty!" Otim spat, and he swung his arm in a wide arc, bringing the lock down on the boy's back.

"No!" an older girl beside Patrick screamed. She stepped forward to help the boy, but Patrick grabbed her arm.

"They'll kill you, too," he whispered.

She attempted to wrench her wrist from Patrick's grip, but failed. "He's my brother," she cried.

Ricky looked around at the rebels, who'd gathered to watch Otim deliver the boy's punishment. Their eyes devoured every strike. As starved as Ricky was for food, Kony's men hungered for the kill.

Ricky flinched with every swing of Otim's arm. When he could no longer bear to watch the lock tear into the boy's skin and break his bones, he fixed his eyes on the blades of grass surrounding his feet. He counted them.

Every single blade.

The tall and short. The straight and broken. The new and dying. And when the boy's pained cries or the sickening thud of the lock striking flesh caused him to lose count, he started over. The small patch of grass where Ricky stood became his whole world. Nothing else existed.

Until it did.

Otim stepped back, and Ricky stopped counting. The blood-ied lock swung from the chain clutched in the wild man's hand, and the boy lay in a small heap at his feet. Otim dropped the chain back in the bag and dragged the boy's limp body in front of the new and old abductees. "Tell them your name!" he de-manded, glaring down at him.

The boy's jaw hung open at a broken angle. He moaned senselessly and choked on the blood spilling from his lips.

Otim walked around the circle of abductees, staring at each boy and girl. "What is his name?" he demanded.

No one answered.

"You!" He pointed to the girl next to Patrick. "What is your name?"

"Sarah," she answered.

"You were taken the same day as this boy. What is his name?"

Sarah looked to her brother. His name was stuttered through her tears. "J-J-Joseph."

"What?" Otim asked, leaning closer.

"Joseph," she repeated.

Otim stepped back and continued to saunter around the cir-cle. "Did I not warn Joseph what would happen if he tried to escape? Did I not warn you all?"

He stopped and drew his gun. Striding to the center of the circle, he pressed the muzzle of his weapon to Joseph's forehead. "Look at me!"

Joseph lifted his broken face and swollen eyes to his former commander.

"I am Otim! Should you try to run away, I will be the one to kill you!"

He released the safety on his gun, and Joseph closed his eyes.

"No!" Sarah cried. "Please, Afande, please don't kill him!"

His gun still pressed to Joseph's head, Otim glared at Sarah. "You are asking me not to kill Joseph?"

"Yes, Afande," she begged. "Please."

"Fine," Otim said, lowering his weapon. "I won't kill him."

Sarah's shoulders and head slumped with relief, and Joseph opened his eyes.

"Trench," Otim ordered, "bring me his sister."

A pained cry rattled in Joseph's throat as Trench pushed past Ricky and grabbed Sarah's arm. He dragged her into the center of the circle, where her little brother lay broken and bleeding. Otim drew the machete from his belt. At the sight of the large knife, Joseph began to sob, and Sarah covered her face with trembling hands.

"You asked me not to kill him," the wild man said, tearing Sarah's hands from her face and shoving the machete into them. "So you will."

Joseph's sister stared in horror at the curved blade. The dried blood of many ran the length of the machete and stained the wooden sheath in rusty streaks.

"Cut him!" Otim said through clenched teeth.

Sarah shook her head.

Otim pressed the muzzle of his gun into the side of her head. "Cut him!"

With one unsteady step, Sarah stood beside her brother. She shook so violently, the panga wavered in her grip as she placed it on the back of Joseph's neck. He stilled beneath the blade. Ricky's breath stilled with him, but his mind raced with questions he prayed he'd never be forced to answer.

*If threatened with death, could I cut Patrick?*

*Could I kill my brother?*

*And if Patrick died, would I have the will to survive?*

"Cut him!" Otim demanded.

"I'm sorry, Joseph," Sarah whispered as she pressed down on the machete. A thin stream of blood ran down Joseph's broken jawline and dripped from his chin. The moment Sarah saw the blood, she lifted the blade. With the panga removed from his neck, Joseph's battered body trembled and swayed.

Otim grabbed the machete and strode around the circle, glaring at the captives, who dared not meet his septic eyes. Ricky glanced over at his brother, and the answer to all his questions ripped through him with unwavering resolve.

*No.*

He would take Otim's bullet before he ever hurt his brother.

Patrick kept his chin raised and his eyes locked on Joseph. An eerie calm, like the surface of the Agago River, washed over Patrick's face as he watched Trench drag Sarah away from her brother, and a new question pressed against Ricky's thoughts.

*Could Patrick cut me?*

"Line up!" screamed Otim.

The abductees scrambled to form a single-file line. Patrick

stood in front. Ricky moved to stand behind him, but Patrick shoved him from the line. Ricky fell. His eyes wide with shock, he stared up at his brother. Patrick's face twitched with anger as he glared down at Ricky.

"Patrick," Ricky mouthed.

His brother turned away.

"Get up," Lujimoi ordered, grabbing Ricky by the neck of his shirt. He dragged him to the back of the line. "Wait your turn."

Ricky's eyes blurred with tears as he stared down the line at Patrick. His brother stood tall and straight, unlike the cowering abductees separating him from Ricky. Hopelessness gripped Ricky with the realization that his brother, who'd protected and loved him all his life, was gone. The LRA had killed him, just as they'd killed his parents and sisters. Numb with grief, Ricky watched Otim walk to the front of the line with his bloody machete.

"Tonight," the wild man announced to them all, "Joseph's blood will not only be on my hands." He stopped before Patrick. "It will also be on yours."

# 14

# SAMUEL

Samuel thrust his crutches into the ground and swung his legs forward. With each step, he increased his pace. He had to escape the man, the drawings, and the nightmares they brought back. He didn't stop until he reached the porch, where the memories crashed into him with such force he fell to his knees.

"Samuel?"

Before he could look up, the big man was at his side, lifting him from the ground. As the man carried him up the porch steps, Samuel stared at the large arms holding him. With one squeeze they could break him, but the man held him with the gentleness of a mother carrying her infant in his obeno. On the porch, he eased Samuel back into his chair and left to fetch the crutches. When he returned, he leaned them against the post. "I'm going to get the doctor. Wait here."

On the dirt field, a new group of children gathered, but Samuel's target, the small boy, remained, watching from the side-line. Samuel's numb, unblinking gaze traveled from the soccer game to a dozen teenage girls gathered around a short elderly woman to the right of the field. The girls stood quiet as the woman showed how to thread the needle on a heavy cast-iron sewing machine. They edged closer to the worn wooden table for a better look as the woman set to work. Her bare feet rocked the rectangular iron grate of the presser pedal up and down with the fluid, unconscious rhythm of decades spent hunched over the machine while her fingers, knotted with arthritis, guided a length of lavender cloth beneath the blur of the needle. The motion lulled Samuel, and he began to rock in time with each swing.

Beyond the group of girls, several young boys crouched beside a low brick wall. Using hand trowels, they spread mounds of burnt red clay on the top bricks. While they worked, a slim man with a cane supervised their progress. With some difficulty, he knelt beside the wall to show the boys how to fit the bricks snugly together, just as Samuel's father had once taught him.

Samuel picked at the frayed edge of his bandage as he watched the boys work. He wound a thread around his finger, tighter and tighter, until the tip darkened to a deep purple and deadened to the touch. He freed it when he heard the creak of the door behind him.

The doctor knelt beside his chair. "I heard you had a fall. Is your leg hurt?"

Samuel shook his head.

"Do you mind if I take a look?"

Samuel removed his hand, revealing the rust-colored stain.

"It needs to be changed," the doctor said, extracting the clasps' tiny metal teeth from the soiled bandage. Placing the clasps aside, he carefully unwound the cloth from Samuel's leg. For the first three rotations, the bandage gave way easily, but as the doctor neared the layers closest to Samuel's injury, the material pulled and tugged at the sticky wound. Samuel bit his lip and looked away.

Once the doctor had finished applying a fresh bandage, he reached inside a paper bag and pulled out a small plastic container of large pills. "You must remember to take one of these antibiotics every day until there are none left. Even if the swelling and redness go away, keep taking them or the infection will return." He placed the pills back in the bag and pulled out a second bottle. "I put some painkillers in here, too, in case the pain becomes unbearable on your way home." He put the bottle away and held out the bag, but Samuel refused to take it, so the doctor placed it on the armrest and, with a pat on Samuel's shoulder, left.

Alone on the porch, Samuel reached into the bag and took out the bottle of painkillers. He poured two into his hand, tempted to take them before his memories resurfaced, but he couldn't afford to break his second rule. Not again. He put the pills back in the bottle, glanced at the door behind him to make sure the man wasn't coming, and then threw the bottle off the porch. He knew he'd regret the decision later, when he escaped the soldier and was hiding in the bush, but he also knew the truth. Nothing could kill his pain and there was no way home.

# 15

# RICKY

"Home."

Ricky's breath caught at the sound of Patrick's voice. It was the first word his brother had spoken to him since their abduction, and he spoke the word so quietly Ricky questioned whether Patrick had spoken at all.

Ricky's eyes swept around the bush, where he and Patrick lay back to back with their wrists bound behind them. Their guards had fallen asleep. When several moments had passed with no sound from Patrick, Ricky's heart sank with the thought that he'd imagined his brother's voice, but as he closed his eyes in despair, he felt his brother shift behind him. Patrick tilted his head back and pressed the side of his face against Ricky's.

"Home," he whispered again, his voice breaking.

The desperation in his brother's voice made Ricky tremble. It was more than Patrick expressing how much he missed their home; it was an assurance for Ricky that they would someday return. For the first time since their abduction, Patrick gave Ricky hope.

But then Trench's words from the previous night reminded him of the truth. *"There's only one way to escape the LRA."*

A wave of grief extinguished the flicker of hope his brother's voice had ignited. In its absence, the day's events recaptured Ricky's thoughts. The terror in Joseph's eyes when he realized the rebels had found him and the surrender in his bowed head when the abductees lined up to deliver his fate. The anguish in Sarah's whispered apology when she cut her brother and the deafening silence when Joseph's cries ceased. An aftershock of emotion trembled through Ricky, and he flinched as he recalled Otim snatching the blade from his hands before he was forced to take a turn.

*"There's nowhere left to cut," the wild man announced. Pushing Ricky forward, he pointed the bloody blade and said, "March."*

As he thought of Joseph, Ricky stretched out his legs until they reached a tangle of thorns at the base of a bush. He scraped his feet back and forth against the curved thorns until they dripped with blood, and then he pressed harder, welcoming the pain that seared through his soles and dulled the image of Joseph's broken body beneath him. When the pain subsided, he peered into the dark and listened to make certain the guards were still sleeping before turning to his brother.

"Danger," he whispered.

Patrick nodded and then repeated his plea. "Home."

"How?" Ricky asked.

They could never speak of home in the LRA. In the five days since their abduction, they had both seen others killed for less.

"Code word," Patrick answered.

Ricky waited for his brother to continue. He knew his brother was trying to think of a word that symbolized everything that was home, but it also had to be a word that would not raise suspicion if overheard.

Ricky's thoughts drifted back again to his home. The image of his mother, her arms outstretched, reaching for him, gripped his heart. He strained against the rope at his wrists, and tears ran down his swollen cheeks, stinging the cuts and abrasions. He ached to run into her embrace, to feel her breath and hear her heartbeat.

And then a word slipped into his head. *Obeno.*

He thought of one day at the marketplace with his mother and family. His mother had stopped at one stall to visit with a friend with a newborn boy. The infant's mother had died giving birth to him, and his aunt had taken him into her home.

*The baby started fussing as they were gathered around looking at him.*

*"Is he hungry?" Ricky's sister Margaret asked, staring down at the crying infant.*

*"Yes," Mama said, "but that is not why he cries."*

*"Why does he cry?" Ricky asked.*

*His mother's friend lifted the baby close to her chest and gently rocked him. "He cries for his mother's touch."*

*"But she's dead," Margaret said.*

Patrick held a finger up to his lips. "Shhh. That's not nice to say."

"Will he always cry, then?" Margaret asked.

"No." Sadness pressed on the woman's words as she caressed the baby's back with her hand. "But he will always miss his mother."

The baby's cries softened as he nuzzled his face into his aunt's neck and closed his eyes.

"Babies need to feel safe and loved," Mama said, stroking the infant's head with her thumb, "just as much as they need sleep and food. That is why mothers carry their babies in obenos."

Betty pulled her thumb from her mouth and pointed to the blanket securing the baby to his aunt. "'Beno," she said.

"That's right," Mama said, touching the toddler's chubby cheek.

Betty smiled with pride and stuck her wrinkled thumb back in her mouth.

Mama helped her friend tuck the blanket around the baby until all of the child that remained visible was the curve of his cheek and the small bump of his nose. "The obeno holds the baby close, so he can feel his mother's breath and hear her heartbeat."

"And that's as important as food?" Margaret asked, unable to hide her doubt.

"Food feeds a child's body, but love and security feed his soul and strengthen his heart, letting him know he is not alone," Mama said.

"Will he always feel alone?" Ricky asked.

"No," the baby's aunt said, resting her cheek against the baby's *head as she rocked him. In her embrace, the infant's tiny back rose and fell in contented slumber. "With our help," she whispered, meeting the children's eyes, "he will know he is loved."*

Ricky opened his eyes, releasing hot tears, which burned down his cheeks. He leaned back and pressed his lips to his brother's ear. "Obeno," he whispered.

Patrick tensed for a moment and then his bound hands groped behind him until he found Ricky's fingers.

"Obeno," he whispered. Then, tightening his hold on Ricky's hands, he said, "Promise."

The word held the authoritative tone their father had often used with them in the classroom and fields.

A rebel near them stirred, and Patrick released Ricky's hands. While they waited for the rebel to settle back into sleep, Ricky turned the word over and over in his mind.

*Promise.*

Promise what? If Patrick ran, Ricky would follow. His brother couldn't doubt that. So what promise was Patrick demanding of him? What did he fear Ricky wouldn't do?

Ricky remembered the look on his brother's face when Otim traded John and Andrew to the other rebel group. Patrick understood that the rebels had separated Thomas from John as soon as Thomas showed allegiance to his brother, and he'd seen Sarah's punishment for speaking up for her brother. The rebels had made it clear they would not tolerate loyalty to anyone but Kony. It was a fact that now Ricky finally understood. A fact he knew Patrick had realized that first day.

Ricky pictured his brother hunched over the broken family radio in their hut, studying its parts and searching for a solution to fix what was broken. From the moment the LRA arrived in their village, Patrick had been watching the rebels with the same stoic determination.

Ignoring the rope cutting into his wrists, Ricky stretched his arms toward Patrick and grabbed his brother's hands again. Patrick hadn't been ignoring him and pushing him away out of anger or indifference; he'd been protecting him, just as he'd always done.

But with that realization came the truth about his brother's demand.

*Promise.*

It hit Ricky like a blow to the stomach. If the rebels separated them into different brigades, their opportunities to escape might not present themselves at the same time or in the same place. Patrick wasn't just asking for Ricky's assurance that they would return home, he wanted Ricky's promise that if he found the opportunity to run, he would take it, even if Patrick couldn't.

Panic seized Ricky. He shook his head. "No," he whimpered, fighting the urge to scream. He would never leave without his brother. He couldn't find obeno without Patrick. It wouldn't exist.

Patrick squeezed Ricky's hands. "Promise," he whispered.

Ricky trembled. He couldn't lose Patrick. His brother was all he had left. He stared at the dark form lying yards away. In the moonlight, Joseph's lifeless eyes stared back. "I can't," he whispered.

Patrick leaned his head back and rested it on Ricky's. "Please," he begged.

The pain in his brother's voice burned in Ricky's chest. Gripping Patrick's hands for support, Ricky closed his eyes and whispered, "I promise."

# RICKY

Patrick and Ricky did not speak another word that night. There was nothing left to say. As the first hint of morning burned through the leaves, Patrick released Ricky's hands, and the marching began. After three weeks, they arrived at the Aswa River in the Gulu district. Struggling to keep pace with the rebels, they stumbled along the riverbank and pressed through fields of elephant grass until they reached the rendezvous point, deep in the bush, where Commander Komakech waited.

Komakech stood taller than the other rebels. His military uniform did not show the wear or stains evident on the lower commanders' camouflage uniforms. It stretched across his broad chest, with braided gold cords that encircled his shoulders and hung beneath his armpits in loose loops. They swayed with each step as he strode before the abductees, looking down at the boys with a regal air.

On his third pass he stopped before Thomas, the tallest of the new captives. "Do you speak any English?"

Thomas shook his head, and Komakech moved on to Patrick. "Do you?"

"Some, Afande," Patrick answered.

Komakech asked Patrick a question in English. Ricky did not understand the commander's words or his brother's response, but Komakech smiled and pointed to Patrick and Otim yanked him from the line. Ricky held his breath as he fought the urge to look at his brother. He could not show loyalty to him in front of Komakech and Otim, but fear that he might never see Patrick again broke his resolve, and he locked eyes with his brother. Patrick shook his head once and looked away.

The LRA commander moved down the line, asking each boy the same question. Ricky envied the boys who now stood beside his brother. He knew a few English words from his schooling, but not enough to answer if Komakech tested him.

The commander stood before him. His long hair reached his shoulders, but did not hang in the knotted dreadlocks most of the rebels wore. Otim, who stood behind him, appeared feral in Komakech's shadow.

"Do you speak English?" the commander asked.

"No, Afande."

And with two words, the brothers were separated.

Otim said he was taking Patrick and the older boys for intelligence training. Their ability to speak English made them ideal LRA spies by allowing them to blend into villages and towns, where they could gather information on the government troops' movements and learn whether the villagers' loyalties rested with Kony or President Museveni.

Trench took charge of Ricky, Thomas, Vincent, and the remaining boys and girls.

"You are going to where the fighting is. When you hear the sound of bullets firing," he said, "don't run. Don't be scared. The bullets you hear are not the ones that will kill you. It is the bullet you don't hear that will kill you. When you hear gunfire and explosions, stand your ground." He stopped before Ricky and shifted his weapon to his other shoulder. "Do not run, or I will kill you. You will not hear my bullets."

He then handed them each an unloaded rifle. Ricky stared down at the weapon that would be all that stood between him and trained government soldiers.

"The AK-47. It is a beautiful machine. You must know how to field strip and reassemble your weapon at any time, even in the middle of a battle." Trench began to take apart his rifle, reciting the name for every part. His fingers moved so quickly, Ricky struggled to keep up. When Trench finished, he put it back together with the same fluid ease. "Now you try."

After hours of practice, Trench pitted the abductees against one another to see who could complete the task in the fastest time.

"Your weapon is worth more than your life," he explained as the boys worked. "You never leave a weapon on the battlefield, the LRA's or our enemy's. If you see a rebel or a government soldier fall, you take the weapon and leave the wounded." He stopped before Ricky. "What do you do if you see a rebel or soldier fall?"

Ricky held out his reassembled gun. "Take the weapon, leave the wounded."

When they completed their last round of competition, their group rejoined the intelligence-training group, and the wild man turned the abductees over to Lujimoi for instruction. The stocky twenty-year-old forced them to march carrying short, curved sticks in place of weapons. They marched until dark, and as they marched, Lujimoi preached to them about their leader, Joseph Kony.

"Ladit Kony's commands are the Holy Spirit's commands," he warned, using the Acholi word for "boss." "Those who refuse to help or seek to oppose him in his holy mission to create a Uganda on the foundation of his holy word are the enemy. Nonbelievers cannot hide. Ladit Kony knows what you're thinking. Even if your lips don't speak it, your mind will." He stepped in front of Ricky, who stumbled back so he didn't crash into the rebel. "The Holy Spirit will read your minds when we meet up with his Control Altar brigade." He poked Ricky in the chest with the puckered stub of what remained of his index finger. "And he will judge you as loyal to him or a traitor."

On the eighth day of training, Trench woke Ricky hours before sunrise. He gave him his clothes and led him and the other abductees before Commander Komakech, where hundreds of rebels stood in the elephant grass awaiting instruction.

"Intelligence scouts discovered government troops closing in on our position," Komakech said.

Standing next to Thomas, Ricky searched the faces surrounding the commander for his brother, but Patrick was not among them.

"Today we fight," Komakech announced. "Prepare for battle." He led them to a clearing in the bush. Mango-sized stones in a curved line created a large circle within the clearing. The experienced fighters stood before thick rows of ashes that marked the only break in the circle. In the center of the circle stood a man the rebels called Teacher.

"Empty all bullets from your magazines," Teacher instructed. "Separate them from your guns, but bring both your weapon and bullets with you into the yard for cleansing."

The rebels with weapons followed his instruction without question.

"No shoes in the yard," Teacher said, continuing his list of rules regarding the ritual.

Ricky had neither a weapon nor shoes, so he waited quietly as the experienced fighters followed Teacher's commands.

When the fighters stood before the circle with their magazines empty and their feet bare, Teacher motioned to the first rebel in line. "Come forward."

One by one, the soldiers stepped through the ashes and stood before Teacher. Ricky's heart raced as the line before him shortened. Whatever the man in the circle was saying and doing to the experienced fighters seemed to infuse the warriors with power. They left the circle with their eyes wide and their chests heaving, eager to fight. The new abductees mimicked the rebels' actions and expressions as they left the yard, but the tremble in their hands betrayed them. Eagerness did not course through their veins, only fear.

When the fighter before Ricky exited the yard, Ricky entered. The ash, silky beneath his steps, stung the cuts and blisters covering his feet. He stopped before Teacher and looked up into his bloodshot eyes.

"The Holy Spirit lives in our leader, Joseph Kony," Teacher said. "If you believe in him and the Holy Spirit, no harm will come to you in battle. Do you believe in our leader, Kony?"

Outside the circle, Ricky thought he heard the click of a gun's safety disarming.

"Yes, Afande."

Teacher dipped his thumb in a bowl and touched Ricky's forehead. The scent of shea nut oil brought images of working in the fields with his mama and sisters flooding forward in his mind. He focused on Teacher's voice, every word, every syllable, leaving no room in his thoughts for the memories to linger.

"Run straight, and no bullet will touch you," Teacher proclaimed. He anointed Ricky, placing the oil in the sign of the cross on his body. "Bullets will turn away from a true Kony follower. Bombs will malfunction before a true believer." His voice rose in strength and volume. "Kony and the Holy Spirit will lead you into battle, young warrior. Fight without question. Fight without hesitation. Fight without fear." He placed his calloused palm on Ricky's head. "You are cleansed. You are blessed with the Holy Spirit. He will protect you in battle."

With the ritual of the yard completed, Komakech divided the fighters into three large battalions, each composed of smaller companies, or coys, that encircled the top commanders' positions on all sides. As two of the newest abductees, the rebels placed Ricky and Thomas with a low-level commander and two other abductees. Their group of five moved ahead of the coy to serve as lookout. Of the five rebels, only the commander held a weapon. Ricky and the others walked into battle unarmed.

Thomas inched closer to Ricky as the group peered through the tall grass. "I'm going to run," he whispered.

Ricky's head swept to either side to make sure no one heard. "When?"

"During the battle. I have to find John."

Ricky had seen the same look of determination in Thomas's eyes when they'd been hunting or fishing near their village, and he knew there was nothing he could say that would change his friend's mind.

Behind them, their commander waved the group forward. "Do not retreat until I say. If you run, I will shoot you."

The battle began with the cry, "Government troops!" and a gunshot so loud Ricky thought it had fired inside his head. Urine soaked through his shorts and ran down his legs as he stood his ground and bullets whistled past him from all directions.

"March!" his commander screamed.

The rapid bursts of machine guns echoed in Ricky's ears as he moved toward the enemy line. Explosions and screams filled the brief pauses between each rattle of gunfire as grenades struck the earth, spraying the air with soil and deadly shrapnel. The wails of the wounded as they lay dying on the field buried the battle cries of the commanders. Ricky's bare feet slipped across the wet grass and muddy earth. With no weapon to hold them steady, his hands covered his head, but did little to shield him from the dirt and blood raining down from the sky.

The boys looked back to their commander as the LRA front line crumbled and the rebels scattered before the approaching government forces. The commander lay on the ground, a hole ripped through his chest. Crouching low, Ricky scanned the battlefield for Thomas, but couldn't find his friend. In the chaos, he grabbed another boy's arm. "Run!" he screamed. The boy pulled free from his grasp, ran over to their fallen commander, and grabbed his weapon. As he turned back to Ricky, an explosion tore into the earth. The concussion of the blast knocked Ricky to the ground and muted everything around him. When the smoke cleared, he stared at the crater where the boy had stood seconds before. Ricky hadn't even known his name.

Another explosion shook the ground, and Ricky sprinted for the bush. As he neared the tree line, he tripped over a fallen branch hidden in the tall grass. Sprawling face-first on the ground, he was scrambling to his knees to keep running when he noticed it wasn't a branch he'd tripped over. It was the body of another rebel.

He rolled the boy over to see his face. Thomas stared back. "Thomas!" Ricky cried. "Hold on!"

The boy who had survived lion hunts and a python attack back in their village convulsed beneath Ricky's helpless hands. Blood spilled from the corners of his mouth and gushed from a gaping wound on his side. With every breath, the blood retreated into his body, but even more sprayed through his lips as he let it go. As Thomas exhaled one last time, a grenade exploded to Ricky's left.

Ricky threw himself over his friend. "Help!" he screamed as rebels ran past. "Please!"

No one stopped. Grabbing his friend by the front of his shirt, he tried to lift him, but his arms, weak from starvation and exhaustion, could not move Thomas's lifeless body. Another grenade exploded in front of them, kicking up dirt and stone. Deafened by the blast, Ricky scrambled back and ran for the protection of the bush.

As he entered the jungle, a group of rebels intercepted him. The commander led him back to camp, where he lined Ricky up with the other abductees. Blood covered Ricky's chest and legs. He ran his hands over his body and discovered the blood was not his own.

As Teacher moved down the line, questioning the fighters, Ricky reinspected himself. It was impossible that he'd escaped the firefight untouched, yet there he stood, not a mark on him. He reached up and touched his forehead. His fingers lingered on the smear of shea nut oil from the yard ceremony. It was still slick, but when he pulled his hand away, it wasn't oil that glistened on his fingertips. It was blood. Ricky wiped his face. More blood smeared across his hand.

"Were you hit?" Teacher asked.

"No."

"Is that the blood of our enemy?"

"No."

"Where is the rebel whose blood this is?"

"He's dead," Ricky said.

"Then he was a nonbeliever," Teacher said, moving past Ricky to address the other surviving fighters. "Those who died on the battlefield today were not true believers of Kony. They died because of their lack of faith. And they were killed by our enemy. The government troops killed them."

"Yes, Teacher!" Ricky responded with the others, but his words were hollow. Anger knotted in his stomach at the truth of his friend's death.

A government bullet may have claimed Thomas, but the LRA killed him.

# SAMUEL

The afternoon breezes no longer carried the heat of day from the compound. It settled, hot and heavy, on the porch and clung to Samuel's skin. His captor returned with two bottles of water. He handed one to Samuel. Samuel sipped his water, noticing how it slid, clean and clear, across his tongue, leaving behind no grit or unpleasant taste. When he finished, he placed the empty bottle beside his chair and pretended to be lost in the game on the field. He hoped the man would go back inside and leave him in peace until the soldier came for him, but the man sat down and joined Samuel in watching the boys play. The longer they sat in silence, the more the index finger of Samuel's right hand twitched.

*Tap, tap, tap, tap.*

*Tap, tap, tap, tap.*

Faster and faster it struck the rusty metal bar. The man glanced over, and Samuel grabbed hold of his hand and shoved it in his lap.

Looking away, the man stood and crossed the porch. He returned with a small circular table. "It's hard to watch others play and not want to join in the fun." He placed the table between Samuel and himself. Painted black squares, faded and chipped with wear, decorated the tabletop, creating a crude checkerboard.

The man sat down opposite Samuel and poured a handful of red and black wooden chips from a small burlap bag onto the table. "I like checkers. It gives me something to do with my hands when I talk." He smiled at Samuel. "What color would you like to be? Red or black?"

Samuel, still holding his trembling hand in his lap, refused to answer, so the man continued. "I think I'll be red today." He arranged the pieces on the board in front of him. Finishing with his side, he reached across the board and arranged the black pieces before Samuel. "That way you get to make the first move."

Samuel did not respond.

"If you don't know how to play, I can show you."

Samuel shifted in his chair, turning his back to the man.

"It's an easy game to learn," the man continued as though he hadn't noticed. "I've taught many children here, and I'm embarrassed to say they usually beat me on the first game. Would you like me to teach you?"

Samuel's hands tightened into fists in his lap. He didn't want to play checkers or draw pictures, and he definitely did not want to talk.

"You are the black pieces," the man said, "so you begin the

game. You can only move at a diagonal, like this." He slid one of his red pieces forward at an angle.

Samuel squeezed his eyes closed in frustration.

"The object of the game is to capture the other player's pieces." The man lifted his red piece over one of Samuel's black pieces and then picked up the black piece. "Pretty simple, don't you think? Though sometimes it can take a few turns to get the hang of it."

Samuel slammed his hand down on the table and glared at the man. "I know how to play! My father and I used to play all the time." He turned away again, angry with the man for not leaving him alone and furious with himself for losing control.

The man returned the pieces to their original squares. "You *used* to?"

Samuel stiffened at the man's question and its implication.

He ran his trembling hand over his head and wished he still had his dreadlocks. For thousands of kilometers, they'd protected him from suspicious glares and accusing stares. During the day, they'd masked his fear, and at night, they'd hidden his tears. They'd been as much a part of him as the machete that once pulled at his waist and the rifle that dug into his shoulder. And just as the rebels had stolen his weapons, his captors had taken his dreads. They'd stripped them from his body, leaving him small and vulnerable, with only his secrets to protect him. And now the man wanted to steal those, too.

Seconds stretched into minutes, and Samuel began to wish

that the man would start talking about checkers again. Anything to end the silence.

"How long has it been since you played checkers with your father?" the man finally asked in a gentle voice.

Samuel drew in a long breath. He dared not look at the man when he answered.

"Three years."

# 18

# RICKY

*Obeno.*

The whisper of home kept Ricky's legs moving forward over unforgiving jungle terrain and hundreds of kilometers.

Determined to put as much distance as possible between his brigade and the government troops, Komakech marched the rebels day and night, stopping for only an hour at a time for food and rest. When they reached Palabek Padwat, near the Uganda-Sudan border, Komakech ordered Otim to take eight rebels on a scouting mission to determine the location of the pursuing government troops while he led the remaining Gilva rebels south, deeper into the Ugandan bush. As Otim moved down the line of rebels, Patrick held Ricky's panicked gaze for a heartbeat, and Ricky concentrated all his thoughts on prayer.

*Please, God. Please spare my brother from this mission.*

Otim studied every face he passed, sniffing out his spies. By the time he neared Patrick's position in the line, seven young rebels trailed behind him.

*Please don't take my brother. Please, God. Not my brother.*

The wild man stopped beside Patrick. "You," he said, pointing to him. "Come with me."

"Yes, Afande." Patrick removed the bundle of sugarcane from his shoulder and handed it to the boy beside him.

As his brother stepped from the line, Ricky stopped praying—no one was listening. Patrick looked straight ahead as he walked down the line, but as he neared his little brother, he whispered, "Obeno."

His voice weak with restrained tears, Ricky answered. "Obeno."

And then Patrick was gone.

In the wild man's absence, Kilama took over the role of disciplinarian. The quiet rebel with the machine gun paced up and down the line, resting one hand on his firearm and the other on the panga tucked in his belt.

As darkness swallowed the jungle, the rebels watched for Komakech's signal that they would be making camp for the night, but it never came. After several hours, the boy marching in front of Ricky stopped without warning. Ricky leaned back with his bundle to avoid running into the boy, a move that nearly put him on the ground.

The boy, whom Otim had ripped from his village two days before, dropped his sugarcane and bent forward. His face, disfigured with fresh cuts and swelling from his abduction, contorted in pain as he pressed his fists into his stomach.

"Pick up the cane," Kilama said, a flat chill in his voice.

The boy wrapped his arms around his waist and fell to the ground.

Kilama grabbed him by the shirt. "Get up."

"My stomach," the boy groaned between labored breaths.

"Are you sick?" Kilama asked.

"Yes, Afande."

A shiver coursed through Ricky at the emptiness in the young commander's eyes. They held no empathy or warmth as they stared down at the boy clutching his stomach. No emotion reflected in their gaze, not even anger or hate. Only emptiness, cold and lifeless.

"Do you need to rest?" he asked.

"Please, Afande," the boy begged. "Just for a minute."

Kilama held a small radio up to his mouth. After a brief exchange, he tucked the radio back in his pocket. "You will rest now."

Lifting his head, the boy had begun to thank the commander when he noticed the panga in Kilama's hand.

"I'll march, Afande," he said, scrambling toward his bundle of sugarcane. "Please."

The commander grabbed him by the arm. "Carry his cane," he ordered Ricky as he dragged the boy into the bush. Ricky picked up the bundle and stepped forward to close the gap left by the sick boy. Behind him, the boy screamed once, and then Kilama, his panga streaked with fresh blood, rejoined the line.

They marched through the night. Ricky fought to keep both

bundles of cane in his arms as he navigated his way through the dark jungle. By morning, fatigue and hunger began to win the tug-of-war for his body. The bundles slid farther down the front of his chest with every forced step as he strained to keep his hold. The muscles in his arms, shoulders, and back burned. But instead of trying to ignore the pain, Ricky embraced it. He focused on it as a welcome distraction from the persistent thirst that scratched his throat and swelled his tongue. It allowed him, for a moment, to forget the unrelenting hunger pangs that twisted his stomach, demanding his attention.

Ricky's foot caught on a tree root hidden beneath the sea of undergrowth that flowed across the jungle floor. He fell and dropped his bundles, bringing the line behind him to a halt. Aware of the punishment such a delay warranted, he crawled forward to his sugarcane. As he pulled the bundles from a tangle of vines and greenery, the muscles in his back twisted into tight knots, paralyzing any movement or breath. He squeezed his eyes closed, praying for the muscle spasms to subside. When they did, he opened his eyes and found Kilama's worn boots standing before him.

"Get up," Kilama said.

Ricky tried to stand, but another spasm cut through his back and he crumpled once more to the ground, struggling to draw breath.

"Are you sick?" Kilama asked.

Ricky shook his head.

"Do you need to rest?"

"No, Afande," Ricky gasped.

Kilama drew his panga, still stained with the sick boy's blood, from his belt. "Get up," he ordered.

Ricky pushed up from the ground, and Kilama pointed his panga at the bundles of cane. Ricky feared that he would be unable to lift the heavy bundles before Kilama decided to use the machete. Digging his blistered fingers into the coarse, braided rope that held the cane together, Ricky hefted the load into his arms and, on shaky legs, stood once again before his commander.

"Now, march," Kilama demanded.

Hiking the bundles higher in his arms to secure his hold, Ricky obeyed.

They marched for six days with little rest or food, aside from wild fruit they plucked from trees and bushes as they wove their way farther south through the jungle. The leafy canopy shielded them from the sun and the military helicopters patrolling the skies, but the jungle concealed other dangers. Pythons, poisonous spiders, and the metal teeth of traps left behind by hunters threatened the barefoot abductees' every step. Their dehydrated, starved bodies strained to balance the sugarcane and pilfered supplies on their heads, backs, and arms. Only the constant threat of Kilama's panga kept their feet moving.

On the seventh day of marching, they exited the bush into a clearing near the Aswa River. Hills on either side of the river embraced the valley in shadows. As the sun broke through the clouds, Komakech held up his hand, and the line of rebels stopped.

"The wind is still," Komakech announced, "and the sun is high. We will stop to rest and cook some food."

The abductees' bodies slumped in relief as they slid the heavy loads from their arms and shoulders and rushed to the river-bank. With cupped hands, trembling with fatigue, they scooped its water to their chapped lips. Ricky drank too fast. When the retching stopped, he eased his hands back into the river and forced himself to take small sips as the water leaked through his fingers.

"You have twenty minutes to cook and eat," Komakech yelled.

Without waiting for further instructions, the rebels set to work. The girls plucked and cleaned chickens they'd stolen that morning from a village in Bolo and sorted small piles of cassava to cook while the boys gathered firewood. Ricky stepped forward to help, but Komakech stopped him and four other boys.

"Spread out around the area and take observation posts."

"Yes, Afande," Ricky said. Ignoring the protests of his stomach, he left the fire and the first real food he'd seen in days.

He found an old tree at the crest of a hill. Scaling it to the top, he leaned back against the trunk and scanned the surrounding land for any sign of danger. After several minutes, the scent of roasting chicken reached the tree, and Ricky's stomach twisted with hunger. As he leaned into the smoky air and inhaled deep and long, savoring the aroma, he spotted a man emerging from the bush. Ricky was too far from the man to determine if he was a government soldier, so he worked his way behind the thick foliage to where he could observe the man unseen.

The man, half concealed by jungle shadows, paused for a moment. The only movement was that of his head, which swept the clearing a full 180 degrees before turning back to the jungle. A moment later, fourteen other figures joined him. Ricky shielded his eyes from the glare of the noon sun, but he could not identify the group as it made its way across the clearing. Though the sun and distance hid their identities, they did not mask the weapons the strangers carried. The silhouette of a panga extended from the first man's arm. The others held assault rifles. As they drew closer, Ricky recognized the tall, broad-shouldered physique and steady gait of his brother leading the line.

He scrambled down the tree and waited for the group. Patrick held his little brother's relieved stare for a breath, but did not say a word as he passed. A line of new abductees, bound together by rope and chain, trudged behind the rebels. Not one looked up at Ricky as they shuffled past his position beneath the tree.

Otim brought up the back of the line. A fourteen-year-old girl stumbled along behind him, her head hung low. Her wrists were bound together in front of her with one end of a short length of rope. Otim held the other.

The wild man gave Ricky a curt nod as he passed, and the girl glanced up at him. Her eyes, swollen from crying, had the same dark beauty that Christine's eyes had once held. Ricky's world tipped at the glimpse of his baby sister in the girl's eyes. Reaching behind him, he steadied himself against the tree.

"Come on," Otim spat. And with a jerk of the rope, the girl followed the wild man.

## 19

# RICKY

Days bled into weeks, and weeks bled into months. Between battles, the Gilva brigade swept through unsuspecting villages in the Kitgum district like a storm, leaving only death and destruction in its wake. And at every village, it left with more stolen sons and daughters. Ricky's fear of Patrick leaving on intelligence missions was numbed by the constant rub of their routine, though he breathed easier when the spies returned and he was reunited with his brother.

One evening, as they moved on from a village in northern Kitgum, gunshots echoed in the distance. Otim's scouts had reported military in the area early in the day. Uncertain of whether the shots signaled villagers or government troops in pursuit, Komakech called for Lujimoi.

"The new abductees are slowing us down," he told the rebel. "I need you to buy us some time. Take thirty fighters and set up an ambush."

"Yes, Afande."

Lujimoi pulled thirty rebels from the line for his mission. Ricky was among them.

Before they left, Komakech issued Lujimoi a warning. "Our scouts spotted the commander with the two-tipped spear in the area. If he is among the troops following us, you know what must be done."

"Yes, Afande," Lujimoi answered, and with a wave of his hand, he signaled for his small battalion of rebels to fall in line. He handed each fighter a rifle and six rounds. After three months on the front line without a weapon, the old AK-47 felt heavy in Ricky's hands. He'd become quite proficient at field stripping and reassembling the weapon during his week of training, but Trench had never allowed the abductees to fire one.

"You will only pull the trigger if you are certain you can hit your mark. Wasted ammunition will not be tolerated."

Ricky took several deep breaths in an attempt to quiet the shaking of his hands as he loaded his weapon. Then, gripping his rifle, he followed Lujimoi and the other fighters back toward the village.

Columns of black smoke stretched to the sky, marking the locations of the homes and families the rebels had set ablaze. Lujimoi stopped them at a cornfield outside the village. The dry season had gripped northern Uganda, leaving many of its fields barren. He ordered the abductees without stolen fatigues to remove their shirts to help them blend in with the scattered grasses and the few remaining bushes dotting the field.

"Spread out in a line!" he ordered. "Find a position three meters from one another."

Brittle stumps of dried cornstalks scratched at Ricky's bare chest as he lay on his stomach and inspected his AK-47 to make certain it would fire when the enemy arrived. He had grown accustomed to the sound of gunfire. At least he now had the means to protect himself. But as he lay in wait, a new thought emerged. Could he set the sight of his rifle on another person? And could he pull the trigger?

Doubt reignited his fear. He had no answer for the questions pressing down on him in the field. He stretched his fingers to break the tension settling in his muscles and forced himself to ponder Komakech's warning about the commander with the two-tipped spear.

At night, Ricky often heard talk of the man with the two-tipped spear. The older rebels spoke of him in whispers.

*Hundreds of rebels have died by his hand. Thousands.*

*He walks across the battlefield firing his rifle with one hand and wielding his spear with the other.*

*Bullets fear him, and grenades fail to explode before him.*

*He made a deal with the devil. In return for invulnerability, he must kill every one of the Holy Spirit's servants.*

*He is a witch. His spear is his source of power. He carries it with him always.*

*He takes no prisoners and leaves no survivors.*

Ricky prayed he would never face the man so terrible that the mere mention of him caused rebels' voices to tremble. With

140

each minute that passed, the image of the magical man with the two-tipped spear grew in Ricky's imagination until he swore he could hear the slow, steady boot steps of the witch approaching.

Clutching his weapon, he peered behind him, concerned that the enemy had skirted around the LRA's position and planned to ambush them from the rear. He saw no one. As he returned his attention to the stretch of field in front of him, a loud bang shattered the silence.

The sound came from the rifle of Okema, the young rebel immediately to Ricky's left.

Lujimoi scrambled across the field straight toward Ricky's position.

"Why did you fire?" he demanded.

Ricky started to explain it wasn't him, but Lujimoi pointed his rifle at Okema.

"It was you," he said.

His eyes wide with shock, Okema, who was no older than Ricky, stared down at the weapon in his hands.

"Why did you fire?" Lujimoi repeated, grabbing the boy and pulling him to his feet.

Okema opened his mouth to answer, but no words came.

Lujimoi threw him to the ground and kicked him in the stomach. "How dare you waste a bullet of the LRA! You will pay for your mistake."

Two older rebels rushed forward to help Lujimoi dole out Okema's punishment. They kicked the boy and struck him with their weapons until he spat up blood. Delivering one last kick, Lujimoi held up a hand, and the rebels stepped back.

"You will fight on every front line without a weapon until you find thirty bullets to replace the one you fired. Do you understand?"

Blood dripped onto the ground from Okema's split lip. Lifting his head, he looked up at his commander. "Yes, Afande."

Wiping the boy's blood from his rifle, Lujimoi addressed the rest of the rebels. "It is a bad omen to have a bullet fire under unclear circumstances. Grab his weapon. We're leaving."

As the rebels fell in line behind Lujimoi, Ricky picked up Okema's rifle and helped the injured abductee to his feet.

Clutching his stomach, Okema limped behind Ricky. Neither boy spoke. Ricky could not find the words to comfort the boy Lujimoi had just sentenced to death. He doubted such words existed.

# 20

# SAMUEL

The man rearranged the checker pieces on the board. "My father taught me to play, too. He was a skilled player, but always lost when we played. I suspect he let me win."

Samuel took one of the black pieces from the table and ran his thumb over the rough edges where the paint had worn away, revealing the pale wood beneath.

"We don't have to play now," the man said, holding out his hand. "But you'll let me know if you change your mind?"

Samuel placed the checker in his palm and returned his attention to the children playing on the field.

A sudden explosion of gunfire echoed across the compound. By the second round, Samuel jumped up, bumping the edge of the checkers table as he scrambled behind his chair.

He pulsed with fear as he crouched low. They'd found him. They'd always find him. He pulled his legs in closer, ignoring the fresh pain searing through his thigh.

More gunfire.

"Samuel," the man called out over the shooting, "it's all right."

Samuel peered around the back of the chair. The man had turned to face him, but remained seated. Beyond the porch, the boys continued to chase the ball across the field, and the woman under the shea tree made no move to rush the children in her care to safety. The razor-wire fence might be keeping them trapped inside the compound, but they could not all be so foolish as to think the fence would keep the rebels out.

"It's not what you think," the man said, picking up the toppled table and checkers.

Another explosive burst.

Samuel ducked back behind the chair and cradled his head in his arms. He pressed his palms to his ears, but could not hide from the sights and sounds of battle replaying in his head. The man eased the checkerboard table aside and knelt beside him. Samuel scrambled back, his eyes wide with fright.

"You have my word. You're in no danger." He handed Samuel his crutches. "Come. I will show you what's happening."

# 21

# RICKY

Okema stole five enemy bullets from the bodies of fallen soldiers during the Gilva brigade's next battle before a sixth bullet caught him above his left eye.

As the government troops pressed forward on the rebels' position, the abductee next to Ricky pried the five bullets from Okema's lifeless hand before running for the safety of the bush. Grabbing the weapon of another fallen rebel, Ricky followed.

As the LRA attacks on villages increased, so did the Ugandan government's efforts to stop the rebels. Patrick spent his nights on patrol, monitoring the government troops, and Ricky spent his days fighting them. With each battle, Ricky searched the enemy lines for the man with the two-tipped spear, afraid of an encounter with the untouchable witch, but he never saw him, and soon questioned whether such a man existed or if the rebels had created him as another tactic to frighten abductees.

The war took a heavy toll on the outnumbered and outgunned rebels. The military had an endless supply of weapons and ammunition at its disposal, while the LRA's supply was limited to what it could scavenge. With each battle, the rebels lost fighters and weapons. Fighters were easily replaced. Weapons were not. After months of fighting on the defensive, Komakech decided the time had come to change tactics.

Early one afternoon, Trench summoned Ricky.

"Put these on," he said, handing him a full army uniform.

Ricky recognized the uniform as Ugandan military. He had witnessed rebels stripping dead and dying enemies of their clothes and boots after victorious battles. Every stolen uniform bore remnants of its former owner: his smell, his sweat, his blood. As he snaked his arms into the large uniform, he hesitated at the sight of a dozen jagged holes and blackened spots mottling the front and back of the shirt. Pushing their origins from his mind, he rolled the long sleeves to his wrists and tucked the cuffs of the baggy pants into the oversized boots. Pulling on the bloodstained military cap, he joined Teacher and twenty-six other rebels, all of whom also wore stolen uniforms. Ricky watched the hundreds of other rebels milling around the camp, surprised they weren't also preparing to fight.

"You've proven yourselves loyal to Kony," Trench said to the boys gathered before him, "both on and off the battlefield. Tonight you will prove your loyalty to the LRA."

Ricky's hands felt cold and unsteady as he held his weapon. For months he'd stood on the LRA's front line with nothing to protect him but his faith in Kony. What further proof of loyalty could they possibly require?

"The Holy Spirit lives in our leader, Joseph Kony," Teacher said as Ricky stood before him. "If you believe in him and the Holy Spirit, no harm to you will come in battle. Do you believe in our leader, Kony?"

"Yes, Afande."

Ricky's voice no longer wavered. With every unanswered prayer to God and every battle he survived without injury, the conviction behind his answer grew. Kony was the only one listening, so every time Ricky entered the yard, he made sure his voice was heard.

After Teacher anointed the rebels, Trench led his troops in a traditional LRA song:

> *Tell me some things good about Jesus Christ, my God!*
> *Tell me something good about my God.*
> *My God, they have shot me because of you; they have*
> *beaten me because of you.*
> *Tell me something good about Jesus Christ.*

Then, in a single line, they moved through the darkness, silent as shadows. Ricky's concern about their mission grew with every step. Never had Komakech sent such a small group of rebels to face the enemy.

After an hour of walking, Trench held up his AK-47 and the line stopped.

"We are going to raid the Pabor Health Center for medical supplies," Trench said. "The hospital is small, but it's in the middle of the village and there will be many soldiers guarding it, so we'll have to overpower them first."

Ricky looked at the small band of rebels around him. Most were no older than Patrick. Komakech sent teenage boys to attack grown men. Men trained by the military and armed with weapons that never jammed or misfired. It was a suicide mission.

"We will be outnumbered," Trench explained, "but we will have the element of surprise." His puckered scar stretched taut against his excited smile. "When we've driven the soldiers away, we'll raid the hospital. You won't meet resistance inside. The hospital treats mainly expectant mothers and malaria patients. No more than ten patients and two or three staff will be present."

Ricky pictured his brother walking through the village, asking the villagers questions about the hospital and the soldiers stationed there, knowing every word they shared would be used to build a plan to attack them. He recalled his brother's ashen complexion and dull eyes when he returned from his last intelligence mission, and Ricky understood. He might have to pull the trigger, but Patrick had to aim the rifle.

"You will have five minutes to grab as many supplies as you can. Leave the people. We won't have time to take anyone before military reinforcements arrive."

This last news eased Ricky's guilt over attacking the village. No parents would lose their children tonight.

The rebels kept to the tall grass, crossing roads but never

following them, as they made their way to the village. When their target was in sight, Trench led them to the nearby bush. "We'll wait until dawn to attack."

Keeping within their line, the rebels lay on their backs with their weapons resting across their chests, awaiting Trench's signal.

For hours, Ricky watched the moon creep across the night sky. At its peak in the star-strewn heavens, it nestled inside a cloud, casting a bright ring of white light onto the hazy veil. Ricky remembered his father's warning that such a sign foretold the death of a chief. Staring up at the haloed moon, Ricky wondered which chief fate would claim tonight—the unsuspecting army commander in the village or Trench?

As the rebels crept into the village, dawn seeped up from the horizon, casting the underbellies of the night clouds in burnt orange and golden hues. Ricky stayed his trigger finger, determined not to be the first to fire. He did not want to make the same mistake Okema had made, nor did he want to suffer the same punishment.

It was Trench who fired the first shot. The second his bullet exploded from the chamber, heralding the raid, Ricky and the others also fired.

The LRA's brazen attack and stolen military uniforms disoriented the soldiers, who outnumbered the rebels five to one. The soldiers posted just inside the village fell before they could raise their weapons.

Screams filled the morning air as parents gathered their

children in their arms and ran for the protective wilds of the surrounding bush. Ricky charged forward, sprinting between huts and dodging terrified villagers and dead bodies. A few soldiers attempted to hold their ground, but were quickly overpowered. The remaining soldiers followed the fleeing villagers into the jungle.

With the area secured, Ricky and Trench rushed into the hospital while Vincent guarded the door.

"Quiet!" Trench warned a pregnant woman. He aimed his weapon at her head and she clasped a hand over her mouth to stop her cries.

"Hurry!" he told Ricky. "They'll be regrouping in the bush. We need to leave before they come back."

The raiders shoved containers of pills into their pockets and grabbed as many boxes of supplies as they could carry. As they exited, Ricky noticed two young rebels among the dead.

Trench and Vincent grabbed their weapons as angry voices and gunfire rose up from the jungle behind the hospital.

Trench motioned to Ricky. "Let's go!"

Ricky quickened his pace to join his commander in retreat, but as he neared the edge of the village, he stopped and glanced back at the two dead rebels. He had trained and fought with them on the front lines since his abduction. Their abandoned, lifeless bodies sparked a memory of a common burial ritual in his village.

"What are you doing?" screamed Vincent as Ricky ran back to the dead rebels. Pulling out his panga, he cut a handful of small branches and leaves from a tree and knelt beside the boys' bodies. The pain and fear of dying remained etched on their young faces.

He placed the branches and leaves on their chests. "May your spirits find peace," he said. "I'm sorry." Then he ran to join the survivors.

# 22

# RICKY

Ricky's participation in the successful raid on the hospital and his courage on the battlefield gained him the respect of his fellow rebels and the attention of his commanders. In the days and weeks that followed, Komakech gave him the title of OP, Operation Post, and put four young rebels in his charge. They had one job, to position themselves several kilometers away from the commanders' position at camp and alert them to any sign of government troops. If they saw anyone they did not recognize, they were to shoot without hesitation.

Late one morning, as Ricky and the four boys kept watch in the tall grass on a hill above the LRA camp, he spotted a large group of armed soldiers walking down the road. He motioned to the boys to stay low, and then he peered through the scope on his AK-47. The scope had been added to his weapon for guard duty.

He recognized Lujimoi leading the coy of fifty rebels, who carried baskets and sacks of pilfered goods from their raid on the center in Pabor. When the last of the rebels disappeared into the bush, Ricky and the boys settled back into their hiding place. For hours, they lay on their stomachs. No one spoke or moved. They only listened and waited.

As the morning stretched on, Ricky's head swam with exhaustion and hunger. He shook it to clear his mind and sharpen his senses, but the jostling only increased his dizziness.

"Obeno," he whispered to himself. "Obeno."

The word led his thoughts from the field where he lay starving and weary and guided him back to his village. Back home.

He pictured Father waving to him from the fields, and his sisters climbing his and Patrick's favorite mango tree. He imagined Mama emerging from the girls' hut, her eyes glistening with tears as she held out her arms, reaching for him.

The rhythmic marching of feet and low murmur of voices broke through Ricky's daydream. He looked around at the young boys in his charge and held a warning finger to his lips. Their eyes widened with fright, but they nodded in reply.

Ricky eased the grass before him apart and peered through the small opening. He didn't recognize the uniformed man leading the steady stream of troops marching down the road.

*. . . Ninety-one . . . ninety-five . . . ninety-nine . . .*

Ricky lost count as more and more soldiers appeared on the horizon. He had one order—shoot anyone he didn't recognize—but he also had only one weapon and four unarmed boys. His finger hesitated on the trigger. He would be no match for an army of that size. He looked to his right, where the boys awaited his decision, and with a flick of his hand, he signaled them to retreat.

Staying low, the boys crept through the grass. Ricky sat up to follow, and a fresh wave of dizziness swirled through his head. He squeezed his eyes closed and took a deep breath, praying the spinning would stop before the soldiers spotted him. When the light-headedness had dissipated, he followed the path of matted grass left by the boys. As soon as they were clear of the troops' view, Ricky led them down the hill and into the jungle.

"Government troops!" he yelled as he entered the camp. "Government troops!"

The rebels jumped to their feet and grabbed their weapons.

"Where?" Komakech demanded.

Ricky pointed back toward the road. "They're right behind us, Afande."

As Komakech scrambled his troops, Otim charged Ricky. "You led them here?" he screamed.

"No. They didn't see us, Afande, but they're headed in this direction."

Otim grabbed the front of Ricky's shirt and pulled him close. "Why didn't you stand and fight?"

"There are hundreds of them, Afande. We wouldn't have stood a chance."

"Of course you wouldn't," Otim snarled. "But the gunfire would have warned us." He pushed past Ricky. "You always stand and fight, you coward."

Komakech positioned the rebels on both sides of the road to

ambush the approaching troops. As the first armed man rounded the corner, Ricky targeted him through his scope. He released a slow, controlled breath and was about to squeeze the trigger when he heard a sharp whistle.

"Stand down!" Komakech yelled. "They're LRA."

When both LRA groups returned to camp, Otim dragged Ricky before the commander.

"Well?" Komakech asked.

"I thought they were government troops, Afande," Ricky said. "I should have known they weren't."

"You should have fired on them," Komakech said, his voice cold and measured.

"But they're LRA."

"Your orders were to fire on anyone you didn't recognize nearing our camp. Did you recognize them?"

"No, Afande, but—"

Komakech held up a hand to stop him. "You ignored a direct order from your commander. You must be punished." He whispered a brief order to Otim and then joined the commander of the visiting LRA group.

Otim smiled. "Now you'll get what's coming to you, coward."

Ricky's mouth went dry. He tried to swallow and failed.

Otim turned to a group of rebels in Trench's coy. "Vincent! Come here."

The bully from Ricky's village well stepped forward. He'd grown taller over their months of captivity, and he'd grown crueler.

"Kneel!" Otim ordered.

Vincent knelt before the wild man. Otim pulled a long piece of sugarcane from a bundle stolen during Lujimoi's raid and beat Vincent across the back. Aware that the wild man would restart the ten lashes if he cried out or reached back to protect himself, Vincent bit his bottom lip until he drew blood. With each strike, his hands shook in clenched fists at his side.

Ricky stepped forward. "Afande, he wasn't even there. Why are you beating him?"

"Because," Otim said, striking Vincent a tenth time, "I want his blood boiling with rage when I give him the cane to beat you. Take off your shirt!"

Ricky removed his shirt and knelt before Vincent. Blood ran down Vincent's back and dripped from the stalk of sugarcane clutched in his hand.

"Your brother can't help you this time, baby." The force of the first blow knocked Ricky to the ground. Vincent did not wait for him to get up before he delivered the second. He struck Ricky countless times. Ricky only felt the first ten. With his punishment for cowardice carried out, Otim ordered Ricky and his coy back to the hill to keep lookout. The boys didn't say a word as they followed Ricky up the steep slope, and they looked away when he cried out in pain each time the strap of his rifle pressed against his raw skin. His back torn and swollen from the beating, Ricky lay on his stomach in the tall grass. Only the sting of pain kept unconsciousness at bay, and only the numbness of months of physical and psychological abuse restrained his tears.

After an hour, the crunch of boots on gravel and muffled voices carried over the grass.

"Obwona," Ricky whispered to the boy closest to the road, "are those our troops?"

The thirteen-year-old peered through the grass but could not see, so he stood for a better look.

"You!" a man's voice yelled. "Stop!"

Obwona's bare feet rushed past Ricky's hiding place in the grass. They were followed by a gunshot.

The moment Obwona's body hit the ground, two other boys scrambled to their feet and ran for the LRA camp. No warning was called out this time as they were instantly gunned down.

Oryema, a new abductee and now the only member of Ricky's charges still alive, looked to his commander with panicked desperation.

Ricky motioned to the boy to follow his lead.

Holding his automatic rifle close to his chest, he crawled toward the top of the hill. When they reached the crest of the hill, they stopped.

"I don't think they saw us," Ricky said, gritting his teeth against the pain. "Run."

Oryema's eyes darted to the torn, bloody flesh of Ricky's back.

"I promise you won't be punished," Ricky said, "but you have to warn Komakech. Tell them we're sure this time. Go. I'll stay and fight."

Oryema crouched low and scrambled down the hill. Ricky's vision pulsed in and out of focus as he stared down at the steep terrain. Behind him, he heard the rustle of soldiers searching the field. He had to move. If he didn't, the enemy would find him. Taking a deep breath, he pressed his weapon to his chest and rolled down the hill. With each rotation, the thick blades of spear grass, jagged rocks, and sharp thorns tore at his exposed wounds.

When he reached the valley, he hid behind a tree and watched the first troops arrive at the top of the hill. He raised his weapon and held his breath, waiting to see if the pursuing soldiers had spotted him. The crack of a gunshot and explosion of tree bark to his left verified they had.

He returned fire, and the soldiers dived for cover. Before they regrouped, Ricky stumbled into the bush. He felt less exposed in the thick woods, but knew the soldiers would soon follow. He pressed forward, determined to find the LRA and praying they wouldn't mistake him for the enemy and shoot.

As he staggered through the jungle, he listened for pursuing soldiers or approaching rebels, but all he heard when he neared the LRA camp was frantic cries for help. He peeked out from behind a tree he was leaning on for support. The rebels had abandoned the camp, leaving behind some supplies and six female abductees. Their arms flailed in the air as they ran in circles in the small clearing.

"What are you doing?" he yelled. "Run!"

They didn't hear him over their own pained screams.

He stepped into the clearing. "Run!"

That's when he heard it—a low, angry hum. Broken on the ground at the girls' feet lay two gray cones, like giant hatched eggs. To save ammunition, the LRA often resorted to using whatever natural weapons they had at their disposal. The hum grew louder. Ricky stumbled back, but it was too late. They were upon him. Thousands of wasps. The retreating rebels had left the destroyed nests as bombs to delay the government troops. The girls, abducted as "wives" for the LRA commanders, were simply abandoned, easily replaced at the next village.

The dark cloud of wasps swarmed Ricky. He swatted at the air, but with every piercing sting, he knew he was failing. If he didn't escape the wasps, within minutes he'd be dead.

The buzzing roared in his ears as they stung his neck, head, and face. Squinting through swelling eyes, he spotted an old canvas bag. He dropped to the ground and rolled toward it with the frantic desperation of a man on fire. When he neared the bag, he grabbed it, pulled it over his head, and continued to roll. Through the canvas, he listened for the buzzing to subside. When it did, he got to his feet and ran to the tree line. Free from the wasps' rage, he removed the bag.

He shouted to the girls to follow his example.

The oldest, one of Komakech's wives, heard him and dropped to the ground. The five younger girls did the same. After several minutes the buzzing stopped, and the girls' screams weakened into sobs.

When Ricky was certain the wasps were gone, he approached the girls, who remained curled up on the ground. Large welts covered their arms, legs, and faces. Ricky could feel the tight swelling of stings on his own lips and around his eyes. In the distance, he heard the sharp pop of gunfire.

"Can you walk?" he asked.

"I think so," Komakech's wife mumbled through swollen lips.

"Which way did they go?"

She pointed toward the bush, where the tall grass lay flat from the rebels' hasty retreat, creating a visible trail. It would be easy to follow. Gunfire echoed in the distance. The government troops would find the camp soon, and Ricky had no doubt they'd find the trail and pursue.

He paced before the girls, scanning the perimeter of the campsite. He spotted a thick, overgrown wooded area to his left and stopped. He could run with the girls. The LRA would assume them all dead. He'd be free.

He gripped his rifle. This was his chance. His opportunity to escape. His promise to keep.

Another round of gunfire broke the silence, and the girls' cries grew louder.

"Patrick," Ricky whispered, "I'm sorry." Then he helped the girls to their feet and led them down the LRA's trail.

# 23

# SAMUEL

**Fighting every instinct, Samuel followed the man toward the** gunfire. As they neared another yellow building, a new sound rose above the noise. Screaming.

Samuel stopped. The man motioned him to follow before disappearing around the corner of the building. Samuel glanced back at the adults and children milling about the compound. They continued with their work and play, oblivious to the attack taking place. He swung forward on his crutches, but his pace slowed with every barrage of gunfire and responding cry. The man stood with his back to Samuel, his attention focused on the scene playing out before him.

On a dirt field, men and women standing in a wide circle beat on large plastic gas containers and metal trays with sticks.

*One-two-three! One-two-three!*

*Ra-ta-ta! Ra-ta-ta!*

Inside the circle, boys wearing long headdresses of elephant grass and carrying sticks made to look like guns and pangas slunk toward a group of boys and girls without costumes or props. The armed children screamed orders and threats as the adults banged on their containers and trays.

*Ra-ta-ta! Ra-ta-ta!*

With each strike, another unarmed child cried out and fell. The mock attack drew Samuel forward until he stood beside the man.

The boys with their grass dreadlocks and stick weapons forced the children who remained standing to their knees. They yelled at their captives, and the adults continued hitting their containers while young girls poured water over the chests, legs, and heads of the children lying still on the ground. The water bled through their clothes, darkening the fabric and ground beneath them.

When the reenactment ended, the children helped one another up and gathered before the adults. An older man collected their grass dreadlocks and stick weapons, and a woman instructed the children to form a circle. The children wiped tears from their faces as they sat down. The adults took seats behind them and placed comforting hands on their backs and shoulders. Samuel counted more than thirty boys and girls seated around the circle.

"Most of these children were abducted from their homes," the big man said. "Some were born into the LRA, but they were all slaves in Kony's army." He grew silent for a moment. "When men join a military, officers train them for months, preparing their minds and bodies for the rigors of war, but even with all that training, what they see and hear and do can be too much for their spirits." He motioned toward the boys and girls on the field. "These activities can be difficult, but they start the healing process, and once former abductees begin to repair their spirits, they can begin to repair their lives."

The man stood there in his clean clothes and calm silence, pretending to understand, pretending to know, but Samuel knew he could never understand. He could never know. He made children draw and act out their nightmares. He studied their reactions and passed judgment. He stared as they cowered behind chairs and listened as they stumbled over words in a feeble attempt to explain their crimes. And for what?

To expose their pain?

To punish their sins?

Hatred burned in Samuel's stomach as he turned to leave, but his anger outpaced his injured leg and limited experience with the crutches, sending him pitching forward. Embarrassed, he fumbled to regain his footing.

The man walked behind him. Samuel quickened his pace but could not outrun the man's easy strides.

"We are just trying to help, Samuel."

Samuel stopped. "You think any of this will help them forget what the LRA did, what Kony took from them?"

The man's shoulders raised and fell in a defeated sigh. "No, but we're trying to help them recover the most important thing they've lost."

"What?" Samuel asked.

"Hope."

# 24

# RICKY

**Six months after Ricky's and Patrick's abduction, the Gilva** brigade joined Kony's Control Altar brigade in its march north to the border with Sudan. In the days and weeks following their abduction, Ricky and Patrick had hoped they might catch a glimpse of Andrew or John marching by in another brigade or hear their voices calling out to them on a battlefield, but after months with no sign of either boy, the brothers knew they'd likely met a fate similar to Thomas's and they stopped looking.

As they marched alongside the Control Altar rebels, Ricky instead turned his attention to finding their commander. He had never seen Joseph Kony, but from the rebels' stories of the leader, he imagined him towering above all others. Only a powerful giant of a man could possess the Holy Spirit.

Yet as Ricky searched the thousands of faces in the Control Altar group, all he found were scrawny rebels looking like those in Gilva: hunger hollowed their cheeks, and years of malnutrition yellowed the whites of their eyes. Filthy, matted hair, hanging in heavy, knotted dreads and crawling with lice, rested on their shoulders, and bug bites and scabies mottled their cracked, ashen skin. They wore bloodstained Ugandan military uniforms stolen from dead soldiers after fierce battles.

As the two brigades trudged down dirt roads and through tall grass, one after the other, Ricky wondered if he now looked like these other wild creatures. He also wore a stolen uniform, but he'd traded his old uniform for one he'd found in a fallen soldier's backpack. It didn't bear the holes of fatal shots or the stains of a dead man's blood. Ricky hadn't bathed in months, and he'd scratched himself raw in an attempt to ease the constant itch. His stomach always ached with hunger, and his skin clung to his hip bones and ribs. He doubted anyone from his village would recognize him if he were to return home.

Home. He pushed the thought from his mind before the image could take form. He couldn't allow his wandering thoughts to betray him, especially with Kony so close. With each step, he focused on trying to determine where the LRA leader hid among the elite group. The Control Altar rebels bore the signs of having been in the bush for years and having fought in many battles. Ricky was grateful his body was not marred like those of the veteran rebels, who were missing chunks of flesh or bore festering sores. Their faith in Kony must have wavered on the battlefield. Ricky's would not.

In some of Control Altar's leaders, Ricky recognized the frantic desperation he'd seen in the wild man's eyes on the day of his abduction. As the rebels trudged along in unison, these men stalked up and down the line with fidgety paranoia, their ferocious gazes burning with the need to kill. The leaders searched for the smallest infractions—a poorly handled weapon, a misstep in cadence, a sideways glance. They sought weakness in the pack on their hunt for the next kill.

Staring straight ahead, Ricky kept time with the rebel in front of him, careful to avoid the predators' ravenous eyes.

When they reached the border, with the addition of the Control Altar group, their numbers had swelled to more than two thousand. After a sparse meal of roasted goat meat and mashed cassava, the rebels gathered in a large field. As they waited for Kony to speak, Ricky searched the crowd for his brother.

"Have you seen Patrick?" he asked Labeja, an abductee who'd been taken a month after Ricky.

"No. Have you seen Kony yet?"

"No."

"I heard he's almost as tall as a giant," Labeja whispered. "And once, he read the mind of one traitor out of a whole battalion. He said the rebel was plotting to assassinate him, so he had him tied to a tree and cut in half."

"They say the Holy Spirit speaks to him," whispered Dominic, another young rebel. "Is that how he reads minds? Do you think he's reading ours right now?"

Dominic's words stopped Ricky's search for his brother. If Dominic was right, Ricky's thoughts betrayed not only himself, but also Patrick. He buried his concern for his brother in thoughts of the LRA commander. *I am loyal only to Kony*, he repeated over and over in his mind, in case the leader was listening.

As though the rebels around him heard his silent praise, a chant rose up from the crowd of thousands.

"Kony! Kony! Kony!"

At the front of the crowd, a circle of tall teenage boys armed with machine guns stepped forward. Mangy dreadlocks rested on the shoulders of their tattered and mismatched soccer jerseys. They wore military pants and boots and trained their weapons on the thousands of chanting rebels. One of the teenage rebels held up his hand. "Sit!" he cried after the group had fallen silent.

The rebels gathered in the clearing took seats on the ground, and Ricky emptied his thoughts. He held his breath in anticipation as the front two guards stepped aside, revealing a man.

Ricky found it difficult to judge the man's height from his seated position in the crowd, but he appeared slight in comparison with his armed guards. He wore camouflage military fatigues and an army-green military cap. Like Komakech's uniform, a braided rope looped loosely around the man's right shoulder, but his rope was blood red. His dark skin hid his features in the shadow of his cap, which covered a head of closely cropped hair. He wore a neatly trimmed mustache and an almost serene expression as he stared out at the crowd. Had he not been standing in the midst of thousands of LRA rebels, Ricky would have thought him a commander in the Ugandan military.

The man walked into the center of the seated rebels, and the cheering resumed. "Kony! Kony! Kony!"

Ricky looked around at the rebels, surprised by their reaction. He'd noticed this man when they first joined the Control Altar group. He'd marched among them, calm and quiet, blending into their ranks with no fanfare. At fifteen, Ricky was almost as tall as the man the rebels now cheered. This man could not possibly be the vessel of the Holy Spirit. He could not be Joseph Kony.

But he was.

"The Holy Spirit is with us tonight," Kony said.

The cheers grew louder.

"The Holy Spirit sees into your hearts. He knows who among you are loyal and who among you are traitors to his cause."

*Kony is my leader. Kony is right and just. The Holy Spirit lives in Kony.*

Ricky repeated his pledge as the LRA commander spoke to his troops.

"You must all fight hard for the Holy Spirit. You must not fear our enemies. There is no room in the LRA for cowards. Cowards should go back to their mothers' wombs."

Cheers rolled across the field until all two thousand rebels were chanting Kony's name again. After a moment, Kony raised his hand, and the voices quieted.

"Our enemy is no longer only within the government troops. Our enemy is in every village and town in northern Uganda. Our own people have betrayed us to our enemies, so now they are our enemies."

Kony paced around the circle, his voice growing in strength and conviction with every step.

"Every person who stands between us and our mission of ripping Museveni from his throne and building a Uganda ruled by the Ten Commandments not only betrays us, they betray the Holy Spirit. And we will strike them down for their betrayal! We will make them pay for their sins! Every man, woman, and child who chooses to fight on the side of the devil will die with him!"

*Kony is my leader. Kony is right and just. The Holy Spirit lives in Kony.*

For three hours the LRA leader preached, his voice ringing with the fervor of a man possessed. His eyes grew large as he stared unblinkingly over the crowd, and his hands shook as he paced before his troops, ranting and raving.

"The Holy Spirit has given me a message for you!" he yelled at the end of his sermon. "A command to punish those who have betrayed his word and his army." He raised his panga, and the rebels silenced their cheers.

Ricky stopped repeating his pledge to Kony in order to hear his holy order. The sky around him filled with thousands of raised machetes, blocking Ricky's view of the LRA leader, but the blades did not shield him from the Holy Spirit's command, screamed into the night.

"Go and kill!"

# 25

# RICKY

Kony's words whipped the death-starved rebels into a frenzy. Armed with guns and machetes, many rushed into the jungle in the direction of the nearest Acholi village to fulfill his commands. The remaining rebels dispersed in search of a small patch of hard ground to claim for the night while Ricky worked his way around the camp, searching for his brother. The thought of Patrick alone in the bush with those blood-crazed rebels on the prowl made Ricky's heart pulse faster with each strange face he passed. After thirty minutes of searching, he spotted Patrick on the far edge of the crowd.

"There you are," he said after he made his way over, his voice ragged with relief.

"What's wrong?" Patrick asked.

He lay down next to his brother. "Nothing. I just couldn't find you. I thought maybe you'd—"

Patrick gave him a warning glance.

"There are just so many of us now," Ricky explained.

"I know. It would be easy to get *lost* in this crowd." He met Ricky's eyes. "Make sure you don't."

Ricky followed Patrick's gaze around the camp and noticed thirty or more armed rebels circling the perimeter. Komakech and Otim were among them, but so were some of the wild rebels who'd stalked them on their march. The starved looks in their eyes told Ricky they had yet to satiate their hunger for blood.

"It would be dangerous to get lost now," Patrick whispered.

Ricky nodded. As he closed his eyes, he heard a rustling to their left. The girl with Christine's eyes, whom Otim had stolen for a wife months before, crept out from the shadows. Crouched low, she moved toward Patrick.

"Go away," Patrick whispered to her.

"Please," she said. "I can't find my brother."

"He's probably sleeping," Patrick said.

"No. I haven't seen him since we got here. He was with you on an intel mission, wasn't he?"

"Yes."

"Did he come back with you?"

Patrick closed his eyes, feigning sleep. "We split up. I went south. Timothy went north."

"Do you think the enemy found him?"

Tears glistened in her eyes, and in his head Ricky saw his baby sister crying as the rebels shoved her into his hut. His chest tightened as he remembered Christine's little hands clinging to the torn folds of their mother's skirt. He looked away before the unbearable pain crushed him.

"I didn't see any troops," Patrick said. "Now go before you get us in trouble."

"He always lets me know when he is back," the girl whispered, more to herself than to Patrick.

All three fell silent, and the girl edged back into the shadows as one of Kony's guards walked past. When the guard was gone, the girl spoke. "Please," she whispered. "The other girls and I are being traded to the Control Altar brigade tonight. I need to know my brother is okay before we go."

"I can't help you," Patrick said, turning away from her. "Now go, before Otim comes looking for you."

At the mention of her LRA husband, the young girl stiffened. Bowing her head in despair, she crept back into the dark.

"Why were you so mean to her?" Ricky asked.

"She needs to act normal. We all do, or others will become suspicious."

"Why is Komakech giving the girls to Control Altar?"

"He doesn't want any of them to form attachments, so they're traded every few months."

Ricky had seen how the rebels treated the female abductees. The girls' burden far outweighed that of the boys. On the front lines, the rebels forced them to fight alongside their male counterparts, often without weapons. As they marched over hundreds of kilometers, it was the girls who carried the bulk of the supplies, and when they set up camp, it was the girls, weak with hunger, who prepared the food for the commanders and rebels before they were allowed to eat whatever remained. But these roles were nothing compared with their main purpose in the LRA.

Every night the female abductees bore a burden the male abductees were spared, a burden so heavy it extinguished the light in every girl taken by the rebels. Ricky shook his head to free himself from where his thoughts were taking him and from where the dwindling evening would undoubtedly end.

"Do you think her brother"—Ricky hesitated and glanced around to make sure no one was listening—"got *lost*?"

"I don't know. All we can do is keep quiet, and hope it's morning before they realize Timothy's gone."

"Patrick," Ricky whispered, his voice tight with fear, "Kony sent rebels into the bush tonight. If they find Timothy, they'll make us cut him apart, like Joseph."

Patrick grabbed a handful of soil and ground the dirt and rocks into his palms. He lowered his voice, urging Ricky to lean closer to hear his words.

"We must pray that if Timothy really did get lost, he's never found."

As Patrick slipped into a restless sleep, Ricky peered up through a jagged hole in the thick foliage far above him. He longed to hide within his brother's embrace from the feeling of loss that burned in his chest in the quiet of night. He began to slide his leg across the ground to touch Patrick's, but the thought of Kony listening to his thoughts somewhere in the surrounding dark paralyzed him where he lay.

Smoky clouds drifted across the moon, and Ricky remembered how Patrick and he would lie by the wangoo and stare up at the night sky through empty glass bottles, searching for the mother in the moon. Mama swore she was there, watching over her children in Uganda, even if they could not see her. For hours, the brothers would peer up through the glass bottles, determined to be the first to find her seated on the moon with a baby nursing at her breast and a child standing at her side. But they never saw her, and as they grew older, they abandoned their quest, leaving the bottles and search to their little sisters.

As Patrick's breathing eased into a slow rhythm, Ricky searched the shadows of the moon for the mother and her children and listened for the sound of Timothy's footsteps crashing through the jungle, driven back to the camp by serpents or Joseph's vengeful spirit, but the only sounds to meet his ears were those of the bush.

The patter of rain tumbling through the canopy of leaves filled the night air. The rhythmic echo of chirping frogs in a nearby swamp accompanied the raindrops' rapid beat. Each sound was a note from a familiar song, a lullaby whispering memories of home, as though Obeno was calling to Ricky from the earth herself. He squeezed his eyes closed, allowing the sounds to wash over him, but before long another song claimed the night.

It began with one voice. The hopeless wail of a girl, pleading for help she knew would never come. Ricky thought of the girl with Christine's deep brown eyes disappearing into the inky black, where Otim waited to trade her. The voice was soon joined by others. For over an hour they clawed at Ricky's sleep from the shadows as dozens of young wives were raped again and again by their abductors. Their pained voices, a chorus of dying souls, cried out from the depths of darkness. Ricky covered his ears, but their pleas echoed in his heart.

As the cries subsided, the rain grew steadier, and Ricky gazed up once again through the jagged hole in the sky. The moon was no longer visible. She hid behind a river of dark clouds, but Ricky knew the mother in the moon was there. He could feel her tears raining down upon his face as she wept for her lost daughters.

# 26

# SAMUEL

The aroma of roasted chicken greeted Samuel and the man before the woman with all the questions had a chance to welcome them.

"Time for dinner," she said as they neared the porch. "I thought you might be ready to eat."

Samuel's stomach writhed with hunger as he took his seat.

Before the man joined him, he bent down and picked up the bottle of painkillers Samuel had thrown off the porch. Without a glance at Samuel or a word about the medicine, he put them in his pocket, smiled at the woman, and patted his stomach. "I know I am."

She placed two bowls on the checkers table.

Samuel did not wait for the man to sit before shoveling handfuls of rice and chicken into his mouth. When he'd raked the last grains of rice from his bowl, he noticed the man and woman watching him.

"Would you like more?" the woman asked.

He lowered the bowl from his lips and his eyes to his lap. His stomach begged for more, but he placed his empty bowl on the table and shook his head.

"I'm quite hungry," the man said. "Would you bring me two more bowls, please?"

The woman picked up Samuel's empty bowl. After she left, the man pushed his bowl of untouched food across the table. Steam, thin as morning mist, rose from the rice. Samuel didn't know when he'd have hot food again, much less a cooked meal. His mouth watered with need, but he refused to reach for the bowl.

"Eat," the man said. "It may be late by the time you arrive in your village tonight. You should eat what you can now."

Samuel's eyes traveled from the bowl to the man and back.

"A growing boy like you needs food." The man patted his stomach again and smiled. "I do not."

Hunger overpowered shame, and Samuel grabbed the bowl. As he ate, the woman returned with two new bowls and a plate of millet bread. Not wanting to see the pity he knew he would find in her eyes, Samuel took a chunk of bread without looking at her. While she and the man talked about a gathering scheduled for the evening, Samuel ate. He ate until he thought he might be sick. And then he ate some more.

"Will you be staying tomorrow night, as well?" the woman asked the man as she picked up Samuel's empty bowl.

"No. I must return to Kampala in the morning, but I'll be back in a week."

Samuel stopped eating at the mention of the Ugandan capital. He forced himself to swallow the thick paste of rice and bread in his mouth as his stomach rolled in nauseous waves. His first instincts had been right. The man worked for the government. He was here to hand Samuel over to the soldier, who would put him back on the front lines. Samuel had reached out to place the last chunk of bread back on the plate when it occurred to him it could be days before he ate again. With the adults' attention on their conversation, he shoved the bread into his shorts' pocket.

The woman, noticing the empty bowls and plate, smiled. "Are you full?"

Samuel nodded.

She collected the dishes and returned to the building.

When the man had emptied his own bowl, he reclined in his chair. Letting his head fall back, he closed his eyes and sighed.

Samuel watched him for a minute before clearing his throat and asking the question that had been rattling through his mind since they'd left the abduction reenactment. "Why do you give them hope?"

The man handed him a new bottle of water. "Because any hope they had was replaced with fear. Fear is a powerful weapon."

Samuel thought about this.

*Machetes dangling from the belts of men.*

*Assault weapons clutched in their hands.*

*Stalks of sugarcane stained red with blood.*

Unable to stop his trigger finger from tapping on the side of the plastic bottle, Samuel placed the bottle on the table and gripped his armrests.

The man glanced at Samuel's finger. "They tell them tall mountains will spring up before them if they try to escape and wide rivers will appear wherever they walk. They warn them the Holy Spirit will send poisonous vipers and the ghosts of those they've killed to drive them back to the LRA. And when they return, they promise to cut them."

A tremble took hold of Samuel's hand. He gripped the armrests tighter.

"And if the abductees manage to outrun the snakes, and mountains, and spirits," the man continued, "the rebels warn them the villagers will greet them with anger and mistrust when they return home. That their own people will condemn them for their sins and punish them for their crimes."

No longer able to contain the anxiety vibrating through him, Samuel tapped his finger against the armrest.

The man placed his hand over Samuel's. "Fear is a powerful weapon, Samuel. But so is hope."

Samuel pulled away. The man's hand lingered on the armrest for a second before returning to his lap.

"I'm sorry," he said. "I don't mean to upset you."

Samuel unscrewed the cap of his water bottle and took a long drink. Fear had kept him alive for the last three years. Its relentless chafing against his mind sharpened his senses, and its persistent whispers warned him of danger. He trusted his fear more than any person, even a gentle giant with words of hope. But the more time he spent with the man, the quieter his fear grew, and that frightened Samuel more than anything.

# 27

# RICKY

"Obeno."

Patrick whispered the word to Ricky every time Otim sent him on another intelligence mission.

"Obeno," Ricky repeated every time he watched his brother leave.

Time slowed without Patrick. During the day, Ricky longed for the chaos of battles, when his survival instinct took control, shutting out doubt's whispers that he'd never see his brother again. He dreaded the monotony of marches and the quiet of night, when fear conjured images of Patrick suffering at the hands of the enemy or dying alone in the bush. With each day that passed, his doubt and fear grew. When the intelligence group finally returned, he searched every face until he found his brother's. Only then could he breathe easily again.

His moments of relief, however, were brief. Komakech's strategy in northern Uganda relied on good intelligence, and the LRA commander depended on Patrick and the Gilva spies to secure that intelligence. As soon as they delivered the information needed for his next attack, the commander sent them on another mission.

One October afternoon at the border between the Kitgum and Gulu districts, the Gilva brigade faced a large number of government troops. The high-pitched shriek of Komakech's whistle signaled the rebels' attack.

"Go! Go! Go!" Ricky screamed. Crouching low, he waved his coy forward as they fired on the first troops to emerge from the bush. For every soldier the rebels cut down, three more stepped from the jungle. Equipped with assault rifles and rocket launchers, they stepped over their fallen comrades in wave upon wave of military might. Ricky had never faced an enemy so numerous or well equipped. Within minutes, the low rumble of helicopter blades joined the din of battle as two gunships swooped in low over the field and opened fire.

"Get down!" Ricky screamed. He and his coy of a dozen young fighters dropped to the ground and covered their heads as a spray of bullets cut across the field in two lines, meters from their position. When the helicopter had passed, Ricky looked to the boys on either side of him. "Anyone hit?"

They shook their heads.

"Stay low and keep moving."

Grenades and rockets exploded around them as they pressed forward, and the summer sky filled with dark smoke and the screams of the injured and dying. Ricky aimed his automatic weapon at the approaching troops and pulled the trigger.

Nothing happened. He ducked back under the grass to strip his weapon and fix the jam. As he worked, the boy next to him had raised his rifle to fire when an enemy bullet struck him in the neck. The twelve-year-old dropped his weapon and grabbed his throat. Blood gushed through his fingers as he fell to his knees. He looked to Ricky and then collapsed in the tall grass.

Ricky crawled over beside him. "It's okay," he said, pressing his hand over the boy's throat. "You'll be okay." But the boy's eyes dimmed and blood no longer pulsed from the wound. Removing his hand from the boy's neck, Ricky ripped several blades of grass from the ground and laid them on the boy's chest. "May your spirit find peace. I'm sorry." Then he picked up the boy's rifle and rejoined the fight.

Over the next twenty minutes, Ricky repeated his prayer and apology over the bodies of six more boys. When the shrill of Komakech's whistle finally signaled their retreat, he'd lost half of his coy. His senses dulled by gunfire and death, Ricky sprinted for the cover of the Ugandan bush.

As he and his remaining troops returned to the LRA camp, the battle continued to rage. Entering the camp, Ricky spotted Patrick. He hadn't seen his brother in five days. The tension of the battle left his body, and his shoulders slumped in relief. Strapping his rifle across his chest, he wiped his bloody hands on his pants and started toward Patrick, but stopped when he noticed Otim.

The wild man spoke to Patrick and then pointed in the

direction of the battle. Patrick stiffened and his jaw tightened, but he nodded once and then continued to listen to his commander.

Ricky walked over to where Trench was packing up supplies. Ricky didn't trust Trench. Ricky didn't trust anyone but Patrick, but he felt less anxious speaking with Trench than with the other commanders. During the Pabor Health Center raid, he had earned the disfigured commander's respect, and over the months that followed, the two had formed a bond of camaraderie on other missions and battlefields. "What's going on with them?" he asked, motioning toward his brother and Otim.

Trench looked up from his bag. "Lapwony is ordering Patrick back to the battlefield."

Ricky cringed. He hated that Otim had started demanding that the abductees call him Lapwony, the Luo word for "teacher." It burned on his tongue every time he called the sadistic wild man the name the villagers had used for his father. Only people who'd earned the respect of a community deserved the title. The abductees did not respect Otim. They feared him.

"Why is he ordering Patrick to go back?" he asked.

Trench shrugged and returned to packing for their retreat.

Ricky inched closer to Otim, but stopped when Patrick noticed him behind the commander.

Otim set down his AK-47, reached into a pouch on his belt, and handed Patrick two grenades. "Return with the number of troops in the next twenty minutes or you'll be punished."

The wild man's command eliminated all doubt and fear in

Ricky's mind. With his hands still sticky with the blood of seven boys, only rage remained. "No," he said, his voice trembling with anger. "You can't send him back there."

Patrick stopped, and Otim turned and glared through his dreadlocks at Ricky. "I don't remember asking your opinion, boy."

In the ten months since he'd first seen the wild man on the road beside his home, Ricky had grown. He no longer had to look up to meet Otim's yellowed eyes. He stared directly into them as he stood toe-to-toe with the man who'd killed his family.

"Walk away," Otim said, turning back to Patrick.

"No," Ricky said.

Otim's chest swelled and his face twisted with hate, an expression that vanished the second he wheeled around to find Ricky's rifle pointing at him.

"Ricky," Patrick asked, "what are you doing?"

Ricky kept his eyes and weapon aimed at Otim. "You're not going back there, Patrick."

Otim trembled with barely contained fury. "Lower your weapon, boy, or I'll make sure every rebel in the LRA takes a cut out of you."

Ricky held his stare. "No."

Patrick stepped forward and grabbed hold of Ricky's gun. "Are you trying to get yourself killed?" he whispered.

Ricky wrestled the weapon from his brother's grip and aimed it again at Otim. "I won't let you go back there."

"It's my mission," Patrick said.

"It's a suicide mission!"

Patrick lowered his voice. "Put down the weapon and let me go."

"No."

"You can't stop me," Patrick said, shoving past Ricky. He took one step, but froze under the chill of metal on the back of his head. Slowly turning, he stared down the barrel of his little brother's weapon.

"If you take one more step," Ricky said, "I'll kill you where you stand."

Patrick's eyes widened in disbelief.

"Are you mad?" Otim asked. "Lower your weapon, or I swear I'll put you down like a rabid dog."

Ricky kept his attention fixed on Patrick as he answered the commander. "If Patrick goes back, he'll be killed, but you know that, don't you?"

"I gave you an order!"

"If you're sentencing my brother to death," Ricky said, "I might as well kill him myself." He swung his gun toward Otim, who stood unarmed beside Patrick. "I might as well kill both of you."

For once, Otim had no reply.

"Ricky," Patrick said, "stop this before it's too late. Let me go."

"No," Ricky said, pointing his gun alternately at his brother and Otim.

The three stood staring at one another for several moments. Ricky's pulse throbbed in his ears, and his breathing grew ragged as a large group of rebels gathered around them to see how the showdown would end.

"What's going on here? I ordered a retreat!" Komakech pushed through the gathering crowd. He stopped when he saw Ricky holding a weapon on Otim and Patrick.

"What's going on?" he repeated, his voice calmer than before.

"This boy's gone mad," Otim said. "He's threatening to kill me and his brother."

"Why?" Komakech asked.

Otim stepped forward to answer, but Ricky pointed his gun at him, forcing him back beside Patrick.

"Lapwony," he said, spitting out the bitter word, "ordered Patrick to return and count the government troops. He'll be killed before he gets to three, and Lapwony knows this."

The rebels surrounding them tightened their circle. Ricky's eyes darted around at the faces watching him, wondering how many he could shoot before they took him down, but Komakech raised his hand and the rebels stopped their advance. He lifted his nose in the air and stared down it at Ricky. "You'd kill your own brother?"

Ricky tightened his grip on the rifle to stop his hands from shaking. Any sign of weakness, and Otim would attack. He raised his chin to answer Komakech. "He's dead if you send him back. Better he die at my hands than our enemy's."

Staring down the length of his weapon, Ricky braced

himself for Komakech's judgment, but the commander laughed, wrenching the rebels' attention from the standoff.

Patrick, Otim, and Ricky gawked at their leader as the deep, crusty laugh rattled in his broad chest.

"Lower your weapon," he said. "Patrick's not going back to the front."

"What?" Otim asked.

The sound of gunfire and explosions rumbled in the distance.

"We've lost enough fighters today," Komakech said. "We'll send out scouts after we've gained some distance."

The second Ricky lowered his rifle, Otim grabbed it. He then pulled the panga from Ricky's belt and pressed the blade to his throat.

"No," Komakech said.

"But he has to die," Otim said. "We must make an example of him."

"We will," Komakech said, measuring up the young rebel before him. "Get the new abductees."

A smug smile slithered across Otim's face as he lowered the blade. "Yes, Afande."

Ricky's mind reeled as the wild man hurried off to gather the forty-six abductees they'd kidnapped from various villages over the last two months. What had he done? In his attempt to spare Patrick a death at the hands of the enemy, he'd sentenced himself to a death at the hands of the rebels. The wild man pushed the abductees in front of the older rebels, who'd congregated to witness Ricky's punishment.

"Everyone's here," he said, returning to Komakech's side.

"Good." Komakech turned to Patrick. "Join the others."

Patrick hesitated. He looked at Ricky, but Ricky dared not meet his brother's eyes. He knew the betrayal and pain he'd see in them would destroy his resolve to meet his death with dignity.

"Join the others," Komakech repeated in a voice that left no room for argument.

"Yes, Afande." Patrick stepped back and stood with the rebels, and Komakech turned his attention back to Ricky.

Slowly circling the young rebel, he raised his voice so all could hear. "I am building an army for Kony. An army of strong, fearless soldiers to fight for the Holy Spirit. There is no room for cowardice in the LRA."

As the commander spoke, Ricky stared straight ahead, his eyes unfocused on the mob of terrified abductees and eager rebels watching him.

"I am building an army of soldiers who will take up their weapons without hesitation, without question."

Panic surged through Ricky's veins with every step Komakech took. His muscles tightened, but he didn't move. He was unarmed and surrounded by eighty rebels with machetes. He wouldn't make it one step before their pangas cut him down.

"I am building an army of soldiers who will charge onto the battlefield to meet our enemy, not run from them."

Komakech stopped so that his face was centimeters from Ricky's. "Soldiers who will stare the devil himself in the eye and not blink."

From the edge of his vision, Ricky saw his brother. Patrick had moved through the crowd so that he stood before Ricky. Tears that Ricky could not shed stung his eyes at the pain etched on Patrick's face. Otim would never give Ricky the chance to explain his actions to his brother and apologize for his weakness. As Komakech stared down at him, Ricky said a silent prayer.

*Please, God, please spare my brother the pain of cutting me.*

Otim's eyes narrowed as he ran his thumb along the edge of Ricky's panga.

*Mama, Baba, please let my death be quick.*

As Komakech turned to give Otim the order of execution, Ricky closed his eyes.

*Patrick, may your spirit find peace. I'm sorry.*

Drawing in a shaky breath, he opened his eyes.

"Rebels like Ricky," Komakech said, slapping a hand on his back, "will help us build such an army."

Ricky's thoughts seized in disbelief.

"Give him back his weapon," Komakech ordered.

When Otim did not act, Komakech repeated his demand. "Give him back his weapon and put more soldiers under his command."

With Ricky's panga still clutched in his hand, the wild man watched Komakech step up to the circle of rebels. The crowd parted, and the commander walked through, shouting a last command over his shoulder as he left. "Pack up. We're moving out."

The rebels scrambled to fulfill his order, and Otim stepped up to Ricky. Leaning forward, he spoke in a low, cold voice. "You may have fooled Komakech with your little act of bravery today, but I've seen where your heart lies, and it's not with Kony." He threw the panga at Ricky's feet and glanced over at Patrick, who was shoving supplies into a backpack.

"You will slip up eventually," Otim said. He pressed his mouth close to Ricky's ear. "And when you do, I'll be there."

# 28

# RICKY

Following the confrontation with Otim, Komakech assigned Ricky more responsibilities. Ricky performed each task under the constant scrutiny of the wild man, aware that the smallest mistake would result in severe punishment. Otim also dissected Patrick's every move, causing Ricky's brother to distance himself further from Ricky. They stopped whispering their secret vow to each other, afraid the wild man might hear. Instead, Patrick would nod once as he passed Ricky, a movement so subtle anyone watching perceived him to be looking at the ground or stretching his neck, but Ricky knew what the head dip meant.

*Obeno*, he repeated in his mind, nodding once in reply.

As the Gilva brigade marched north through Gulu district, Komakech called Ricky to the front of the line. "I have a new assignment for you."

"Yes, Afande."

"I want you to move on ahead of the brigade and scout the next village. Look for any sign of the enemy or armed villagers.

We don't want to march into an ambush. Locate any food or supplies we can use, and find potential targets to abduct. We lost many rebels in the last battle."

Ricky thought of the dozens of boys and girls they left dying in the bush with no one to bury their bodies or mourn their loss.

"I'm counting on you to find us replacements, and Commander Kony is counting on you to help build his army."

"Yes, Afande," Ricky said. He looked back at the long line of rebels. He couldn't spot Patrick, but saw Otim watching his conversation with Komakech.

"Go," Komakech said, slapping him on the back. "And make sure you stay out of sight."

"Yes, Afande," Ricky said, eager to escape the wild man's threatening glare.

As he ran through the jungle to the next village, Ricky reviewed his mission.

*Look for any sign of the enemy or armed villagers.*

*Locate food and supplies.*

*Find potential targets to abduct.*

*Stay out of sight.*

When he reached the edge of the jungle, he peered through the bush. The village was small, but many people milled about, putting wood on a fire and preparing food for dinner. The smell of cooking meat made Ricky's mouth water, but he pushed his hunger aside and scanned the area for signs of danger.

The villagers wore civilian clothes, and he spotted hunting

and fishing spears outside several huts, but no weapons. It would be an easy village to raid. Komakech would be pleased.

Finishing his surveillance, Ricky turned his attention to a group of young boys fishing in the river. The boys weren't tall, but they were lean and strong. They showed no apprehension about wading deep into the murky waters with their fishing spears. Ricky judged them to be in their early teens, the perfect age to strengthen Kony's army.

Ricky watched the boys and remembered running home from school to finish his chores so he could rush off to meet his friends at the Agago River. A wistful smile touched his lips as he recalled long days spent swimming and fishing with Patrick and their friends, but the smile withered with the realization that even if Patrick and he escaped, they would never fish with Thomas again or hear him tell of his epic battle with the python. They'd never collect sticks for the wangoo with him or go hunting for edible rats. Thomas was now just a memory. Nothing more.

Ricky pressed his hands against his legs as the image of his friend's blood gushing between his fingers formed in his mind. When it faded, he wondered if Andrew and John had met similar fates. He thought back to the last time they were all together, sitting on the side of the road, laughing at Andrew's and Thomas's antics and waiting for news from the market. And then the smiling man on the bike had appeared.

In the river, one of Ricky's targets splashed his friends. The boys threw down their fishing spears and started wrestling in the water. Their laughter reached Ricky in his hiding place, and a realization, heavy and cold, pressed on him. They were unaware of the evil coming for them, just as unaware as Ricky and his friends had been when they waited on the side of the road eleven months before.

Glancing behind him, Ricky listened for the approaching rebels. The bush was quiet. In his need to distance himself from Otim, he'd run faster to the village than he'd realized, but he knew Komakech and the others were not far behind.

*I will not be the smiling man on a bike*, he thought as he stepped from the bush. The moment he was free from the jungle, he ran.

"Run!" he screamed at the boys in the river. "Run!"

The boys froze. Water dripped down their faces into their open mouths as they gaped at the wild man running toward them.

Ricky waved his arms in the air. "Run! The LRA is coming."

The mention of the LRA shocked the boys into action. They scrambled up the riverbank and sprinted for home.

Ricky followed them into the village. "Run!" he yelled, pointing away from where the LRA would be arriving. "Go!"

Whether it was in response to his appearance or his warning, the villagers abandoned their food and, grabbing their children, fled for the safety of the bush. Ricky raced through the small village, throwing open every hut door.

"Go! Now!" he yelled when he found families huddled inside.

When he'd driven all the villagers from their homes, he ran

back to his hiding place by the river. He ducked behind a tree at the edge of the jungle and took several deep breaths. He could look winded from the run; Komakech would expect it, but he couldn't afford to look nervous. Komakech might dismiss it, but Otim would not.

Three minutes after he returned to his scouting spot, he heard the rustle of bodies pushing through the foliage and stood to greet his commander.

"What did you find?" Komakech asked.

"It's a small village, Afande. I spotted some fishing and harvesting tools, but no weapons."

"Excellent. Let's get ready to move in."

"But, Afande," Ricky said, "there are no people."

Komakech stopped. "What?"

"Someone from another village must have warned them we were coming."

Otim, who'd been listening to the exchange, stepped up beside his commander. "Strange. We've never had that problem before. I wonder who could have warned them."

Ricky kept his attention on Komakech. "I don't know. When I arrived, they were already gone."

"The military is sending troops into villages all over northern Uganda to warn them of our presence," Komakech said. He turned to his junior commander. "I want you and some of your rebels to go on ahead and find out where government troops are headed and what they're telling the people in the villages they pass. We may have to change tactics. We'll meet you in Kitgum in five days."

"Yes, Afande."

Otim left with four rebels, including Patrick, who nodded once as he passed Ricky. Ricky nodded and watched with guilt as his brother left. As grateful as he was for being free of Otim for five days, he worried for his brother's life under the wild man's command.

After the intel group disappeared into the jungle, Komakech pushed past Ricky. "Are you sure there's no one?" he asked, marching into the village.

"As far as I can tell, Afande. By the looks of it, they left in a hurry." Hoping to lessen the anger simmering in Komakech's cold eyes, he pointed to the food by the fire. "But they left many supplies and food."

"Take everything you can carry," the commander ordered. "We'll find people at the next village."

As the rebels looted the homes, Komakech sent Ricky down the river to scout the next village. The commander was enraged when he and the rebels arrived an hour later to find the second village as abandoned as the first. Over the next three days, the Gilva commander's anger grew as the rebels acquired more supplies, but few teenagers in their raids. Frustrated, he decided Ricky would be more valuable training the handful of abductees they did capture than scouting empty villages.

With Ricky no longer scouting before raids, the number of abductees sent for training grew. Komakech attributed the increase in new abductees to his decision to press east, away from where government troops were patrolling. But when they joined Otim and his spies in Kitgum two days later, the suspicious glint in the wild man's eyes told Ricky he believed the change had less to do with the enemy and more to do with the removal of Ricky as scout. On the front line, Ricky noticed another disturbing trend. Komakech was no longer sending him teenagers to train.

He was sending him children.

# 29

# SAMUEL

After dinner, a group of young girls emerged from a building to the left of the porch. Dressed in lavender skirts that hung below their knees and matching wraps tied snug around their chests, the girls followed a woman across the clearing toward Samuel and the man. The woman wore a similar dress, but a bright yellow ruffle encircled her waist. As they approached the field, the boys playing soccer stopped their game.

Samuel shifted in his chair, bracing himself for more simulated gunfire.

The man smiled but didn't say anything.

A group of older boys, dressed only in blue shorts and thin headbands, joined the girls on the field. Three long black feathers tucked in the backs of the bands stood tall above the boys' shaved heads. Leather straps, like those of the rebels' assault rifles, rested across the boys' bare chests, but they did not secure weapons. They held small drums.

The woman with the yellow ruffle spoke to one of the boys,

who nodded and ran over to Samuel. He held out his drum, and Samuel noticed he was missing two fingers.

"Do you want to play?" he asked.

Samuel wedged his hands between his knees, and the boy looked to the man for help.

"Thank you, Charles," the man said. "Will you be practicing for a while?"

"Yes, before the others arrive."

"That's a fine idea. Samuel and I may join you later." He reached out and took Charles's maimed hand in his. "I look forward to enjoying your performance tonight."

A proud smile appeared on Charles's mouth as he ran back to rejoin the group.

"What others?" Samuel asked.

"We have some guests joining us later," the man said. Samuel waited for him to explain further, but the man clapped his large hands together and asked, "Do you sing?"

"No."

"Never?"

Samuel did not reply.

The door behind them creaked, and the boy turned, expecting to see the woman with all the questions, but instead he found himself staring into the startled eyes of a girl he hadn't seen in three years. Her name had faded from his memory, but not her light brown eyes and dimpled chin. The last time he'd seen his sister's friend, she was eleven and rebels were tearing her from her mother's arms.

She wore a lavender outfit, but unlike the girls in the field, she also had a pale green and white gingham cloth tied around her waist. The cloth, which bulged in front, secured the small, rounded body of a sleeping infant.

"Amina."

The man's voice broke the shock holding the girl in the doorway, and her name shook free memories of Samuel's childhood spent sculpting clay animals in the garden and playing tag on the walk to school.

"Have you brought us more bread?" the man asked.

She nodded and gave the man his bag and then handed Samuel one. "For your trip home."

Samuel's palms became slick with sweat at the mention of returning home. Amina knew he could not return, so why was she keeping his secret? She stared at him for a moment without saying another word and then, placing a protective hand around her baby, she joined the other girls gathered on the field.

"Do you know Amina?" the man asked.

Samuel shook his head.

"She came to us six months ago after escaping the LRA. She was pregnant and very scared."

The weight of the man's words pressed Samuel back in his chair. "Why didn't she return to her village?"

"Amina is very ill. She will stay with us here, where we can care for her until she is well enough to care for herself and her baby."

Samuel watched Amina talking with another girl. Her tan

eyes flitted to the porch and quickly looked away. The girl wrapped an arm around Amina and pulled her into a hug. Amina rested her head on the girl's shoulder.

"Will she get better?" Samuel asked.

"There is no cure," the man answered, "but there are medicines that will help."

"What's wrong with her?"

"Amina not only escaped the LRA with a child. She escaped with AIDS."

Samuel watched his childhood friend kiss the top of her sleeping infant's head. He'd seen others succumb to this disease that ate away at them until nothing but skin and bones remained. Amina, with her round cheeks and strong arms and legs, looked nothing like the walking skeletons he had seen in the bush.

"Why hasn't she gone home?"

"She wasn't ready."

"So you let her stay?"

"Yes."

Samuel watched Amina stroke the top of her baby's head with her thumb. "Until when?"

"Until she is."

# 30

# RICKY

Within a month, the Gilva brigade's ranks swelled with children. At camp, the new abductees, stripped naked to prevent escape, huddled together for warmth. On marches, their stolen military uniforms hung off their small frames and tripped up their steps, an infraction Otim was quick to punish.

For every ten children the LRA abducted, only six survived the first week. The rebels left the dead behind. The living, they sent to Ricky.

One afternoon, Komakech brought Ricky a group of new abductees to train. The youngest, an eight-year-old boy named William, weighed no more than fifty pounds and barely reached Ricky's waist.

"Afande," Ricky said, holding a machine gun he had taken from a dead government soldier a few weeks earlier. "He is too small. He won't be able to carry a weapon this big."

"He will learn," Komakech said, grabbing the weapon and forcing it into the frightened boy's small hands. "We will make him a man, a fierce fighter, loyal only to the LRA and Kony."

William's wiry muscles strained to raise the weapon to his shoulder like the older abductees. He lifted it as far as his bare stomach before his muscles gave and the machine gun dropped below his hips. Ricky restrained the urge to help the child. He knew the commander's anger over such insubordination would be unleashed on not only him, but also William.

Komakech took the panga from his belt and glared down at the terrified child. "Lift that gun, boy."

William's arms shook as he hefted the heavy weapon back to his stomach, inching it higher until it pressed into the hollow of his shoulder.

"See there," Komakech said, a hint of smugness in his voice. "With proper motivation, even the smallest child can be trained for battle." He smiled down at the boy, whose arms trembled under the weight of the gun still perched on his shoulder. "The government troops may not be so quick to pull the trigger when they see our new front line."

Three weeks later Komakech tested his new battle strategy when their brigade clashed with government troops in Gulu. Confident in his plan, he marched his youngest soldiers to the front line. William dragged his weapon behind him like a toddler dragging a toy. Ricky's coy followed as the second line. The children's steps grew slower as they neared the raging firefight. They flinched at every explosion and shrank further into themselves with every step. With the government troops in range, Komakech stopped his group of twelve abductees.

At the appearance of Komakech's child soldiers, a whistle

sounded across the field and a loud voice called out, "Hold your fire!"

The government troops stopped firing and looked to their commander for direction. Disbelief mutated into disgust as the military leader stared at the LRA commander and his human shields.

"Ready your weapons!" Komakech ordered from the safety of his position behind his small soldiers.

Eleven children lifted their guns. William failed to raise his, so Komakech walked up behind him, grabbed the stock of the weapon, and pressed it to the boy's shoulder. "Hold it steady!"

William wobbled as he fought to keep the weapon level.

Stepping back behind the boy, Komakech raised his own weapon and yelled, "Fire!"

Eleven guns discharged. The government troops returned fire, and two boys fell.

"Fire!" Ricky ordered, hoping his troops would help draw the soldiers' attention away from the children in Komakech's coy.

"Fire!" Komakech yelled again.

Nine children obeyed. William, his machine gun still shaking in his hands, stood frozen in position.

Komakech aimed his own weapon at the back of William's head. "Fire!" he repeated.

William glanced back at Komakech's weapon and, squeezing his eyes closed, stretched his small index finger toward the trigger. Barely reaching it, he pulled back and held. The weapon discharged with such force that the slight boy was jolted back. He kept his finger on the trigger as he stumbled backward, leaving a spray of bullets in his wake.

A stunned Komakech suddenly found himself in front of his soldier boy. With his eyes still squeezed closed and his finger holding down the machine gun's trigger, William emptied the rifle's magazine into the commander. An agonized scream tore from Komakech's throat as bullets ripped through his thighs and groin.

The moment their commander fell, the boys stopped shooting and scattered. As William ran past, his weapon bouncing across the ground behind him, Ricky's coy looked to him for their orders.

"Retreat!" he yelled over the gunfire.

His troops turned and sprinted for the bush. Ricky made it several steps before he stopped. Otim would seize any opportunity to punish him and his boys if they left a weapon on the battlefield. Ducking low, he ran back to his fallen commander's side. Keeping his own assault rifle firing at the enemy line, he grabbed the AK-47 still clutched in Komakech's hands and yanked. The commander's hold on the weapon did not release. Ricky yanked harder, but a pained cry stopped him. Komakech was still alive.

*Take the weapon. Leave the wounded.*

His commanders, including Komakech, had drilled the LRA's number one battlefield rule into his head for over a year. Blood soaked the commander's pants from his waist to his knees. His entire body convulsed, and his eyes, wide with shock, stared unseeing at the ground before him.

"Take the weapon," Ricky repeated, grabbing the gun. "Leave the wounded." He stared into Komakech's unfocused eyes. The commander's breaths stuttered from his lips in a broken rhythm.

"Leave the wounded," he repeated. Then, looping an arm under Komakech's shoulders, he dragged the dying commander off the battlefield.

# 31

# RICKY

The Gilva brigade left Komakech, two of his wives, and several guards, including Vincent, in an LRA sick bay, one of several low-lying huts hidden throughout the jungles of northern Uganda. The sick bays, which the LRA used as crude infirmaries for injured rebels Kony deemed worthy of saving, offered little more than shelter to the wounded fighters. Ricky doubted Komakech would survive the night, but he knew the commander's chances were better than little William's. When he returned to camp that evening, he was shocked to find the boy still alive. After the senior commanders retired for the night, the low-level commanders gathered to guard the new abductees. Lying in the darkness, Ricky listened to their whispered conversation.

"Do you think he'll live?" one asked.

"He will not. He left most of his blood on the battlefield."

"If his wives are unable to keep him alive, Kony will have their lives as well."

"They took fifteen rebels from my coy to guard him. They better not replace my fighters with his baby soldiers."

Ricky recognized the cold voice of Otim among the others. The scrape of rock against metal accented the wild man's words. "We all told him the boy was too small for the front line, but he wouldn't listen. Death is now the price he must pay for his arrogance."

* * *

In Komakech's absence, Kony sent a commander named Oloya to take charge of the Gilva brigade. Oloya was barely twenty-one years old, but he'd proven himself a strong fighter for the LRA and loyal to Kony. Under Oloya's charge, the tactics of the Gilva brigade changed from resistance to retreat in the face of an approaching enemy.

Ricky received praise for returning with Komakech's weapon and saving the high-ranking commander, and Oloya gave him greater responsibility both on and off the battlefield. Despite his strenuous routine and severe malnutrition, by the time Ricky reached his sixteenth birthday, he'd caught up to his brother in height. Though Ricky persevered under the dangerous conditions of the bush, not every rebel was so fortunate. Three weeks after Komakech's shooting on the battlefield, a severe bout of dysentery incapacitated William.

"May your spirit find peace," Ricky whispered as the rebels left the eight-year-old boy whom Komakech had deemed the perfect warrior for Kony's army alone in the bush to die. "I'm sorry."

During his many, many months in the LRA, Ricky had marched thousands of kilometers. The soles of his feet had grown so thick and calloused, no rock or thorn could penetrate them. As the rebels carried out Kony's orders in the Kitgum district, the wet season finally ended, and Ricky enjoyed sleeping on dry ground for the first time in months. After several days, however, his gratitude changed to dread with the realization of the dangers Patrick and he faced in the approaching dry season.

Days stretched into weeks with no rain. The lack of fresh water forced the rebels to quench their constant thirst with any liquid they could find. The juices of wild fruits and leaves, water squeezed from muddy soil, and urine became their sole sources of hydration on the long, hot marches.

As drought gripped northern Uganda, the lush, green blades of elephant grass that swayed and bowed to them in the wet season shriveled to brittle, parchment-yellow stalks that creaked and crumbled beneath their feet. Wildfires ravaged acres of farms and fields, leaving the earth scorched and the rebels with few places to hide. Smoke hung like a dusty shroud over the land. Ricky's eyes stung with every blink, and his nose burned with every breath.

When they found a small swamp, they pulled out their pangas and hacked at reeds edging the area. Ricky cut several reeds and threw them to the boys in his coy. "Find water and drink," he commanded.

Stepping through the mud, the rebels stuck their reed straws in small puddles of water and drank. The dirty water collected on their tongues and in their throats. Ricky himself gagged trying to swallow the sludge. He pressed the mud to the roof of his mouth with his tongue and sucked any liquid he could from the clump of damp soil. When mud clogged the reed's hollow center, he threw it aside and scooped handfuls of the dirty water into his parched mouth and empty jug before Oloya ordered them to march again.

Four weeks after the Gilva brigade left Komakech in the sick bay, Ricky's right leg began to burn. It was not the aching burn of fatigue or the cramping burn of dehydration. The pain was constant and radiated upward with every step. Several days later, as the rebels sat in the bush awaiting Oloya's orders, Ricky noticed a bump on the top of his right foot. The swollen area was tender and hot to the touch. He knew he hadn't been injured. They'd been in only a handful of firefights since Oloya had taken charge, and Ricky had walked away from each battle unscathed.

Lujimoi noticed Ricky inspecting his foot. "What's wrong?" he asked.

"My leg feels like it's on fire, and it itches terribly."

Lujimoi prodded the swelling with his finger. "It's infected. It needs to be cut."

Ricky clenched his teeth to keep from crying out as Lujimoi pressed the blade of his panga into the raised skin. Placing the machete aside, Lujimoi pressed down on either side of the cut. Yellow pus oozed along the crude incision and ran down the sides of Ricky's foot, but the relief was immediate.

"Thank you," Ricky said. "That feels better."

"Don't thank me yet," Lujimoi said, wiping away blood and pus.

"What are you looking for?" Ricky asked.

"The guinea worm."

Ricky stiffened. He'd seen the results of guinea worms in his village. Men and women who'd somehow ingested the eggs were often left crippled by the parasites, which grew up to a meter long inside their bodies and then burrowed their way out through their victims' legs and feet. Revulsion choked off his words. "You think it's a guinea worm?"

"I know it is. I've had a few myself."

Ricky winced as Lujimoi pressed two fingers harder on both sides of the cut.

The rebel pointed to a thin white thread that poked out of the middle of the wound. "See. There it is."

A wave of nausea swept through Ricky. He closed his eyes and waited for the feeling to pass before speaking. "What do I do?"

"You can only pull it out a little bit each day, but wait until evening, when it's cooler. It's easier then, and the worm won't break."

Fighting the urge to grab the worm and yank it from his body, Ricky looked away from his foot. He knew if the fragile parasite broke, it would burrow back into his leg, only to re-emerge somewhere else.

"When you've pulled it out enough," Lujimoi said, "tie it off to a small stick, so it can't crawl back in during the day. Then each night, pull it out another couple of centimeters."

"What about when we're marching? Won't it break off?"

"Probably, but yours is on the top of your foot, which is better than if it were on the bottom. And if it does, it'll eventually pop out again."

Ricky shuddered at the thought of having a worm burrowing through his leg and foot for months.

Knowing that if he looked at the worm poking out of the top of his foot he wouldn't be able to resist the urge to grab it and pull, Ricky kept his head up and his foot out of his sight line. "So you've had a guinea worm before?"

"I've been cut fifteen times for guinea worms," Lujimoi answered. "Of course there's no telling if it was fifteen different worms, or the same worm just burrowing in and out of my leg."

Lujimoi laughed. Ricky did not.

"But you got them all out," he asked, afraid the rebel, who'd been with the LRA for six years, would tell him his body was still a breeding ground for the parasites.

"Eventually, but there could be another one waiting in my next drink of swamp water."

The rebel laughed again at Ricky's obvious unease. "Don't let a little worm get to you," he said, punching Ricky on the shoulder. "Out here, it's the least of your worries."

## 32

# SAMUEL

The boys and girls danced in a circle, their arms pumping in the air and their bare feet drumming the earth to the rhythm of the woman's clapping.

As Samuel watched Amina, he remembered the night of his abduction.

*My family sleeping.*

*A door opening.*

*Feet kicking.*

*Hands grabbing.*

*Bodies dragging.*

He tightened his hold on his chair. His breaths came too shallow, too short.

*My mother pleading.*

*My sister crying.*

*Blood spilling.*

*Homes burning.*

*Tears flowing.*

*The world blurring.*

His hands and feet prickled with numbness. It was happening again. Just like that night.

*My father kneeling.*

*Praying.*

*My hands trembling.*

*A gun shaking.*

*A voice screaming.*

*My finger squeezing.*

*A bullet firing.*

Samuel had to regain control before the man saw. The boy slid his hand under the table until his fingers found the rough edge of his bandage. He curled his fingers over it and pressed down until he felt the cloth dampen, and then he pressed harder. Only when the pain burned away all remnants of that night did he stop. Closing his eyes, he took a deep breath to slow his heart. Then he drew a second and waited for feeling to return to his hands and feet.

"Samuel?"

He opened his eyes to find the man staring at him.

"Are you all right?"

He nodded.

The man didn't look convinced. He reached for Samuel's crutches. "Why don't we go for a walk?"

He led Samuel behind the ring of buildings, to the farthest point in the fence outlining the compound, where a small clearing with two stools lay tucked behind a coppice of trees. The only sounds that reached the secluded spot were the murmur of distant voices and the hum of insects hidden in the leaves.

"I come here when I need a quiet place to talk, or think, or just be," the man said when Samuel caught up. He motioned to the stools.

Samuel laid his crutches on the ground and took a seat. Reaching down, he broke off a blade of grass and stretched it tight, feeling its waxy ridges glide beneath his fingers. "Do you think the fighting will ever end?"

The man sat down. "Two generations of our children have known nothing but war and fear their whole lives. I have to believe someday it will end."

Samuel thought back to life in his village. War and fear had always been there. When he was three, war kept him awake at night, crying with hunger after the young men of his village abandoned the fields to join the military's fight against Kony. When he was five, war stole his education when rebels attacked his lapwony for his bike and left the teacher dead on the side of the road. When Samuel was six, fear forced his sister and him to walk sixteen kilometers every evening to the nearest city center to seek sanctuary on the floors of churches with hundreds of other children. For two years, when the sun began to set, fear chased him from his home until one evening after his eighth birthday, he refused to leave, and fear found him asleep in his hut.

"Unfortunately, every time the military strikes a blow to the LRA, the rebels strike back." The man ran his hand over a patch of grass and wildflowers beside his stool. "And when two elephants fight, it is the grass that gets trampled." He pointed beyond the fence, where wild grass and weeds grew in the neglected furrows and tangled undergrowth encroached on the borders of the abandoned farmland. "Our country used to be rich with fertile fields and strong people, but look what decades of fighting have done. It's left our country barren of life and hope. The more troops the military sends to remove the LRA, the deeper Kony's army burrows into northern Uganda."

Samuel slid the blade of grass back and forth between his fingers. "Like a guinea worm."

The man's eyebrows rose in surprise. "Why do you say that?"

Samuel shrugged.

The man waited.

Samuel twisted the blade of grass between his fingers until it kinked into a bumpy knot. "When the guinea worm comes out, if you pull too fast, its tail breaks off and the rest goes back into the body." He glanced at the man, who nodded, encouraging him to continue. "Just like the rebels. When they come out of hiding, the military strikes, and the LRA brigades break apart and retreat back into the jungle to grow stronger and plan their next attack."

The man crossed his arms on his chest. "So you think the government's tactics with the LRA don't work?"

Samuel froze. He was foolish to criticize the government, especially to a man who worked for it. He shredded the blade of grass with his fingertips.

217

"You can be honest with me," the man said.

Samuel dropped the bits of grass on the ground. "Kony is still out there."

"That's true. So, if military strikes don't work, what do you think would?"

"I don't know."

"Well, if the LRA is like a guinea worm, maybe that's how we need to extract it from northern Uganda, by using a gentler, more patient approach. If we can get Kony to agree to a cease-fire to talk, at least no children will be dying on battlefields." The man handed Samuel a new blade of grass. "And if we can get the elephants to stop fighting, maybe the grass will grow again."

"Do you really think that's possible?"

The man smiled. "When I talk to intelligent young people like you, Samuel, I think anything is possible, even the impossible."

Embarrassment squirmed through Samuel. He couldn't remember the last time anyone had paid him a compliment. He'd forgotten how to accept them, so he said nothing.

# 33

# RICKY

Five months after Komakech's shooting, the senior commander, along with his wives and guards, rejoined the Gilva brigade. His injury left him with a permanent limp, and his once-strong build had withered, causing his uniform to sag from his shoulders.

Oloya ordered a female abductee to give the commander a new uniform to replace his ill-fitting one. He then apprised Komakech of the changes that had taken place in his absence and handed control back to his superior.

The rebels marched north to the Sudan border to rendezvous with Kony's Control Altar brigade. During the LRA leader's speeches, Ricky cheered louder than the rebels around him to drown out the whispers of *obeno* Patrick and he had shared. When Ricky sensed Kony watching him in training or around camp, he pushed his successes on the battlefield to the forefront of his mind to shield his betrayals in the villages from the Holy Spirit's penetrating eyes.

They spent two days with Kony before the LRA leader ordered them south to attack the villages of the Kitgum district. As the Gilva brigade left with a new batch of wives for its commanders, including a few they'd traded to Kony's brigade the previous year, the rains began again.

It rained for weeks as they marched both day and night. The morning it finally stopped, Ricky woke in a puddle so deep the rainwater lapped at his ears. Komakech ordered the rebels to strip off their wet clothes and lay them out in the narrow blades of sunlight cutting through the jungle canopy. While they sat in silence, waiting for their clothes to dry, a man stepped out from the bush. Ricky glanced up, but before he could get a good look at him, the man turned and ran back into the jungle.

"Was that a civilian?" Otim asked.

Ricky shrugged.

"I didn't see what he was wearing," Lujimoi answered.

"It was only one man," Komakech said, untroubled by the stranger's sudden appearance. "If he comes back, we'll kill him."

Thirty minutes later, as the rebels pulled on their damp clothes, Ricky heard movement in the bush.

The first shot struck Vincent as he reached for his shirt. The bullet entered through his stomach and exploded from his back. As he fell forward, a second bullet struck him in the forehead. Before he hit the ground, the jungle surrounding the rebel camp erupted in gunfire, and government soldiers rushed out from between the trees. A dozen rebels died where they sat.

The surviving rebels scrambled for their weapons and

returned fire as they fled into the bush. Ricky's instincts took control while his brain tried to catch up to the chaos around him. He spotted Patrick sprinting into the jungle and moved to follow, but soldiers blocked his path. Ducking low, he ran in the opposite direction. Bullets pursued him as he darted for the trees, and a cold pain tore through his left calf. He stumbled and fell twice, but kept running.

The government troops spread out in pursuit of the fleeing rebels. Ricky and six boys from his coy followed Lujimoi through the jungle. As they ran, a bullet hit Lujimoi in the back and he went down.

"Help me!" he screamed as Ricky and the others ran past.

Realizing not one of his rebels was going to stop, Lujimoi ripped a grenade from his belt and lobbed it toward the boys. The throw fell short, but the explosion knocked Ricky to the ground. The others ran on without him. The concussion of the blast muted the sounds of the ambush and blurred Ricky's vision. He squeezed his eyes closed and shook his head to clear it. Behind the ringing in his ears, he heard the muffled sound of gunfire. He looked up and spotted one of Otim's wives, the girl with Christine's eyes, tripping through the undergrowth.

"Run!" he yelled. With the explosion still echoing in his ears, his voice sounded distant in his own head. "Run!" he yelled louder.

She was within meters of him, her hands reaching out for help, when a bullet struck her from behind. She arced forward, and her chest was torn open.

Lujimoi's wails screeched through the gunfire as the girl

crumpled to the ground. Ricky crawled over to where she lay and grabbed her outstretched hand. She convulsed, and little Christine's eyes, wide and scared, stared up at Ricky. She didn't make a sound as her life poured onto the earth. She'd cried every night for over a year as she faced life as an LRA abductee and wife. She had no tears left for death.

Releasing the girl's hand, Ricky scrambled between the trees, his feet catching in the tangled underbrush that covered the jungle floor. He headed in the direction the rebels had fled, but rapid gunfire and explosions diverted his route. Ricky was weak from exhaustion and a lack of food. His vision grew wobbly, but the sound of bodies crashing through the bush behind him urged his legs forward.

After several minutes, the sounds of pursuers and gunfire faded, and Ricky stopped. His finger gripping the trigger, he swung his machine gun from side to side, aiming at the shadows shifting in the trees around him. The acrid scent of gunpowder cut through the dank stink of mud and moss that permeated the jungle. Behind him, the *pop-pop-pop* of guns echoed in the distance. Ricky had to find Patrick. He'd raised his weapon to lead the way when he noticed the warm trickle running down his left calf.

Taking a shaky breath, Ricky started to look down, but stopped when he remembered his brother's advice in the fields when they were young.

*Don't look. It makes the pain worse.*

Turning his head to the right, he closed his eyes and urged his hand behind his knee and down the back of his leg until he felt wetness. Lifting his hand, he dared a glance. Blood dripped from his fingers. Taking another deep breath, Ricky looked down at the two wounds on his calf. Blood trickled from the first, a small, clean hole where the bullet had entered. Just behind, blood gushed from a large, jagged crater where the bullet had torn through muscle on its exit. Pulling off his shirt, he bandaged it securely and then pressed on through the bush in search of his brother.

When he caught up to what remained of the Gilva brigade, he found Patrick speaking with Otim near a group of wounded rebels. Patrick's eyes widened with concern when he noticed Ricky's limp and the bloodied shirt tied around his calf. He stepped forward to help, but Otim stopped him.

"Kilama was hit," the wild man said. "Carry him."

"Yes, Lapwony."

Glancing back at Ricky, Patrick walked over to where Kilama lay bleeding out from three wounds to the stomach. He tried with little success not to inflict more pain on the injured commander as he maneuvered him onto his back. Bent forward under the weight of the man, Ricky's brother fell in line with the rest of the rebels. Kilama cried out with every step.

As they marched through the jungle, the rain began again. It continued well into evening, but Komakech ordered them to keep walking. For three days they marched in the rain, stopping only for a few hours to rest. And for three days, Kilama cried out to his mother in Luo, the language of the Acholi.

Aside from the tortured screams of the young rebel's daily

night terrors, it was the most Ricky had ever heard Kilama speak. As he limped behind his brother and the injured rebel, he longed for Kilama's silence.

When they stopped on the evening of the third day, Ricky searched for lum alele. Finding a small patch of the wild grass his mama had used on his cuts when he was little, he grabbed a handful and tucked it into his mouth. His mouth was sticky with thirst. It took several minutes of grinding the bitter grass between his teeth before he produced enough saliva to create a small amount of juice. While he chewed, he carefully unwound the bloodied bandage from his leg. Using the rain, he wiped away the congealed blood and dirt and inspected the wound left by the bullet. It was a bright, beefy red. Angry scarlet streaks spread out from it like the legs of a venomous spider. The skin was tight and hot, and his knee had swollen to the point that it was no longer distinguishable from his thigh. He spat the lum alele juice in his hand and trickled it over the wound, careful not to waste a single drop. Then, overcome by exhaustion, he curled up on his side and closed his eyes.

Every night since his abduction, nightmares had plagued Ricky's sleep. They were not the nightmares of his childhood, filled with strange images born of fear of the unknown. His were the memories of a child solider. Memories forged in the harsh light of day and reborn in the shadow of night. Ricky prayed every night for dreamless sleep.

But that night, a high fever infected his sleep, creating visions so sharp and real, Ricky believed he was awake. Painful scenes burned across his fevered mind with an intensity that caused him to cry out in agony.

*His parents and sisters tied to the post in his hut, pleading for help.*

*The flames of a burning bundle dancing in Otim's eyes.*

*A black river swallowing a string of weeping children.*

*Pieces of Joseph's body strewn on the blood-soaked earth.*

*A man with a two-tipped spear standing over Patrick's lifeless body.*

*Otim pressing his rotting mouth against the lips of the girl with Christine's eyes.*

*Kony preaching the word of the Holy Spirit from atop a mountain of broken bodies.*

*Thousands of children armed with pangas and guns, shaking their weapons in the air.*

*Kony turning his blood-red eyes to Ricky and giving his child army one command: kill.*

Ricky woke with a start at the sound of his own screams, but soon realized his was not the only voice crying out. Another voice filled the night air; the same broken voice he'd heard crying out for three days.

Looking in the direction of the cries, Ricky saw Patrick tending to Kilama, whose unseeing eyes stared up at the night sky as his ashen lips repeated his pleas to his mother over and over.

Ricky's teeth chattered. He didn't know if he shivered with cold, fever, or fear, but he could not stop the trembling. The rain had continued to fall as he'd slept, leaving the rebels lying in deep puddles. He inspected his leg and found his wound submerged in the muddy water. Gritting his teeth, he eased it from the puddle and laid it atop his uninjured leg. With Kilama's words repeating in his mind, he closed his eyes and prayed along with the dying commander.

When he woke, the rain and Kilama had fallen silent. The rebels welcomed the reprieve from both and fell in line when Komakech called out the order to march. Ricky's leg had swollen during the night to the point that he could no longer keep pace with the rest of the brigade. He tried to catch up, but his leg gave way and he fell.

Komakech walked over to where he sat on the ground. "You are no longer of use to us," he said, his right hand resting on his gun.

"No," Ricky said, tightening the bandage around his leg. "I am fine." Yellowed pus ran down his shin as he pulled on the frayed ends of the filthy scrap of shirt. Fighting to remain conscious, he turned his head away from the sight and the warm stench of rotting meat oozing from the septic wound.

Patrick stopped and took his time readjusting Kilama's limp body on his back so he could eavesdrop on the conversation.

"You're in no shape to fight," Komakech said. "You can barely walk."

"I can, Afande. I just tripped."

"The enemy is following us. We can't afford to stop every time you fall."

"I can walk." Ricky pressed up from the ground, careful to

put the bulk of his weight on his right leg. As Komakech watched, he stepped forward. Pain seared through his leg and exploded behind his eyes. He bit the insides of his cheeks to prevent a scream from escaping. The edges of his vision blurred and the world tilted as his knee buckled and he crumpled again to the ground.

He clawed at the wet earth, trying to push himself upright as Komakech drew his weapon. From the corner of his hazy vision, he saw Patrick slide Kilama from his back.

"You are no longer of use to the LRA," Komakech repeated.

Ricky blinked rapidly, fighting to clear his vision and mind.

"Do not follow us," Komakech said. He turned to leave, but stopped when he saw Patrick standing directly behind him. "Grab Kilama," he ordered.

"Kilama's dead," Patrick said in a voice as lifeless as the rebel he'd carried for four days.

Komakech glanced over at the young commander's motionless body sprawled in the grass. "Then leave him."

Patrick pointed to Ricky. "I can carry him, Afande."

"No. He's slowed us down enough." Slinging his weapon over his shoulder, Komakech walked toward the front of the line.

"Afande!" Patrick called out.

Komakech stopped and turned his cold stare on Patrick. Ricky's head swirled with concern for his brother. Few rebels openly questioned Komakech's orders, and those foolish enough to do so did not live to question him again.

As the commander walked back to Patrick, his hand came

to rest on the hilt of his panga. Sensing a kill was near, several rebels, including Otim, gathered close, their wild eyes darting back and forth between the commander and the young rebel.

"Afande," Patrick said again, swallowing hard but refusing to look away. He lowered his voice so only Komakech and his brother could hear. "Ricky is a good fighter. He will be of use to us again."

Komakech did not answer. His piercing glare cut into Patrick, but Patrick did not relent.

"I could help him to the sick bay. It will not delay us long, Afande."

"You scouted last night," Komakech said. "What were your findings?"

"We spotted government troops not three kilometers away, closing in on both sides."

"Then you know there is no time to get him to a sick bay."

"But, Afande," Patrick began to argue.

Komakech held up a hand to silence him. He then stared down at Ricky, his eyes narrowing as he made up his mind.

Otim stepped up beside him. "If we leave the boy alive, he could be captured."

Komakech nodded at the truth in the wild man's statement.

Otim took the nod as approval, and a cruel smile spread across his face as he pulled his panga from his belt. "I will make sure the boy never gives away any information."

"I can walk," Ricky insisted.

The rebels watched as he struggled to his feet, using his gun as a crutch. He managed one step before the pain forced him to his knees again.

Komakech reached into his pocket. "Stay hidden," he said, handing Ricky three shriveled cassava roots. "If you're still alive when we come back this way, you'll rejoin us."

"But, Afande!" Otim protested.

Stepping around Kilama's body, Komakech signaled Otim and Patrick to follow. Otim's smile twisted into an angry sneer as he tucked his panga into his belt. "Doesn't matter," he spat. "You won't survive the night. That infection will eat you alive if the animals don't."

Turning away, he marched along the line of waiting rebels, barking orders as he made his way to the front.

Patrick stared down at Ricky. "Stay alive."

Ricky reached a trembling hand out to his brother. "Patrick," he pleaded.

Patrick grabbed his hand and squeezed. "Obeno," he said. Then he let go and turned to leave.

"Wait!" Ricky screamed, dragging himself through the grass. His leg burned with such intensity that he feared the pain would consume his whole body in flame, but he kept crawling. The periphery of his vision blurred, and pinpricks of light spotted his shrinking view of the retreating rebels. "When will you be back?"

If Patrick answered, Ricky did not hear. The only sound he heard before unconsciousness smothered him were the muffled footsteps of his brother walking away.

# 34

# RICKY

A fog, thick and heavy, cocooned Ricky's mind. His eyelids fluttered open, only to cringe closed when a large raindrop splattered on the bridge of his nose. Mud, thick and wet, clung to him as he rolled onto his side, and a burning pain, like thousands of razor-sharp blades, pierced through his left leg. He cried out and collapsed onto his back.

The rain fell through wide gaps in a woven grass roof sagging right above his face. The roof balanced on four wooden posts burrowed deep in mud that reeked of urine and excrement. Panic took hold as he remembered the rebels' stories about how government troops tortured prisoners of war. Squinting against the rain, he looked around the small enclosure for any clue to where he was and who was holding him captive. He found nothing.

No longer able to ignore the burning in his throat, Ricky parted his chapped lips to allow the raindrops to fall onto his swollen tongue. As the patter of rain slowed, he remembered the cassava Komakech had given him. He shoved one in his mouth and ground the shriveled root into a gummy paste. He tried to swallow, but the cassava stuck in his dry throat. Gripping his neck, he rolled onto his stomach, thrust his fingers into his mouth, and clawed at the paste. Each second without air pulsed in his ears, until his suffocating heartbeat was all he could hear.

*Not like this*, his mind screamed. *I can't have survived everything to die alone, like this.*

He hooked his finger deeper into his throat. His body convulsed with dry heaves until the paste broke free. As he pulled in a wheezy gasp, Ricky heard movement behind him. Fighting to remain conscious, he peered into the dark jungle, and his breath seized again.

He was not alone.

A pair of eyes watched him struggle from the shadows. The weak light filtering through the gaps in the leaves glistened off the unblinking eyes as they crept closer. From their height, Ricky couldn't tell if they were human or animal. He felt around him for his machine gun.

*Take the weapon. Leave the wounded.*

For over a year Ricky drilled the LRA's rule into every new abductee that Komakech brought to him. Now, as he lay wounded and vulnerable, he wished he hadn't been so convincing in his teaching. His mind raced. If it was a leopard, there was no doubt the rotting stench of his leg had drawn the predator to him in hopes of an easy meal. Fresh adrenaline surged through his veins. He might be hurt, but he would not be an easy kill for any animal or man. He groped around for a branch or rock, anything he could use as a weapon, but the ground was bare.

Terrified, he watched a man step out from the jungle. The stranger's dark, oily skin clung to his thin frame and glistened with sweat. His eyes, sunken in his gaunt face, never left Ricky as he inched cautiously toward the lean-to. He wore only a ripped pair of camouflage pants, stained with dirt and blood. Long, gnarled dreadlocks rested on his shoulders.

Ricky drew back as the man crouched in front of him.

"Drink," the man said, holding out a jerrican.

Ricky grabbed the can and pressed it to his cracked lips. The surge of water in his throat triggered another coughing fit and a bout of vomiting. When it passed, Ricky forced himself to take small sips. His head pounded with every swallow, but he dared not close his eyes against the pain with the stranger still watching him. Uncertain of when he would be getting more water, Ricky fought the urge to drain the entire can. Taking one last sip, he handed it back to the stranger. "Thank you."

"You're welcome."

Ricky attempted to pull himself from the lean-to, so he could sit up and face the man.

"Let me help," the man said.

Too weak to resist, Ricky allowed the stranger to lift him into a seated position. The jungle swayed around him, and he closed his eyes until the world righted itself once again. "Thank you," he said, his voice weak and scratchy, "again."

"I'm Onen," the man said.

"I'm Ricky. Did you bring me here?"

"No. Some rebels did."

Ricky inspected the crude lean-to more closely. It was smaller, but similar to the sick bay where he'd left Komakech months before. "Are you here to protect me?"

"No." Onen lifted his right pant leg, revealing a large wound on his thigh. The puckered skin around his injury boasted the pale coloring of new skin, not the violent red of Ricky's septic wound. "I'm here to heal." He lowered his pant leg. "They said when they brought you here that I can rejoin them the next time they return."

"When was that?" Ricky asked.

"About a week ago. You've been unconscious until now. The few times you stirred I gave you water and I've tried to keep your wound clean, but it doesn't look good. The rebels promised they'll bring medicine for the infection."

Ricky's breathing eased. At least the LRA would be return-ing. "How long have you been here?"

"Three months, I think. It's hard to keep track of time out here."

"Have you been alone the whole time?"

"Yes. Until you arrived." He handed Ricky the water can again. "Even though you've been unconscious, I was glad to have you here." As he watched Ricky drink, his voice quieted. "It's not good to be alone. I'd started to pray for death."

Ricky stopped and looked up at Onen, surprised by the man's admission.

The corners of Onen's lips lifted in a lifeless smile at the confusion furrowing Ricky's brow. "At least in death, you're not alone."

# 35

# SAMUEL

Samuel followed the man back to the porch, but stopped short of his chair when he spotted a crowd entering through the main gate.

Samuel stiffened. "Are those the 'others' you were waiting for?"

The man held out his hand for Samuel's crutches. "Yes. They're local villagers."

Samuel refused to give him the crutches and instead rested them beside his chair. He wanted them as close as possible if he had to run.

The man sat and took the painkillers from his pocket. "Is your leg sore from the walk?"

It was, but Samuel could not afford to dull his senses now. Not with so many strangers approaching. He shook his head.

The man placed the bottle back in his pocket and smiled at the villagers.

Dozens of men, women, and children traveled up the dirt

road. They squinted in the sun that stretched their shadows into a dark army gliding behind them. The woman with the questions greeted the crowd and directed them to the porch, where the man welcomed them with a friendly smile, a firm handshake, and warm words.

Samuel shifted in his chair as the villagers crowded along the porch. He kept his head low and glanced at their faces as they passed behind him. His breath caught at the sight of one villager. The elderly man crossed the porch with the aid of a crudely carved walking stick. Samuel recognized the stick. It was the same one his LRA commander had used to beat the villager four weeks earlier. Samuel remembered the old man's eyes, cloudy with cataracts, staring up at him from the ground where he lay, begging for mercy. The rebels had spared his life, but were not so merciful to his wife.

As the elderly man neared Samuel, he paused. Samuel gripped the seat of his chair to stop his finger from tapping as the villager's milky eyes studied his face. He hoped his shaved head and clean clothes were enough to mask his identity, but the tears in the old man's weak eyes and the quiver in his wrinkled chin told him they were not. Samuel stared down at his lap and waited for the *clump, clump, clump* of the man's walking stick to fade before speaking.

"Why are they here?" he asked when the big man rejoined him.

"They were invited here, so that they may see," the man said.

"See what?"

"What they can no longer see. Anyone can look," the man said, "but few can see."

Samuel's brow furrowed in confusion and anger. "The villagers are here to punish the children, aren't they?"

"No," the man said softly. "I told you. They're here to see."

As if the man's words were the signal the children had been awaiting, the sound of voices and the beating of drums filled the air. Clouds of red dust curled around the girls' bare feet and swirled with their lavender skirts as they danced. The boys' heads bobbed in unison, and their feet stomped to the rhythm as they sang out in voices strong and joyful.

"Though life is full of strife, we love peace and nothing less!"

Their energy swelled across the field and onto the porch, where it was met with the sound of clapping. Samuel turned to see several villagers moving along to the rhythm. Mothers released their toddlers so that they might dance with the performers.

Samuel looked over at the man. A broad smile graced his rounded cheeks as he clapped his large hands to the beat and sang along. When the song ended, the villagers applauded and left the porch to join the children on the field, where they thanked them for their performance and asked questions about life in the Friends of Orphans center before the woman with the questions led them on a tour of the complex. Samuel and the man remained on the porch.

"Sometimes," the man said, "the harsh realities of life can blind us to the beauty and promise in our world." He motioned to Amina and her baby. "When we see a child mother, we see only shame. We must look closer and see courage."

Amina rocked her baby and spoke to a mother whose toddler sat at her feet patting on a drum.

The man pointed to an older boy, who was speaking with the elderly villager with the milky eyes. A jagged scar carved a line from the boy's forehead to his chin, and a gaping hole occupied the spot where his right eye should have been. "When we look at a face scarred by war, we see only pain. We must look deeper and see strength."

The elderly villager reached out and took the boy's hand in his.

"And when the world looks at the former abductees and child soldiers of the LRA," the man said, "they must look past the crimes they were forced to commit and see them for who they truly are."

Samuel's eyes stung with regret. He looked down, so the man wouldn't see. "Who are they?"

The man placed a hand on his shoulder. "Our children."

# 36

# RICKY

As night and rain fell once again across the jungle, the two abandoned rebels sought refuge under the cover of the sick bay. No longer able to see Onen, Ricky struggled to keep his fevered mind focused on the man's voice floating in the darkness around him. Disjointed and separated by ever-growing silences, Onen's words finally evaporated in a fog of sleep.

When Ricky woke, it was still night.

"Onen?" he whispered.

The only voices that replied were those of the bush. The incessant chatter of frogs in a nearby swamp and the haunting calls of guinea fowls protecting their nests echoed in the night air. While Ricky waited for Onen to wake, he remembered Patrick telling Komakech that he'd spotted the enemy closing in on the brigade's position from two directions. Delirious, Ricky envisioned Patrick and the Gilva rebels dying in a firestorm of bullets. His heart raced with the realization that if Patrick and the rebels were gone, no one would know where to find him. He would die alone in the sick bay.

*No! Patrick is not dead. He'll come back for me. I need to be strong. I need to stay alive. I'm not alone.*

He squinted in the direction where Onen slept. He shuddered violently with fever and his throat scratched with thirst, but the knowledge that he was not alone and that the LRA would be returning quelled his fears. As he slipped back into unconsciousness, memories of home replayed in his dreams.

\* \* \*

When the first rays of dawn crept through the grass roof, Ricky wiped away his tears and peered into the dark shadows of the sick bay. Onen was not there.

"Onen!" The name clawed through his parched throat.

No one answered.

Weak with dehydration, Ricky looked for the jerrican. He spotted it in Onen's corner of the sick bay. Careful not to drag his injured leg through the mud, he crawled over to the can and found Onen had refilled it while he slept. He mumbled a quiet thanks and lifted the can to his lips. He sipped the muddy water, trying to ignore its foul odor and the nagging thought of guinea worm eggs. After several sips, he leaned forward to return the can, but stopped when he noticed a small brown sack sitting in the mud. With unsteady hands, he opened the bag and found a dozen cassava roots and a jar of antibiotic ointment.

Dropping the sack, Ricky scrambled to the mouth of the sick bay. The LRA had returned, just as they'd promised.

"Onen!" he yelled, his eyes scouring the surrounding trees for movement. "Patrick!"

Seconds pulsed by with no answer, and Ricky realized the rebels were gone, and so was Onen.

"Patrick," he whispered, crawling back into the sick bay, but he knew his brother couldn't hear him. No one could. As he lay, sick and alone, in the bush, Onen's words echoed in his mind.

*It's not good to be alone. I'd started to pray for death. At least in death, you're not alone.*

Ricky stared up through the gaps in the roof. For hours, he prayed to his parents to watch over Patrick and him and to guide them home. He prayed until day faded to night, and then he cried. Great sobs he could release only when no one was watching or listening. As he wept, shadows were cast across the full moon and swam in his tears, and for the first time in his life Ricky saw the mother in the moon.

The next five days Ricky spent trapped in a cycle of fever-induced nightmares and isolation-induced fear. His paranoia grew with each passing day, and the image of his brother dominated his hallucinations and haunted his sleep.

*Sorrow darkened Patrick's eyes as he stared down at Ricky. Behind Patrick, a shadow slithered out from the jungle. It crept up Patrick's leg and pulled him toward the trees. He struggled against the force, but more shadows appeared from the darkness, winding up his legs like vines. He said Ricky's name, but the shadows wrapped around his throat, choking off his voice. Ricky clawed at the ground, trying to reach his brother, but his hands sank into the earth that oozed red with blood. The shadow snakes devoured Patrick's body and face, until all that remained were his lips. As they opened to form the word Ricky had clung to over the last twenty-two months, the snake entered Patrick's mouth, and the shadows swallowed Ricky's brother.*

Ricky woke screaming for his brother, but his concern for Patrick curdled into paranoia as he lay motionless in the sick bay, listening for any sign that his cries had alerted the enemy to his presence. When he was convinced no soldiers were coming, he focused on his other deadly enemies: thirst, hunger, and infection.

He administered the antibiotic ointment to his wound twice a day. He funneled the rainwater dripping from the grass roof through curved leaves into his jar and disciplined himself to stretch his water and four remaining cassava roots as long as possible.

## 37

# RICKY

The medicine killed the infection within two weeks, but it took longer for Ricky's leg to heal.

During his recovery in the sick bay, the rebels visited three times. Whenever Ricky heard the rustling of bodies pressing through the jungle, his pulse quickened in hopes that Patrick would appear, but it was always the same two rebels, Otoo and Onek. They stayed for less than five minutes, leaving Ricky with another sackful of supplies and a heart heavy with disappointment.

Ricky had been in the sick bay for four weeks when Otoo and Onek finally arrived to tell him it was time to rejoin the Gilva brigade. Throbbing pain radiated through his leg with every step, but he could walk with a limp and fire a weapon, and that was all that was required of the LRA's fighters.

Hobbling through the LRA camp, Ricky was shocked by the number of unfamiliar rebels in its ranks. Panic rose in his chest as he searched the hundreds of strange faces for the one face he needed to see. As he limped toward a group of rebels to ask about his brother, Patrick emerged from the jungle, and relief welled in Ricky's eyes, but he blinked back the tears when he spotted Komakech and Otim.

He nodded once to his brother, and Patrick nodded back before packing up weapons for their march. Otim's eyes narrowed at the brief exchange between the brothers and he leaned in to whisper something to Komakech. The commander did not respond, and the wild man stalked off to torment a group of young girls.

"How is your leg?" Komakech asked Ricky.

"Better, Afande." He shifted his weight onto his left leg as proof.

"Good. I have many new fighters for you to train." He led Ricky over to where Trench guarded a group of young boys. The children, tethered to one another by a length of rope, huddled together naked on the ground. Not one looked up as Ricky and Komakech approached.

Komakech handed Ricky a new automatic rifle and a panga. "Intel reported that government troops are approaching from the west. You have twenty-four hours to get them ready for the front line."

Weeks of convalescence had weakened Ricky's body, but his fighting instincts reawakened with the firing of the first bullet one day after his return. Nearly two years spent fighting, day and night, against man and nature for survival had armed Ricky with the keen senses of both predator and prey. He could smell gunpowder carried on the wind from battles being waged beyond what his eyes could see or ears could hear. In the silence of the bush, he heard the tension of an impending ambush. In the tightening of a commander's jaw or the darkening of his eyes, he saw a beating before the commander drew back his hand or foot. At night, as he slept, his muscles tensed and twitched in preparation for the next day's battle. His senses were always alert, always anticipating the next fight to stay alive.

During Ricky's long absence from the Gilva brigade, the government had increased its pressure on the LRA, and the rebels retaliated with ambushes in an attempt to delay the soldiers' advance. Now Komakech selected him to accompany Otim and forty other rebels on an ambush.

"Put this on," Otim ordered, throwing Ricky a new military uniform.

The shirt hung from Ricky's shoulders, and the waist of the pants slipped beneath his bony hips. Grabbing a length of rope used to tie abductees together, he fashioned himself a belt and hurried to catch up with the wild man.

Otim led the rebels to the Aswa River, where they hid behind the tall grass lining the bank and waited for the military troops' arrival. As the sun dipped behind the trees of the bush, casting the field in shadows, the first soldier stepped out from the jungle.

Ricky secured his grip on his weapon, but Otim signaled for the rebels to hold their position.

Ricky counted dozens and dozens of soldiers. There were too many coming too fast. He braced himself in anticipation of the signal to fire. He was a bullet in the chamber awaiting Otim's pull on the trigger, but the signal did not come from the wild man. It sounded from across the field with the shrill cry of a military captain's whistle. The rebels had been spotted.

The trigger pulled, Ricky exploded from the grass. After so many days of silence in the sick bay, the din of artillery deafened him, but he pressed forward, weapon raised. Dozens of government soldiers leading the charge ran for cover. An enraged military captain screamed threats at the fleeing soldiers, forcing them back to the front.

Ricky's leg, still weak from his injury, wobbled as he moved across the field. He quickened his pace so he wouldn't fall behind the LRA line, but his leg gave out and he stumbled. Still firing, he glanced to his left. No one was beside him. He looked to his right and found an empty field. Confused, he whirled around to see the rebels retreating. With the rebels fleeing behind him and the government troops advancing before him, Ricky fired a volley of shots across the field to give himself a second of cover and then ran for the riverbank, where he crouched low behind the bushes and tall grass.

A whistle blew twice. "Spread out!" a voice screamed. "Don't let them get away!"

As the soldiers followed the rebels across the field, Ricky crept along the riverbank in the opposite direction. If they found him, he had two options: fight or surrender.

Keeping his finger on the trigger, he stayed low and snuck from one clump of tall grass to the next.

After several meters, he lay down behind a small cluster of bushes and waited for the soldiers' voices and gunfire to fade. When the shadows of the bush bled into night and the only sounds Ricky could hear were the chirps of river frogs, he came out from behind his cover and continued his walk.

The riverbank terrain, which had been difficult to navigate with his bad leg in daylight, proved impossible in the dark. So after several steps, Ricky decided to wait out the night. Concerned the government troops might come back and search the brush lining the river, he lifted his rifle above his head, waded out into the Aswa, and climbed on top of a large flat rock. With his AK-47 cradled in his arms, he curled up and slept.

The next morning, he returned to the field and pilfered enough ammunition from the dead soldiers' weapons to protect himself while he waited for the rebels to return. When they didn't, he weighed his options. He could try to find them or wait for them to return. The throbbing pain in his leg told him he would never catch up with the rebels, which left staying put. Ricky had kept himself alive in the sick bay by collecting rainwater and foraging for berries. He could survive alone again while he waited. But as he stared into the shallow waters of the river, a thought occurred to him. What was he waiting for?

This was his opportunity to keep his promise. The promise he and Patrick had made the night of Joseph's death. The promise they'd repeated to each other for so long.

He stumbled as he stood, but, finding his footing, he glanced back in the direction the rebels had fled. Guilt tore through him at the thought of leaving his brother, but he'd already broken his promise to Patrick once. He couldn't do it again.

"Obeno," he whispered through his tears, and then turning away from the LRA, he began his walk home.

Uncertain of his location, Ricky headed for a nearby village to ask for assistance. He found several huts with embers cooling in the fire pits and tools abandoned in the fields, but no people. He walked from hut to hut until he came to one on the outskirts of the village where a woman worked in a small garden with her four children. Slinging his weapon over his shoulder, Ricky started up the dirt path toward the family, but the moment the woman spotted him, she grabbed her children and ran.

"No, no, no!" Ricky yelled after them. "I'm not a bad person!" But they didn't stop.

Grabbing a handful of shea nuts from a bag the children abandoned in their retreat, Ricky continued on to the next home, where he got the same reception. After watching another two families run away, Ricky decided to change his approach.

He walked to the next homestead under cover of the bush, using the same stealthy methods he'd used in hundreds of raids. An older man worked outside the main building with his teenage son, repairing a broken fence. They wore tattered, worn clothes and knelt on the ground to work, making it impossible to tell who was taller. But by the way the pant cuffs cut into the son's skinny calves, Ricky thought that if the boy wasn't already taller than his father, he would be soon. A shadow of hair shielded the boy's bowed head from the sun, and a ring of short, curly white hair encircled the older man's head like a halo of thin clouds. The father wore a pair of scuffed glasses that slid down the bridge of his nose every time he leaned forward to show his son how to adjust a slat or nodded in approval of the boy's efforts.

Crouched low behind the bushes and trees, Ricky moved as close as possible to the pair without being detected. He couldn't hear their conversation, but something the boy said made the father laugh. It was a warm and genuine laugh that made Ricky's chest ache. He'd seen many fathers and sons since his abduction, but he hadn't seen a smile born of happiness or heard a laugh laced with love in two years. Every smile he'd encountered during his time with the LRA was spawned by cruelty and every laugh festered with hate.

Grief burned in Ricky's chest as he stepped out from between the trees lining their property. At the sight of the tall, armed teen, the father shoved his son behind him. The two stood staring at Ricky, their eyes wide with fear.

"Okwer!" a woman's voice called from inside the main building. "Could you get some water from the river?" No sooner had the question been asked than a woman stepped out of the house with a wooden bucket in her hand. A young girl of fourteen followed her outside. Seeing Ricky, the woman dropped the bucket and wrapped her arms around her daughter.

"I'm not here to hurt you," Ricky said. "I promise."

"We know of Kony's promises," the man said. "They bring

nothing but death and destruction to our land and people." He stepped back, pressing his family toward the safety of their hut. "You will not take my children."

"I'm not here for your children," Ricky said. "Please. I just want to go home."

Ricky's plea stopped the man, who scanned the bush surrounding his home. "Where are the other rebels?"

"I don't know. They left me behind during yesterday's battle."

"We heard the gunfire," the man said. "Many of our neighbors fled, but we couldn't." He motioned to the soiled bandages wrapped around his wife's right foot. "Do you think they'll be back?"

"The military drove them downriver."

The man studied Ricky. His suspicion of the young rebel was evident in his defensive stance before his family. Ricky didn't blame him. He knew his appearance invited distrust and fear. He'd caught glimpses of his warped, muddied reflection in the surfaces of rivers and swamps when he'd bent down to drink. His hair hung in bunched dreadlocks to his shoulders. His face had grown gaunt, and his eyes had yellowed with malnutrition. Scabies mottled his skin, and his hair and clothes crawled with lice. The military uniform he wore, the assault rifle lying across his back, and the panga at his belt were constant reminders of the violence the LRA wrought.

"I won't stay long," Ricky said. "I just need to know which way is my home."

"Odong," the woman said, "I think he's telling the truth."

The man looked back at his wife. "Amito, he's a rebel."

She placed a hand on her husband's arm. "He's someone's son."

Odong's glasses slid down the bridge of his nose as he nodded. He pushed them back up and turned to Ricky. "Where are you from?"

"Pader."

"That's a week's journey by foot," the man said.

Ricky's shoulders sagged. "Thank you. Could you tell me which direction I need to go?"

His brow furrowed in thought, Odong stared hard at Ricky and then nodded.

"I will," he said. "But you'll need strength for the journey. When was the last time you ate?"

"A few days."

"Come," the man said, motioning Ricky into the hut. "Once you are fed and rested, I'll take you to the main road and show you the way home."

# 38

# SAMUEL

Following the visitors' tour of the compound, Samuel watched the man bid the villagers good night at the main gate. The old man with the milky eyes shook the man's hand and glanced back to the porch where Samuel sat. The boy knew the old man couldn't see him from such a distance, but he felt the weight of his pallid stare. It was too heavy for him to bear, so he looked to the field, where several boys gathered for one last game before the sun set.

When the man returned, he began rearranging the pieces on the checkers table. "So can I convince you to play a game now?"

Samuel stared down at the board. His thigh ached with swelling, and his head throbbed with confusion. It had been a close call with the old villager. He'd heard stories of the punishments awaiting rebels who returned to their villages, and he knew no amount of singing or dancing would make up for his crimes.

"Well," the man said, "what's it going to be?"

"One game," Samuel said.

The man clapped his hands together and rubbed them with eagerness. "Excellent. You're first."

As the man finished setting up the board, Samuel watched Amina and the other girls talking under the shea tree, and a thought occurred to him. Even though Amina was sick, she was smiling and laughing. The big man knew Amina's crimes and still he accepted her and her child. If his sister's best friend could trust the man's words and promises after everything that had happened, perhaps Samuel could, too. Maybe he didn't have to leave with the soldier. Maybe, like Amina, the man would let him stay at the compound until he was ready.

He took a deep breath and wiped his sweaty palms on his shorts. "Do you think . . ."

"Yes?"

Samuel diverted his gaze to his lap. Staring at the bandage on his leg, his courage faltered.

"What is it, Samuel?"

Samuel picked at the frayed edge of the wrapping. "I was just wondering if . . ."

Something behind him caught the man's attention, and before Samuel could finish his sentence, the man stood. "Excuse me. I'll be right back."

He walked to the end of the porch, where the soldier waited.

Panic gripped Samuel. He wasn't ready to go. Not now. Not yet. He hadn't found the words or courage to ask if he could stay.

The two men spoke for several minutes. Samuel tried to read their lips, but turned away when both men looked in his direction.

While he watched the children on the field, he thought of what he'd say when the man returned. Maybe if he told the man what had happened, that he had had no choice, he'd let him stay. Maybe if he explained that he never wanted to hurt anyone, he'd understand.

Samuel took a deep breath to calm his nerves as the man returned. He had to ask his question before the soldier took him away.

"There's been a slight change in plans," the man said, sitting down again.

Samuel watched the soldier climb into a military truck. The engine turned over, and the vehicle rumbled up the dirt path to the entrance of the compound.

A flicker of hope burned in Samuel's chest. Maybe he didn't have to ask the man to let him stay. Maybe the man knew.

"Your trip has been delayed. Orders came in from Kampala to interview some people about an LRA attack that took place in a nearby village a few weeks ago." The man paused. "Not far from where you were found."

Fear smothered the faint hope Samuel had nurtured when he'd allowed the thought of staying to take root in his mind.

"It was the third LRA attack in that area in less than two months," the man explained. "We believe the rebels who attacked the villages were the same rebels you stumbled upon when hunting."

Reeling from the news, Samuel sat back in his chair and pressed his trembling hands into his lap.

"Don't worry," the man said. "Your ride will be back soon."

Samuel nodded. Just minutes before, when he'd thought the soldier was there to take him from the man and the compound, he'd been desperate to stay.

Now, as he considered the number of witnesses who could identify him as part of the raiding party on their village, he was desperate to leave. He'd broken his third rule. He'd allowed the man and the seemingly normal lives the former abductees enjoyed within the safety of the fence to lure him in with their lies and empty promises. For a moment he'd convinced himself that just maybe he'd found a place where people would understand, but he'd been a fool. No one would understand. No one ever could.

The man handed Samuel his last bottle of water. "So what was it you wanted to ask me?"

Samuel watched the soldier's truck disappear down the road. "Nothing."

# 39

# RICKY

While the family prepared dinner, Ricky went into the surrounding jungle and took off his military uniform so his presence wouldn't raise concerns among the other villagers. He hid them under a bush with his panga and rifle. He fidgeted with the ragged shorts and T-shirt Amito had given him as he walked unarmed toward the family's house.

*What if he was being set up?*

*What if they'd summoned the other villagers for help?*

*What if they'd sent word to the military that Ricky was there?*

But as he neared the home, he saw Amito laying out bowls of porridge and Odong waving to him.

As they ate, the couple asked Ricky about his family and how he'd come to be in the LRA. Silence was his only response, so they steered the conversation to talk of preparing the fields for the coming dry season. Though his stomach writhed with hunger, Ricky declined a second helping of food and quietly listened as Amito and her daughter discussed the best way to transport water from the river to their fields, while Odong and his son made plans for salvaging their meager crop.

Following dinner, Amito examined Ricky's leg, and the couple insisted Ricky stay with them until the wound had properly healed.

"I don't want to cause trouble for you," Ricky said.

"Nonsense," Amito said. "You need to be well rested and strong for your journey to Pader. You will stay with us until you're ready."

"Thank you," Ricky whispered, afraid if he said anything more, he would cry.

Odong gave Ricky a scrap of mat and his son Okwer's small hut to sleep in for the night. After the family retired to the main house, Ricky paced inside the hut like a caged animal until he could no longer stay indoors. Careful not to wake the family, he crept back to the bush and slept beneath a tree.

He woke before dawn and searched the main road for tracks of people passing through the area as he'd slept. Bare footprints alone meant civilians. Left destitute from years of looting and fighting, the people living in the war zone could no longer afford shoes. Boot prints in large numbers meant military. Many boot prints and footprints etched in the dirt meant LRA. Under the hazy light of the morning sun, Ricky scanned the stretch of dirt road. Finding only a handful of bare footprints, he headed back to the homestead and snuck into Okwer's hut.

After Odong and his family awoke, he helped them around the homestead, tending the fire, fetching water from the river, and tilling the fields. When the handle of Okwer's hoe broke, Ricky sat down with the boy to show him how Patrick used to fix his broken hoe. Removing the splintered pieces of wood from the steel ring of the blade head, Ricky ran his thumb over the pitted core of the wood. "See these holes?"

Okwer nodded.

"Weevils burrow into the heartwood of larweco trees too easily, making it weak and prone to breaking. When I broke my hand hoe, my brother carved me a new handle from a pobo tree. He said pobo was strong enough to withstand great pressure and abuse, but also smooth enough to not cause injury to the person using it." He pointed to a coppice of pobos, long, reedlike saplings, at the far end of the field. "Cut me a sturdy piece, and I'll show you."

While Okwer scrambled off to fetch wood for a new handle, Ricky thought of his brother. Patrick wouldn't know he was alive and safe. Staring down at the broken tool, he felt a powerful need to return to the Gilva brigade. To return to his brother.

If he left now, he might be able to catch up with them. It would take days, but he was certain he could track them, just as he had with the girls when they were left behind. Once he found the rebels, Patrick and he would get another chance to escape. They had to. And then they could leave together.

"Is something wrong?" Okwer asked.

"No," Ricky said, shaking himself free from his thoughts. "Sorry, I just forgot what my brother told me to do next." He ran his calloused fingers over the wood's coarse bark, and the memory of Patrick grabbing his hands and whispering against his ear surfaced.

*"Promise," his brother had begged. "Promise."*

"Do you want me to get my father to help?" Okwer asked.

"No," Ricky said, carving a small notch in the outer bark with the blade of the hoe, just as Patrick always had, and carefully peeling back the bark to reveal the smooth, strong sapwood underneath. "I remember what I'm supposed to do now."

That night after everyone retired to bed, he snuck back to the bush and thought about the family who'd welcomed him into their home. They shared the same love and respect for one another that Ricky's family had shared. Ricky knew the warmth and security this family had offered him would be difficult to leave, but he had to go. He'd promised Patrick he would find their obeno and he had to be there when Patrick returned home. As he stared up through the tree branches at the stars glinting in the night sky, he prayed to his parents that his brother would soon escape the LRA, and he prayed to God that the people of his village would welcome Patrick and him back with the same kindness and understanding that this family of strangers had shown.

\* \* \*

The next morning, as Ricky and the family sat by the fire and spoke of his plans for the journey to Pader, Ricky heard movement in the bush behind them. Before he could react, rebels from the Gilva brigade emerged with their weapons drawn.

"Stay seated!" Otim ordered as his troops spread out around the family.

Ricky tried to catch Odong's eye to let him know he did not plan this ambush, but the father kept his attention on the wild man, who'd stopped before his daughter. Abalo cowered under the wild man's depraved glare and leaned into her mother's embrace as Otim ran the tip of his tongue over his gray teeth.

"How much time do we have?" he asked a rebel standing behind him.

His weapon drawn, Patrick stepped up beside the commander. His eyes collided with Ricky's and his breath caught, but he quickly turned his attention away from his brother. "The government troops will be upon us within ten minutes, Lapwony."

"Take forty rebels into the village. Grab whatever food and supplies you find. Meet us at the main road in five."

"Yes, Lapwony." With a backward glance at Ricky, Patrick and forty young rebels sprinted into the village.

Otim then pulled Odong to his feet. "Are you hiding any weapons here?" he snarled in the old man's face.

"No."

Otim pulled out his panga. "If I find out you're lying to me, you'll watch your children die."

Amito and Abalo began to cry.

Otim walked over to Okwer and looked back at Odong as he pressed his panga under the boy's trembling chin. "You're not lying to me, are you?"

Two years before, Ricky had been powerless to stop Otim from torturing and killing his parents and sisters; he would not sit by and watch the wild man destroy another family. He stood up next to the man who'd taken him into his home. "He's not lying, Lapwony. There are no weapons here."

Otim stepped back from the boy.

"Ricky!" Trench yelled. "We thought you were dead. Where have you been?"

"I fell behind in the ambush. I didn't hear the call for retreat."

"There was no call," Trench said. "We all ran as soon as we saw him."

"Who?" Ricky asked.

"The man with the two-tipped spear. Didn't you see him leading the troops?"

"No," Ricky said. "I only saw hundreds of soldiers running across the field. By the time I noticed you'd retreated, you were way ahead of me. This family agreed to take me in until you returned."

Overcoming the initial shock at seeing the rebel he was certain he'd left dead on the battlefield, Otim found his voice. "Where are your uniform and weapons?"

"I hid them in the bush."

"Go get them," Otim ordered.

Reluctant to leave Odong and his family with the wild man for long, Ricky hurried to the spot where he'd stashed his belongings and quickly pulled on his military fatigues. Tucking his panga in his belt, he slung his rifle over his shoulder and rushed back to the homestead, but the wild man was gone.

"Where's Otim?" he asked.

Trench pointed toward the road. "He took the battalion to rendezvous with the rest of the Gilva brigade. I was ordered to wait for Komakech's battalion to come through to report what we found here, though there's not much to report." He adjusted his rifle's shoulder strap. "If it weren't for finding you, this raid would have been a complete loss, except for the boy and girl, of course, but I think Otim's already claimed the girl."

Dread settled in Ricky's stomach as he turned to see only Odong and his wife sitting by the fire. A large welt swelled under the old man's eye, and his glasses lay broken on the ground.

"They took the boy and girl?" Ricky asked.

"Of course," Trench said, surprised by the question.

"When will Komakech be coming through?"

"Any minute now."

Ricky glanced back at Odong holding his wife as she wept. "I'll wait with you," he said. "So I can also report to Komakech."

The Gilva commander emerged from the bush minutes later, followed by what Ricky guessed were two hundred rebels. He stopped when he saw his favorite fighter. "You're alive! I told Otim you'd find your way back to us. What happened?"

Aware that every minute Okwer and Abalo spent with Otim put their lives in greater danger, Ricky quickly relayed the events of the last two days to the commander, careful to leave out the part where he planned to escape for home.

"Afande, if not for this family, I would have been caught by the military or worse. I owe them my life. We should not take their children. The woman is injured, and the man is too old to work his fields on his own."

"Where are the boy and girl now?" Komakech asked Trench.

"At the rendezvous point."

"Go retrieve them," Komakech said.

"Yes, Afande."

As Trench ran toward the road, Ricky knelt before Odong and Amito.

"Thank you," Amito cried, clutching his hand in hers.

"Thank you," Ricky said. "For everything."

"I'm sorry we couldn't do more," Odong said.

Ricky picked up his glasses and wiped the dirt from the lenses. "You did more than you know," he said, handing them to the old man.

"Yes," Komakech added. "You've proven yourselves loyal to Kony by harboring one of his best fighters. You and your family will be spared."

Odong and Amito said nothing to contradict Komakech's assumptions regarding their actions as the commander turned to leave, nor did they try to stop Ricky when he followed.

# 40

# RICKY

Several weeks after Ricky's stay with Odong and his family, the rebels targeted a homestead in the Kitgum district. After pillaging the family's belongings and abducting the mother and daughter, Komakech ordered the rebels to stay the night at the homestead and leave early in the morning.

Ricky's injured leg throbbed from the constant marching, and his limp had become more pronounced with every step. A good night's rest would help reduce the swelling and the chances of Komakech ordering him back to the sick bay. Leaning up against a tree near the main house, he fell asleep, only to awaken an hour later.

"Get up," Trench told him. "Otim wants us to scout ahead."

Cringing against the pain in his leg, Ricky grabbed his rifle. They walked in silence for several kilometers, but as they neared a bend in the road, Ricky stopped and put a hand on Trench's arm. The rebel turned to ask Ricky what was wrong, and Ricky held a single finger up to his lips. In the silence of their still-ness, they heard it, the rhythmic crunch of marching.

Trench leaned in and whispered, "Quick, we'll have to ambush them." He pointed to the tall grass by the side of the road. "You wait here." He then pointed in the direction of the approaching troops. "I'll go ahead twenty meters and hide back in the bush, so they won't see me when they come around the bend. Don't fire until I do. When you hear gunshots, jump out, and we'll have them trapped from the front and back."

"Yes, Afande."

Ricky hid behind a grouping of small shrubs at the side of the road while Trench ran ahead to his post. Minutes crept by. Ricky's muscles tensed in expectation of the crack of gunfire, but the only sound he heard was the crunch of footsteps grow-ing closer to his position. He shifted his gun to the perfect angle to take down as many of the soldiers in the front as possible while Trench fired upon the soldiers in the back. It was a good plan. He couldn't understand why Trench wasn't firing. The sol-diers were now well past the rebel's position. If they waited much longer, they'd lose their advantage. Peering through the scrub, Ricky spotted the men marching his way and suddenly understood why Trench remained hidden.

A thin man led the troops. He stood shorter than the sol-diers following him, but he held his head high and walked with the confidence of a man untethered by doubt or fear. Several ribbons adorned his full military uniform, but it was not his uniform that made Ricky pause. He had faced military captains on the battlefield before. It was what the captain carried that made Ricky sink lower behind the shrub. In one hand, the man held an AK-47. In the other, he held a two-tipped spear.

The captain's confident gait and his troops' relaxed postures revealed they did not suspect an ambush. Ricky had little time to think. The captain would be upon his position within five strides. Ricky's eyes narrowed on his prey, and his muscles bunched in preparation for attack.

As he waited to strike, Ricky sensed his father's voice, a voice he'd buried deep inside him to keep it safe from Kony's reach, whispering from his past about a man who escaped the LRA.

*When given the choice, he chose life. Because he never willingly took a life, God spared his.*

Ricky was not on the battlefield facing an enemy determined to kill him. He had a choice. He could remain hidden like Trench and let the men pass. If he chose to spare their lives, perhaps God would spare his.

Ricky let his father's voice fill his mind, but as the captain with the two-tipped spear neared his position on the side of the road, other voices crowded his thoughts. Frightened voices, cowering in the dark of night.

*Hundreds of rebels have died by his hand. Thousands.*

*He made a deal with the devil. In return for invulnerability, he must kill every one of the Holy Spirit's servants.*

*He takes no prisoners and leaves no survivors.*

They grew louder, warning that if Ricky let this man pass,

God might spare his life, but the witch would never spare the lives of the rebels asleep at the homestead, including Patrick.

With that one truth, his father's voice fell silent.

*I have no choice*, Ricky thought as he opened fire on the man with the two-tipped spear and his troops.

Four soldiers fell in the first volley of bullets. The witch man was not among them. He'd jumped to the other side of the road at the first shot. Jamming his spear into the ground, the captain raised his AK-47 and fired above the bushes where Ricky hid.

Ricky ducked lower. He couldn't believe he'd missed the witch man. He'd been directly in Ricky's sight. As he fired and missed the captain again, the fragment of a fevered nightmare cut through his thoughts.

*A man with a two-tipped spear standing over Patrick's lifeless body.*

"No!" he screamed as he stood and took aim at the captain.

From their positions on opposite sides of the road, the witch commander and boy soldier fired upon each other while the soldiers who'd survived Ricky's ambush retreated and Trench remained hidden.

*The rebels will have heard the gunfire and escaped*, Ricky thought as he fired again. *I will die, but Patrick will live.*

The captain, having mistaken Ricky's first barrage of gunfire as the work of many rebels, yelled at his retreating troops in Kiswahili while he fired at Ricky.

"Shoot them! Get them! Fire! Go in front, go!"

Shots sprayed to Ricky's right and left. He fired back, and the captain's right leg buckled. Bullets struck the ground at Ricky's feet, kicking up rocks and dirt that stung his legs as the captain's weapon dipped forward. Jumping back, Ricky fired again, and an inarticulate scream ripped from the witch's throat. As inky black spots seeped through the captain's uniform and expanded across his chest and stomach, the captain glared at Ricky in disbelief. He'd been ambushed by a single rebel. A child.

Fury surged through the captain in a primal scream as he ripped his spear from the ground and raised his AK-47. He struggled to keep the weapon level as he staggered forward. Ricky stepped back, but the captain's leg failed him again and Ricky lowered his weapon as the untouchable witch with the two-tipped spear sank to the ground.

Screaming and gunfire followed the captain's death as the troops, who'd retreated at Ricky's first shot, regrouped and rushed forward to aid their fallen leader. Grabbing the weapons of three dead soldiers and the captain's spear, Ricky sprinted for the jungle. He stayed under cover of the bush, and despite the jolt of pain each step sent through his left leg, he ran until he found the Gilva brigade. The rebels had heard the gunfire and retreated several kilometers from the homestead.

"Don't shoot!" he called out. "It's me, Ricky!"

"Ricky?" Komakech said, surprise warping the name into a question.

Trench stood next to the commander. His eyes widened as Ricky emerged from the jungle. "How did you escape the witch?" he asked. "I saw him on the road and then I heard gunshots."

"I didn't escape him, Afande," Ricky said, handing Trench the military guns. "I fought him."

Trench stepped back. "You fought him?"

"Yes, Afande."

The commanders fell silent and stared at the young rebel, either unwilling or unable to believe his claim.

"The witch is dead," Ricky said, handing Komakech the two-tipped spear.

Komakech grabbed Ricky by the shoulder and turned to his troops. "Ricky looked the devil himself in the eye and did not blink! He killed the witch with the two-tipped spear!" Otim's eyes narrowed on Ricky as Komakech held his hand up in the air. "He is now a senior fighter!"

The commander stepped back and smiled like a proud father as the rebels gathered around Ricky. The questions came fast and furious, with every rebel vying for Ricky's attention.

"What did he look like?"

"Did his eyes glow red like they say?"

"Did he try to stab you with his spear?"

"How many bullets did it take to kill him?"

Ricky answered their questions, eager to speak with Patrick, who waited at the back of the pack. As the crowd dispersed, many praised Ricky for his courage while others attributed the tremendous feat to his strong belief in Kony.

Finally alone, Patrick reached out to pull Ricky into an embrace, but stopped when he noticed Otim watching. Instead, he nodded once and patted Ricky on the shoulder. "Good job, my big little brother."

# 41

# SAMUEL

Samuel slid a black piece to an open space on the checkerboard. "What happens now?"

"Now it's my turn," the man said.

"No. I mean what happens now with the children?"

The man moved one of his red pieces toward Samuel's checker. "When they are done here, most will return to their villages."

Samuel slid another piece forward. "Don't you worry the villagers will punish them for what they did?"

"No," the man said, taking his turn. "Sometimes the elders ask to perform a cleansing ritual, but that's only done with the child's consent and under the staff's supervision."

Samuel pressed a piece forward, but seeing that the man's next move would put him at risk, he slid it back and moved another checker. "You said some stay."

The man moved his piece to the square Samuel had predicted. "A few stay to get the extended care they need, but they're free to leave whenever they want."

Noticing the right side of the board opening up, Samuel slid a piece in that direction. Within three moves, he made it to the man's side of the board. "King me."

"Well done," the man said. "And here I thought it might take you a while to get the hang of this game again."

After the man's turn, Samuel used his kinged piece to chase the man's red checkers around the board, capturing several. "But they don't all return to their villages?" he asked, forming a small pile of red checkers in front of him.

"No. Some choose to build their lives somewhere new."

The man zigzag jumped two of Samuel's pieces in one move, ending in a space at the far end of the board. "King me, please."

A frown tugged at Samuel's mouth as he crowned the man's checker, but it disappeared when he saw that he could retaliate by jumping a red piece left unprotected in the man's bold move.

They played in silence after that, both concentrating only on the next move. Every time Samuel captured one of the man's pieces, the man claimed one of his. If the man's father really had let him win as a child, it was not a practice the man had adopted as an adult. He was playing to win, but so was Samuel. After ten minutes of tense play, only three of the original twenty-four pieces remained. Two blacks and one red.

While he waited for the man to admit his defeat, Samuel sat back and watched the boys on the field. "So some never go home?"

The man looked up from studying the board. "Home is not

always a place on a map." He slid his checker into one of the open spaces.

"But you said some child soldiers never go back to their villages," Samuel said as he captured the man's last piece.

The man smiled as though he'd won. "True. But I didn't say they never find home."

# 42

# RICKY

Between Ricky's promotion and Patrick's reliability on his intel missions, the brothers' status within the Gilva brigade shifted from dispensable abductees to valued rebels. Except for Otim, the commanders no longer scrutinized their every movement, allowing them more freedom and a hope for escape. The time was drawing near. Ricky sensed it. They just needed the opportunity.

On a cool May morning, the rebels broke camp before dawn. In a routine move, Komakech ordered Trench to take Patrick and two other boys ahead of the brigade to scout the area surrounding the next village. As Patrick passed Ricky, he slowed his pace just enough so that for a few steps he fell in line with his brother's stride. The change in cadence was so subtle, done thousands of times over their twenty-eight months of captivity, that Ricky did not have to look to know his brother was with him.

"Obeno," Patrick said under his breath.

"Obeno," Ricky replied.

Every other time, Patrick always left Ricky's side the second Ricky had repeated their code word, but that morning he walked alongside Ricky a few steps more before kicking up his pace. Ricky watched his brother run ahead to the edge of the jungle, where Trench waited. Before he entered the bush, Patrick glanced back and, raising one hand, nodded once.

Ricky nodded back, but his brother was already gone.

That afternoon, when the small group of spies rejoined the 250 Gilva rebels making camp in the bush, Patrick was not among them. While Trench reported to Komakech and Otim, Ricky sat down near the other two spies from Patrick's group and took out his panga. He busied himself with sharpening the weapon as the rebels picked through the leftover goat and cassava the female abductees had prepared. Ricky's hand shook with concern for Patrick as he ran the flat stone along the edge of his blade. Before he spoke, he glanced over his shoulder to make sure Otim wasn't watching, but the wild man's attention remained focused on Trench. Turning back to the rebel spies, Ricky cleared his throat. Both rebels looked up from their food.

"Keep eating," Ricky said through still lips. Without argument, they looked back to their goat meat, but Ricky knew he had their attention. "Where's Patrick?" he asked, never taking his eyes off his machete.

"We don't know," one of the rebels said.

"We split up to investigate the jungle surrounding the village," the other whispered. "Patrick was supposed to meet up with us within an hour, but he never showed."

"Did you look for him?"

"Yes, but we spotted military troops patrolling the area he was scouting, so Afande ordered us to retreat."

"Was he captured?"

"We don't know," the first rebel said. "We didn't see him with the patrol troops, but there may have been more in the area."

"Did you hear any gunfire?"

"No."

The youngest rebel, no older than thirteen, glanced over at Ricky. His gaze lingered on the panga in Ricky's hands before returning to the hunk of cassava resting on his leg. "Afande thinks he ran," he whispered.

Ricky closed his eyes and let the rebel's words wash over his raw nerves like a balm. Patrick had kept his promise. He would find obeno, and he'd let everyone there know that Ricky would be home soon, too. The thought calmed the tremble in Ricky's hand, and he immediately began planning his escape.

"Ricky!"

All three rebels flinched at the anger in Otim's voice. Ricky tucked his panga in his belt and ran over to where his commanders waited.

"Do you know where your brother is?" Komakech asked.

"I thought he was with Trench," Ricky replied.

"No," Komakech said. "He's gone missing."

Otim stepped forward. "It looks like your coward of a brother has run."

Ricky kept his face emotionless.

"What do you have to say about that?" Otim prodded.

Ricky stared at the wild man and knew what he must do if he had any hope of joining his brother. The knowledge that his brother was finally free strengthened his conviction and voice. "If that's true, he's a traitor."

Otim's eyes narrowed. "Perhaps cowardice runs in his family. I remember the way your parents cowered before death."

Ricky's hand tightened around his panga, but he kept his face free of emotion, thinking only of Patrick.

Otim pressed his face closer to Ricky's. "I remember how they begged for mercy."

"That's enough," Komakech said. "You are dismissed, Ricky."

"Yes, Afande," Ricky said.

As he walked away, he overheard Otim. "I don't trust him, Afande. If his brother ran, he will follow."

"Keep an eye on him," Komakech replied. "If it looks like he's even thinking of running, stop him."

Fear prickled on the back of Ricky's neck at the satisfied smile he knew without looking accompanied the wild man's response.

"Yes, Afande."

# 43

# RICKY

After Patrick's escape, Ricky followed every order, never giving his commanders the slightest reason to question his allegiance. He pretended to hate his brother and tried to prove himself a trustworthy soldier to fortify Komakech's trust.

After several weeks, he was put in charge of night deployment, monitoring the rebels as they slept. From his new position, he was able to study the sleep patterns of the commanders and abductees. His heart ached to return home to his brother, but he had to be patient. He could not leave without doing something first.

"I'm planning to escape," he whispered one night as he walked the perimeter of the LRA camp with two of the young boys in his coy.

His words caused James to stumble. Regaining his footing, the twelve-year-old glanced over at Peter, whose eyes reflected the same shock at Ricky's statement.

They walked in silence for several minutes before Ricky spoke again. "I want you to come with me."

The boys stared straight ahead, refusing to look at their commander. Ricky had anticipated their resistance to his offer. The boys had been with the LRA long enough to suspect such a proposal as a trap. The LRA regularly had rebels approach new abductees with an offer of escape to gauge their susceptibility to such temptation. Ricky had seen many abductees fall prey to the cruel scheme. The children's words against the LRA and their willingness to run earned them a swift death sentence at the hands of the other abductees. James and Peter were responding just as they should to such a statement, with silence.

After they completed their patrol, Ricky lay on the wet grass, searching the night skies for the mother in the moon. When she finally crept out from behind a cloud, he thought of his parents' spirits and prayed for their protection. He'd taken a great risk speaking to Peter and James of his plan. There was no trust in the bush. To prove their allegiance to the LRA, the boys would be wise to expose Ricky's plan to Otim and secure their survival for another day.

Panic swelled in his chest at the thought of James and Peter betraying him. He could convince Komakech he was testing the boys' loyalty, but he'd never convince the wild man. His muscles tightened with an urgency to run. Fighting the paranoia threatening to seize control, Ricky glanced over to where James and Peter lay. James was curled up on his side with his eyes squeezed shut, but Peter stared back at Ricky. Ricky could sense the conflict raging behind the boy's dark eyes, and he knew that regardless of the risk, he had to be patient. If he escaped and left Peter and James behind, they'd be punished, and any hope of escape for them would be destroyed. Looking back to the moon, Ricky decided to wait until they were ready, and he prayed Patrick would forgive him for taking so long to join him.

Each day when the boys joined Ricky for patrol, he whispered to them about escaping. It took weeks of whispers before he earned the boys' trust, and then days of planning and waiting for the perfect moment to run.

Finally, an opportunity arrived. One evening after sunset, Ricky began his usual routine. He moved around the perimeter of a swampy area to see if it was safe for the brigade to set up camp. As he walked, he discovered a good spot in the tangled vegetation where he and the boys might slip away unseen. Completing his surveillance of the area, Ricky returned to his coy. He glanced at James and Peter as he passed and with a subtle nod told them the direction of their escape route. Ricky then informed his commanders that the location was secure, and hundreds of rebels spread out to claim their pieces of damp ground for the night.

During the noise and confusion, Ricky met James and Peter at the designated spot. Without a word, they slipped into the tall grass and got to work, pressing down the grass for over fifty meters to create a secret pathway. At one point, Ricky heard voices nearing their position. Crouching down, he raised a finger to his lips, and the boys sank lower in the grass. A pair of rebel guards stopped several steps from where Ricky and the boys hid. Every muscle in Ricky's body tightened with dread in anticipation of the first shot. Closing his eyes in silent prayer, he held his breath, afraid the slightest sound would reveal them.

The two rebels discussed the next village the LRA planned to strike and how they hoped to take new wives there, and then they continued walking. Ricky and the boys remained hidden in the grass until the guards' voices and footsteps had faded. Then Ricky motioned for the boys to finish trampling down the grass. With the task complete, the three slipped back into the LRA camp and continued their surveillance of the brigade just as they'd done every night for three months.

Several hours later, Ricky signaled the boys. Silent as shadows, they crept into the bush, careful only to step on the path they'd prepared hours before. The scratch of tree branches swaying in the night breeze froze Ricky midstep. He glanced back at James and Peter. The moon reflected off their eyes in watery pools. A rustling in the grass to their left seized their breaths, and Ricky held a finger to his lips. The boys, too terrified to move, did not nod back, but kept their wide eyes locked on Ricky's face. A single tear captured a glint of moonlight as it slid down James's cheek. The rustling moved closer and Ricky's muscles tensed, preparing to run, but the sound changed direction and scurried away.

Ricky knew they had to move, but doubt rooted him to the ground. If they returned to camp now, they could slip in unseen, and no one would ever know of their plan. Another tear ran down James's cheek. Ricky knew the consequences if the rebels caught them. Their deaths would be slow and painful. He was risking the boys' lives, but he knew by running they at least had a chance for a life and freedom, a chance that did not exist for them in the LRA.

Motioning for the boys to follow, Ricky stepped from the flattened path and entered the sea of elephant grass separating them from the road.

The Aswa River ran near the rebel camp, giving Ricky a rough idea of their location. Home was east, so Ricky led the boys west in hopes of confusing the rebels once they finally realized the boys and he were gone. Ricky and the boys walked for over five kilometers before turning north and then finally eastward for home.

With every step, Ricky listened for the sounds of pursuit, but they did not come.

They trudged along a muddy stretch of road for hours until the morning sun appeared before them. Ricky wanted to put as much distance as possible between the LRA camp and themselves, but the harsh light of day made him anxious.

As they walked, they came across a man approaching from the opposite direction.

"Good morning," Ricky said.

The man nodded, but his eyes lingered on Ricky and the two boys for two strides too long. Ricky's skin crept with nervousness as they continued down the road. James and Peter, sensing his unease, stopped talking. When the man was out of sight, Ricky stepped off the road. The boys followed. He walked into the bush until the trees and grasses were dense enough to conceal them, and then he sat down.

"What are we doing?" James asked.

"Hiding," Ricky said.

"But shouldn't we keep moving?" Peter asked. "The LRA will know by now that we're gone. They'll send rebels to hunt us down."

"It's too dangerous to travel by day," Ricky explained. "That man believed I was LRA."

"How do you know?" James asked.

"I saw it in his eyes. He was scared of us . . ." Ricky took in the wild, filthy appearance of the young boys and knew that after more than two years with the LRA, he looked wilder. "He was scared of me. We must travel only at night." He paused for a minute to consider the proposal he was about to make, a proposal he'd determined was necessary the moment he'd seen the fear and suspicion in the man's eyes. "And we must split up."

"Split up?" James asked.

"What do you mean?" Peter asked.

"It's too risky for us to travel together," Ricky said.

"But we don't know how to get home," James said.

"We'll get lost in the dark," Peter added.

"The stars will guide you home," Ricky said, "and the moon will light your way."

Panic rose in James's voice. "But the LRA will find us."

"You have a better chance without me," Ricky said. "You still look like children."

"But what happens when we get to our villages?" Peter asked. "They'll know we were with the LRA."

Tears welled in James's eyes. "Do you think they'll arrest us? Or kill us?"

"They know what I did," Peter said, the words trembling on his lips. "They saw me cut my uncle."

Ricky grabbed Peter's hand and held it tight. "They saw the LRA force you to cut him."

"Do you think they'll understand?" he asked.

Ricky stared down at Peter's hand. Even after months of hunger, his fingers still retained the pudginess of a child's. Ricky thought of Christine's hands reaching out as she begged him to pick her up and swing her through the air. He remembered the last time he'd seen her little hands, clinging to Mama's skirt as the rebels forced his family into the hut. He closed his fingers around Peter's, snuffing out the memory before it rekindled and consumed him.

He then examined his own hand, thick with calluses. The skin, ashen and puckered from dehydration, bore the scars of countless battles. For so long, his hands had fired guns and swung pangas. They'd looted burning villages and cinched ropes around the wrists of terrified children. They'd directed attacks and signaled retreats. On the battlefield, they'd protected the injured and stolen from the dead and dying. Ugandan soil and dried blood burrowed deep beneath his fingernails and occupied every crack and crease of his skin. His were no longer the hands of a child. They were the hands of a soldier. How would anyone ever understand what they'd done? How would he?

He looked at the boys. They'd discard their military gear in the night, so they wouldn't draw attention on the road. Dressed in only the shorts and shirts the LRA abducted them in, James and Peter appeared smaller and more vulnerable. He reached out and grabbed hold of James's hand. "You will make them understand."

"Do you think the people of your village will understand?" James asked.

"I don't know," Ricky admitted, "but it's my home, and my brother is there. And even if the others can't understand what I've done, Patrick will, and he'll forgive me."

The boys huddled together for warmth and security. For hours, they held hands and prayed for one another's safety. When night arrived, they left the bush and returned to the road. Standing at a crossroads with tears running down their cheeks, they hugged. The young boys' small bodies trembled in Ricky's arms.

"Stay safe," he whispered, letting them go. "And reach home well."

Then, turning away, he looked to the stars and headed toward home.

# 44

# SAMUEL

"You can't stop playing without giving me another chance to win," the man said, resetting the board. "Are you up for one more?"

Samuel checked the road, but saw no sign of the soldier's truck. On the field, the children had halted their game to speak with the elderly man who'd instructed them in building the brick wall earlier in the day. With nothing else to occupy his time, Samuel scooted his chair up to the table. "I guess."

The man swung the board around, so the red checkers sat before Samuel. "This time I go first."

Samuel tried to concentrate on the game, but the man's words about finding home distracted his play, and in four moves, the man captured one of his pieces.

"You're not going to let me win, are you?" the man asked.

Samuel slid another piece away from one of the man's checkers. "No."

"Good."

As the man focused on the game, Samuel allowed his thoughts to return to the last time he'd been home. Before he was shot and left for dead. Before he was a killer and thief. A rebel and prisoner.

Before the night the rebels came to his village and found his family sleeping in their hut. Before the rebels shoved a gun in Samuel's hands and threatened to kill his mother. Before Samuel pulled the trigger and watched his father fall. Before.

He was a student and classmate.

A cousin and friend.

A brother and son.

But that was before, and sitting on the porch across from the man, *before* felt as distant and unreachable as home.

Having completed his turn, the man looked up from the board. "Your move, Samuel."

## 45

# RICKY

It took Ricky three days to reach his village. Three days of hiding in the bush and three nights of walking, with only the stars for guides and his thoughts for company. The rustling of tall grass and the murmurings of passing travelers often left him paralyzed along the roadside or in the bush, but two forces urged him forward.

The first was fear. Cruel and taunting, it whispered, louder and louder, quickening his heart and pace.

*They're coming for you. They'll find you. And then they'll kill you.*

The second was hope. The promise of home glinted in every distant star. Hope pulled Ricky up from where he lay exhausted and starving in the bush. It encouraged him to keep walking, to reach his brother. To find obeno.

When he arrived at his village on the morning of the third day, Ricky headed straight to his family's homestead, looking for his brother.

The fields sat empty of the cattle Father had tended, and wild grasses and weeds, stretching high above Ricky's head, claimed the gardens Mama had so meticulously maintained. A mango seed Patrick and he planted as young boys had grown into an even taller, stronger tree in their absence. Its sturdy branches, covered in thousands of thin, pointy leaves, easily bore the weight of the heavy fruit hanging below them in thick bunches. From the outside, his sisters' hut and the main building showed the signs of years of neglect: broken windows, faded, peeling paint, rusted tin roofing, and rotted doors and window frames.

As Ricky neared the spot where Patrick's and his sleeping hut once stood, he froze. All that remained was the crescent shape of a low, broken wall. Tall grass and wildflowers encroached on the hut, growing all around it and spilling out from inside the broken circle. In the center stood a charred stump, the remnants of the post to which his parents and sisters had been tied.

No stone marked this spot where his family had perished. No engraved words preserved their names or their place in the world. But the horror of that day and the brutality of their deaths haunted every crack of blackened wood and piece of crumbling brick. Everywhere Ricky looked, he saw their spirits.

*Margaret. Her tears darkening Baba's shirt.*

*Betty. Her bare feet stumbling along the dirt path as the rebels forced her into the hut.*

*Christine. Her dark eyes peeking out from the protection of Mama's embrace.*

*Baba. His strong arms tightening around his daughters.*

*Mama. Her hands reaching for him. Her eyes holding him one last time.*

The memory, thick and dark as smoke, forced Ricky to his knees, where he gripped his head and pressed his palms to his ears to shut out the anguished screams of his family piercing his mind. When he could no longer bear to hear their cries, he lifted his arms and voice to the sky and joined them. The horror and grief he'd been denied the day the rebels killed his family tore from his body, where it had festered for so long. He cried until his voice broke, and then he curled up on the ground before the burned remains of his family and home and sobbed as wave upon wave of sadness crashed over him.

When he at last found the strength to stand, he entered the neglected farmhouse where his parents once slept. He couldn't understand why his brother wasn't there to greet him. He considered checking for him at the well or in the village, but hesitated when he remembered the LRA commanders' warnings about how villagers treated former rebels. He decided it would be best to remain at the homestead until his brother returned. Then they could face the villagers together.

Sitting beneath their mango tree, he waited.

As night fell and Patrick had still not returned, Ricky sensed something was wrong. Leaving the tree, he crossed the small field separating his family's homestead from their neighbor Okot's property. He lifted his hand to knock on Okot's door, but paused as his anxiety over how his old neighbor would react to his reappearance wrestled with concern for his brother. He glanced back at his homestead, hoping to see Patrick walking up the path, but the path was empty.

He knocked twice. When there was no answer, he lifted his hand to knock again, but stopped when he heard a slow shuffling inside the hut. He stepped back as the door swung open.

Ricky had last seen Okot the day the LRA arrived. The old man's face and posture revealed that the years since that day had not been kind. His fragile shoulders curled forward, rounding his back and stealing centimeters from the man who had once stood as tall as Ricky's father. In his right hand, he clutched a wooden cane.

The elderly man squinted into the darkness surrounding his hut. Realizing that Okot could not see him, Ricky stepped forward, and Okot's eyes widened.

After several seconds of silence, Ricky cleared his throat. "Excuse me, Afande," he said. His voice, raw with thirst and grief, sounded strange to his ears, so he cleared his throat again. "Excuse me for startling you," he said. "Have you seen . . ."

His voice trailed off as the image of Okot grabbing his seventeen-year-old son and running for the bush as the wild man beat Thomas by the road flashed across his mind.

While he struggled to reclaim his voice, Okot peered nervously into the darkness surrounding his hut.

"I'm alone," Ricky said.

With a suspicious grunt, the old man straightened his posture and steeled his gaze. "Who are you? What do you want?"

Ricky stammered out his name. "I'm looking for my brother."

The elderly man brought a trembling hand to his lips. "Ricky?" He studied the boy's features for proof of his claim.

"I'm looking for Patrick," Ricky said. "He escaped Kony's army three months ago. Have you seen him?"

"Yes," the old man said. "He was here."

"Was? Where is he now?"

Okot's eyes darted back toward the darkness. Ricky turned to see what he kept looking at, but there was nothing behind him.

"Please," he said. "Where did my brother go?"

A slight tremor took hold of Okot. Ricky stepped back so he wouldn't frighten him. "Where's Patrick?" he asked in a softer voice.

Okot refused to meet his eyes as he gripped his cane. "He was ill."

Ricky stepped forward. "Patrick's sick? Where'd they take him?"

Okot positioned himself behind the door. "I don't know. You should go home and wait there."

Desperate for answers, Ricky moved to follow the man inside. Okot pressed the door closed, but Ricky stopped it with his foot. "Please. I need to go to him. He needs to know I escaped, and I'm home. I know it will make him feel better."

Okot looked beyond Ricky into the night and shook his head. "It's too late."

Ricky knew the old man was right. Wherever they'd taken

him, the doctors would never let him in to see Patrick at such an hour. He would have to wait until morning. Maybe by then, Patrick would have returned. He pulled his foot back from the doorframe. "What should I do?" he asked.

"I don't know," Okot said. "I'm sorry." And then he closed the door.

Disappointed and uncertain where else to go for help, Ricky returned to his family's homestead. He tried sleeping on the floor of his parents' room, but in the quiet of night, fear's whisperings grew louder and more insistent.

*They're coming for you. They'll find you. And then they'll kill you.*

Unable to silence their warnings, Ricky walked deep into the surrounding bush, where he hid until morning.

At the first blush of sunrise, Ricky returned to his family's homestead, hoping to find Patrick. Instead, a small gathering of village elders greeted him.

"Ricky," an elder said. "Okot told us you had returned."

"I'm looking for Patrick," Ricky said. "Okot said he'd be here. Where is he?"

"We will explain where your brother is," a second elder said, "but first we have some questions for you." He motioned for Ricky to sit.

Anxiousness crept through Ricky. For a moment he considered running, but the elders made no move to apprehend him, so he eased down to the ground. For an hour, he sat across from the six elders, answering question after question about his time in the LRA, hoping each one was the last, but the questions kept coming.

"*What happened to you in the bush?*"

"*How did you manage to escape?*"

"*Where are the other boys who were taken with you?*"

"*Are they still alive?*"

"*What punishments did you receive?*"

"*Did you kill people?*"

With each question, Ricky's concern for his brother grew. Had Patrick received a similar interrogation? And if so, did they find him guilty and punish him? Is that why his brother needed medical care?

"Please," he interrupted. "Where is my brother?"

The men looked at one another. The oldest nodded and in a quiet voice, heavy with burden, told Ricky of Patrick's arrival three months earlier.

"When Patrick first entered the village, there was great fear among us."

Ricky thought of the change in Patrick's appearance while in the LRA. As a rebel spy, his brother had to keep his hair short so he could blend in with the people in the villages he scouted, but it did little to disguise the nightmare he'd experienced in Kony's army. It clung to him. Ricky imagined how frightened the villagers, who'd lost sons and daughters to the LRA, must have been when they saw a filthy, lice-infested wild man coming toward them.

Self-conscious about his own appearance, Ricky pushed his

dreadlocks from his face and adjusted the soiled, tattered T-shirt hanging from his bony shoulders. He'd worn the shirt ever since Patrick had given it to him following a raid on a village near the Sudan border. His muscles ached to tear the stolen shirt from his body, but he didn't want to give the elders, who were scrutinizing his every move, any reason to think he'd gone mad. He stared down at his bare feet, thick with calluses from years of marching, and recalled the shock in his neighbor Okot's eyes when he'd opened his door and found Ricky standing there.

"You thought he was LRA," he said.

"We thought he was a ghost," the head elder admitted.

Surprised, Ricky looked up.

"A week after you and your brother were abducted," the elder explained, "we heard news you'd both been killed by the river, so when we saw your brother, looking as he did, walking into the village . . ."

"You were afraid," Ricky said.

"At first," the elder admitted, "but when we realized it was Patrick and that he had survived, we were happy to see him. Just as we are happy to see you. We fed him and asked him questions about his time with the LRA."

Relief flooded through the boy. They'd welcomed his brother, just as he'd prayed they would.

"We needed to know if Patrick had gone mad during his time with the rebels," another elder added.

One by one, Ricky looked at the faces of the men seated

before him. They were faces he'd known since birth. Men who'd told him stories by the village fire and taught him how to fish in the river. Men who'd named the well after him and whose broken watches had littered the floor of Patrick's and his hut. These men knew him and his brother, yet as they observed Ricky's reaction to their words, their bodies tensed with fear and their eyes followed his every move as if he were a snake preparing to strike.

Ricky understood why the men were afraid. They wondered if he and Patrick had returned as bloodthirsty animals, unable to escape what they'd done in Kony's army, too violent and dangerous to stay there.

Ricky recalled Otim's frantic pacing the day of the abduction. He remembered how the wild man had demanded to know how many people he had killed, and how angry he had become when denied the taking of the lives he had wanted to claim at the market. Ricky could still see Otim's eyes searching the faces of every abductee for his next kill. He remembered the commander's rotted smile as he ordered the abductees to cut Joseph well after the boy had taken his last breath, just so he could see his blood flow. Ricky flinched at the thought of the red-eyed rebels in Kony's Control Altar brigade. How their hands had trembled with barely contained excitement as they grasped their pangas and howled with delight at Kony's order to kill.

Ricky sat very still, hoping to lessen their mistrust as he tried to determine what judgment they had passed on his brother when he returned, and what judgment they were forming on him now.

"We had a responsibility to our people," the elder continued cautiously. "You understand, don't you, Ricky?"

"Yes," Ricky replied, struggling to keep his voice calm. "And what did you find?"

"Patrick answered all our questions, and we took him back into our community."

"Then where is he?" Ricky asked.

The five men looked to the head elder. "Patrick had difficulties adjusting to being back," he said. "He lived alone here on your family's compound, but only during the day. At night he would go off into the bush."

The same thing Ricky had done . . . Tears swelled in his eyes as he thought of Patrick, alone in the bush outside their home, not knowing if his younger brother would ever escape the LRA and join him. "Where is he?" he asked quietly.

"He spoke to no one," the elder said, "and took no offers for work. Most days he spent here at your farm."

Ricky closed his eyes, sending tears spilling down his cheeks. "Where is Patrick?" he whispered.

The elder, unable to look Ricky in the eye, continued. "Life is fragile."

Ricky's hands began to tremble. "Where is Patrick?"

"And for some, the damage is too great."

"Where is my brother?" Ricky asked in an angry whisper.

The men stiffened. They glanced nervously at one another

and then looked to the head elder. The old man, who'd regaled the village children for decades with tales of the past, took a deep breath and then met the eyes of the young man sitting before him. "The damage was too great for Patrick."

Unable to speak, Ricky looked at the men sitting across from him, praying someone would tell him the elder was wrong. They averted their eyes.

"Your neighbor Okot found him," the elder explained.

The image of his neighbor's face the night before flashed across his mind. The shock. The anxiousness.

"Okot said Patrick was alive," Ricky argued. "He said Patrick was ill. He said I should wait here for him to—" Ricky shook his head. "No. Patrick promised we'd find obeno again. He promised. And I'm here now and I want my brother. Where is my brother?"

The elder motioned to Ricky and Patrick's mango tree standing guard along the path to their homestead. "I'm sorry, Ricky. I truly am." His words, spoken gently, struck like lightning. "A few weeks after he returned home, Patrick took his own life."

# RICKY

**Scrambling to his feet, Ricky ran into the family homestead** and slammed the rotted door to shut out the elders' words.

Lies.

Patrick did not survive twenty-seven months in the LRA to come home and take his own life.

Ricky paced the length of his parents' room.

The Gilva brigade was far from Pader when Patrick escaped. It would have taken him weeks, maybe months, to travel such a distance by foot, and only if he didn't get lost on the way.

Ricky glared out the window at the elders slowly walking back to the village.

They were wrong.

They were old and confused.

They didn't know Patrick like he did.

His brother had kept his promise. Ricky knew this. Patrick was on his way back to Pader, and Ricky would wait as long as it took for his brother to find home.

Pacing, he came to the wall where his brother and he had marked their height each year on their birthdays. Fighting back tears, he ran his fingertips over the final thin scratch marks they'd carved on the white wall. He now stood much taller than Patrick's last mark.

His head dipped forward under the weight of all they had lost over the last two years, and he noticed a new carving scratched into the wall below their names and marks.

Trembling with grief, he dropped to his knees as the five faint letters, etched in shaky lines, severed his last strands of hope.

*Obeno.*

* * *

Following the news of his brother's suicide, Ricky spent his days prowling the homestead and his nights sleeping in the bush. He survived by scavenging for food in the jungle or from a few untended fruit trees and plants on the farm.

Okot, who'd lost both of his sons to the LRA, checked on him frequently. One afternoon, as Ricky lay curled up asleep on a shady patch of ground near the charred remains of the hut where his family had perished, the elderly neighbor nudged him with his cane. The boy jumped up, his hands held in front of him to fend off an attack. When he saw it was Okot, he dropped his arms and collapsed back onto the ground.

"Come," the old man said, tossing a hand hoe in front of Ricky. "I need help in my fields."

Ricky stared down at the carved handle of the tool. He ran his fingers over the smooth surface of the pobo wood and thought of Patrick.

"I will give you some food for your help," Okot said, and then, without waiting for Ricky to answer, he turned and hobbled toward his small patch of farmland.

As they worked tilling the neglected soil, Ricky caught the old man studying him. Beneath bushy gray eyebrows, Okot's eyes followed Ricky as he dug up weeds and deepened furrows.

When Ricky left that night for the bush, his neighbor stood in the doorway of his own hut and watched. And when Ricky returned to the family's desolate farm in the morning, Okot met him with a bowl of rice and his hand hoe.

They continued this way for many days, with Okot finding Ricky every morning on his farm and Ricky following him into the fields. Occasionally Okot would ask Ricky basic questions about the planting or sowing, but usually they worked in silence. One evening, he helped Ricky shave his head clean.

Aside from the few words he spoke with Okot, Ricky moved among the rest of the villagers as a silent presence, not of their world and not of the next. Other than the occasional villager who asked him to work as a day laborer, most people shunned Ricky.

One day as he walked through the village to fetch water for Okot, he heard a small voice.

"Hello."

He turned to find a little girl, no more than four years old, standing behind him. She wore a hand-me-down shirt that hung to her ankles. Her smile revealed a handful of baby teeth. No fright or suspicion hid behind her dark brown eyes, and no pity or guilt weighed down her words.

"Hello," he said.

"My name is Ayuki," she said, pulling on her shirt-dress. "What is yours?"

Before he could answer, a woman scooped the child into her arms. As she hurried off with her daughter, she scolded the child. "I've told you not to speak to strangers, especially madmen like him."

After that, Ricky walked to the well through the bush.

He mostly kept to his family's land, guarding the small plot of ground that remained of his past while praying for some hope for his future.

He did not know what else to do.

As days stretched into weeks, Ricky found himself thinking more and more about the girl at the river on the day of his abduction. When he closed his eyes, he could picture how every muscle in her slight body had strained to keep her brother and sisters above the water. At night, hidden deep in the bush, he could hear the echo of her desperate pleas for help and the rebels' cruel laughter. And when he stared at Patrick's and his mango tree, bending low over the path to their home, he remembered the calm look of surrender that washed over the girl's face the moment before she let go and gave herself to the river, as if her spirit had already slipped beneath the dark waters and her body was simply following. Ricky envied her peaceful resignation to the fate that lay before her. In that moment of surrender, she spared herself years of pain and torture at the hands of the LRA and a lifetime of grieving for loved ones lost too soon.

In the LRA, there was little time for thought and grief. There was only time for survival and fear, but now back at his village, all Ricky had was time. Time to think and grieve over all he had lost.

With each passing day, the swirling currents of grief and depression grew stronger. They tugged and pulled at Ricky, threatening to drag him under. Ricky thought of how easy it would be to simply let go. His heart ached from the constant strain to remain above. He was weary and yearned to surrender to death's pull, to silently and peacefully slip beneath its dark waters.

All he had to do was let go, just for a moment. If for one breath he could relax his grip on life, then he would finally, after thousands of kilometers of marching and years of fighting, be at rest, like the girl from the river. Like his parents and sisters. Like Patrick.

But each time Ricky tried to surrender to death's pull, his spirit strained harder. Fueled by images of his family and the sacrifices they'd made for him, Ricky's broken, tattered spirit fought to survive.

So every night, shivering alone in the dark, Ricky prayed to God and his family. "Mama . . . Baba," he begged. Tears flowed from his swollen eyes until they stung. "Patrick, please," he cried. "I'm the only one left. Please, send help."

But what arrived was not what he'd asked for.

Three months after his escape, Ricky sat on the ground at a neighbor's compound with a few other day laborers from the surrounding villages, receiving instructions on a construction job. He struggled to focus on the job leader's words as the ghost of his brother continued to haunt his thoughts. He remembered Patrick taking his hand and leading him from the cassava fields the day he cut his leg.

*"Just hold on. It's going to be fine," his brother had said, looking down at him. "I promise."*

Loud shouting jarred him from his thoughts and awakened dormant instincts. Ricky scrambled to his feet, but the chill of a gun's muzzle on the back of his head and a familiar voice froze him in his tracks.

"Remain seated!" Trench commanded. "Anyone who stands up or tries to run will be shot dead."

Ricky glanced around him. Rebels of the Gilva brigade emerged from the bush surrounding the compound. There was nowhere to run. He slowly lowered himself to the ground and sat hunched over in the dirt, his head hung low as the armed men circled their group. As each man passed, he peeked up at them and recognized every face. Fear, harsh and taunting, whispered in his mind.

*They came for you. They found you. And now they'll kill you.*

Louder and louder it repeated, until it blocked out every sound, every thought.

Avoiding eye contact with the rebels, Ricky weighed his

options. There were but two: death by gunfire or death by panga. Images of the LRA discovering Joseph flashed before his mind.

*Patrick,* Ricky thought, *thank God you are not here for this.*

His muscles tightened, preparing to run and draw the rebels' gunfire, but it was too late. The rebels yanked him to his feet and tied him to the other day laborers. Ricky kept his head bowed and his eyes on the ground. After the rebels tied the men together, they forced them to march.

They marched for over a kilometer. Ricky kept his head down and hunched his shoulders to hide his face and height. At a crossroads, Trench whistled, and the entire line of rebels and abductees stopped.

"We wait here for the others!" Trench announced. "They'll be taking over the lead."

"What others?" one of the day laborers behind Ricky whispered.

Ricky glanced back at Omwony, a twenty-year-old from the neighboring village of Pajule, but did not answer, afraid to speak the words, afraid that saying them would bring his fear to life, but it was already alive and marching toward their small group of rebels at the crossroads.

The wild man's agitated pace stood out in stark contrast to the disciplined, orderly marching of the rest of the approaching rebels. All of the rebels and abductees in Ricky's line turned to watch the larger coy. All except Ricky. He lowered his head and averted his eyes as his old battalion neared. Otim paid no attention to the new abductees as he passed. He was busy talking with an intel rebel, who'd brought news of military troops approaching from the east.

It was a girl who recognized Ricky. One of Otim's wives, no older than fifteen. She'd been taunting the new abductees as she marched past with a baby strapped to her chest in a filthy rag.

She stopped when she neared Ricky, who turned his face away, pretending to look at a group of rebels to his left. She leaned in closer to get a better look. Ricky turned his face farther away, but could feel the heat of her skin. The hot stench of her breath wafted past his nose, and her mouth spread into a venomous smile. Her laughter, loud and crazed, brought the rest of the rebels to a halt.

"Did you really think you could leave the LRA?" she yelled. "Did you really think you could escape?" She poked him hard in the side of his face. "If we get you, we will always have you, even if you run away."

Her questions brought others over to see the target of her taunts. Ricky recognized every face that stared at him, but it was the icy hatred burning in Otim's glare as the rebel commander pushed through the gathering crowd that told him death had finally found him.

The wild man leaned in, toward Ricky's face. "Look who it is. I knew we'd find you, boy." He raised his panga and cut the rope tethering Ricky to the other abductees. Grabbing him by the shirt, he dragged him to the side of the road, where the mob of angry LRA rebels waited. They pulled and tugged at his clothes, ripping them from his body.

Stripped naked, he stood before Otim, his head bowed in numb acceptance of his fate. As the wild man took his assault rifle from his back, Ricky did not protest. He knew the commander had been waiting for his chance to make an example of him ever since their standoff over Patrick returning to the battlefield. No amount of begging for mercy would save him now.

Otim paced with slow, deliberate steps before Ricky while he waited for more rebels to join the mob. With his witnesses gathered, he delivered the first blow, a strike to the stomach with the butt of his rifle that put Ricky on his knees.

Stepping back, Otim addressed his audience. "Kill the traitor." He looked down at Ricky and spat in his face. "Make it slow and painful."

The rebels rushed in like a pack of hyenas. Boys and girls he'd trained and fought alongside clawed and pushed one another to get to him. Their hands tore at his flesh, and their feet punched his face and body. The strikes fell over and under one another, giving Ricky no time to register the pain of one blow before the next struck.

"Traitor!"

"No one leaves the LRA!"

"Coward!"

"Beg for Kony's mercy!"

The rabid voices swelled into a frenzy as rebels punched,

kicked, and struck Ricky with their guns and the broad sides of their pangas.

*Let go*, Ricky implored his spirit as the rebels struck him over and over. *Please surrender.*

But his muscles tightened, curling his body into a protective ball on the ground, and his arms instinctively wrapped around his head. As the world blurred and the voices grew distant, Ricky remembered the day of his abduction. Fuzzy images pulsed in his vision. The wild man and rebels beating him on the side of the road. The rocks and dirt tearing at his knees as they dragged Patrick and him up the path to their home. And he remembered a voice calling his name.

*Ricky!*

Mama's voice reaching him in the darkness, begging him to come to her.

The kicks and strikes continued, hitting him in the head, back, face, and stomach. Feet stomped down on his arms and legs.

*Ricky!*

His mind retreated, pulling him to her voice, to the whisper of a memory calling him home.

*Please*, his mind cried. *Please let go.*

The assault continued, with more than fifty rebels joining in the beating. On the verge of unconsciousness and praying for death, Ricky heard a voice over the vile screams and taunts of his attackers.

"Stop!" the voice commanded. With one word, the screams were silenced and the strikes ceased.

"What is going on?" the voice asked.

"It's a traitor," Otim explained. "He escaped from our ranks months ago with two other boys."

"Let me see him," the voice ordered.

The mob parted, and Otim dragged Ricky to his knees. The moment he let go, Ricky's battered body gave way, and he crumbled to the ground. Lying bloodied and beaten in the dirt, Ricky heard the crunch of gravel in front of him. Peering up from the ground, through eyes swollen nearly shut, Ricky saw the blurred outline of his former commander, Komakech.

Komakech stared down at the naked, half-dead boy huddled in the dirt at his feet. His stoic expression gave no hint of the thoughts forming beyond his dead eyes as one of his favorite soldiers lay bleeding on the ground.

"Where are your clothes?" he asked.

With a trembling hand, Ricky pointed to the mob.

Without looking away from the boy who'd saved him on the battlefield, Komakech ordered the mob to return the clothes to Ricky.

"But, Afande," Otim began to argue.

"I said, return his clothes to him," Komakech repeated, slower this time.

When the rebels did not move, Komakech raised his voice. "Now!"

The girl who'd revealed Ricky to the rebels scrambled forward and dropped the clothes at Komakech's feet.

As she scurried back into the mob, Komakech turned to

Otim. "And give him back his weapon. I want him reinstated to his former position immediately."

He turned to the rest of the rebels who encircled Ricky. "Government troops are closing in on our position. We will be marching all night. Let's move out." Looking down at Ricky one last time, Komakech left, signaling for the rebels to follow.

At their commander's departure, the crowd dispersed and fell back in line. Only Otim stayed behind.

"You heard him," the wild man said to Ricky. "Move."

Disoriented, Ricky pulled on his clothes and struggled to his feet, stumbling and falling several times in the process.

Otim did nothing to help. "I said, move!" He shoved Ricky toward the line of rebels. Ricky fell forward, fighting to stay upright as the world tilted and swayed before him.

When they finally caught up to the coy, Otim grabbed an assault rifle from a younger rebel. "Here's your new weapon," he spat, jamming the stock into Ricky's stomach. Ricky doubled over, unable to suppress the vomit rising in his throat. Otim laughed as the boy heaved. "Welcome back."

# 47

# SAMUEL

The tapping of Samuel's finger against the armrest increased as he watched the road for the soldier's vehicle. Evening was settling over northern Uganda, and Samuel feared if they didn't leave soon, the soldier would decide to stay the night. But Samuel needed to leave now, before he changed his mind.

The man poured the checkers into the small burlap sack and moved the table back to the edge of the porch. When he returned, he sat in silence, watching Samuel for several minutes before clearing his throat and speaking.

"I know what you've done, Samuel."

Samuel squeezed his hand into a tight fist to stop his twitching finger and hide his fear. From the corner of his eye, he watched the man for any sudden movements, but the man remained still.

"I understand what you've been through and know how you feel."

Samuel's fear twisted into anger. "No. You don't."

The man folded his large hands in his lap. "Then why don't you tell me?"

"There's nothing to tell."

The man's broad chest rose and fell in a long breath. "Yes, Samuel. There is."

The man turned to face him, and Samuel drew back in his chair. As the man's knowing eyes burrowed into him, Samuel braced himself for the man's accusations, prepared to deny every one, but the man asked just one question.

"May I tell you a story?"

For over an hour the man spoke. He told Samuel of a village and a family, of brothers and nightmares, and the mother in the moon. He spoke of rebels with pangas and children with guns. He explained how one choice can change a life and one word can give hope. As evening deepened, he wove a story of Ricky's journey to find home, a mango tree, and the inescapable fate of a child soldier.

When the man paused to take a drink of water, Samuel stared down at the bandage wrapped around his thigh. The fresh blood had dried, leaving a dark brown blotch. "So after all he did, all he sacrificed, the LRA still found him."

"Yes," the man replied, "but they weren't looking for Ricky when they found him in his village."

"It doesn't matter," Samuel said, his voice quiet with defeat. "They weren't looking for Joseph when they found him, either."

"But unlike Joseph, Ricky was spared."

"Why?" Samuel asked, "Because he was a good fighter?"

"Maybe," the man admitted, "but I believe that because he saved Komakech's life on the battlefield, the LRA commander spared Ricky's life."

Samuel laughed the hollow, jaded laugh of a man beaten down by life. "You think Komakech cared about Ricky?"

"No. But when you have been in death's grasp and someone pulls you free, that isn't something you soon forget. I think Komakech felt he had a debt to pay, and by sparing Ricky's life, he paid it."

"How is that paying him back? Ricky was worse off than before he escaped."

"Perhaps," the man said, "but he also had something that he didn't have before his first escape."

"What?"

"Nothing to lose."

# 48

# RICKY

When he was interrogated, Ricky swore that despite what Otim believed, he had not escaped, but left to track down Patrick and bring him back to the LRA. When they questioned him further about his brother, Ricky told them Patrick had not yet returned home. The lie appeased Komakech and reinforced his trust in his favorite fighter. The commander assigned Ricky to the Third Battalion and reinstated his previous position, training and indoctrinating new abductees, including Omwony and the other day laborers.

Over the next four days, the stab of pain that accompanied every breath dulled and the swelling on Ricky's face receded, leaving behind crusty scabs and mottled bruises of muddied green and rotten yellow. He played the part of the perfect rebel, obeying every command and carrying out each order with the fervor of a loyal Kony fighter. Yet, as he supervised the new abductees' formations and taught them to march, he carefully observed the direction in which the battalion was traveling and counted each step they took away from his village. When he preached of Kony and his ability to read minds and know hearts, he thought only of his family and the promise he'd made to Patrick. And as he threatened the abductees with stories of venomous snakes and vengeful spirits pursuing them should they be foolish enough to run, Ricky dreamed of obeno and planned his next escape.

After four days of marching and training, the Third Battalion joined other battalions of the Gilva brigade and made camp deep in the bush, and Ricky came to a decision. Tonight he would run.

Seated behind the abductees, Ricky stared out at the thousand rebels milling about the camp and allowed the reality of his situation to settle on his numb mind. The LRA had changed in his absence. The rebels no longer mirrored the controlled, cold cruelty of Komakech. Their barbarism now reflected the chaotic, unfettered brutality of Otim. Their hunger for torture and killing was insatiable, and he knew a second escape would not be forgiven. Komakech had repaid his debt to Ricky. He would not show mercy again. If the LRA found him, the most Ricky could hope for was a swift death, and that was a death Otim would never grant him.

But what the wild man did not understand was that with Patrick gone, the LRA had taken everything from Ricky, including his fear of death.

Ricky stood and addressed the abductees in his coy. "There are beehives in the trees not far from here. I saw rebels eating the honey when we passed. I need help fetching some to bring back to camp."

Several of the abductees volunteered to assist him, but Ricky waved their offers away. "I only need one person to help." His gaze settled on Omwony, the day laborer from Pajule. Although he was three years older than Ricky, Omwony seldom spoke, even before the abduction, and had no experience surviving in the bush. If the rebels didn't claim his life in the next few days, the jungle would.

"Omwony, come with me."

The young man struggled to his feet and shuffled after Ricky. They pressed through the tall grass until they came to a cluster of small trees. The evening air vibrated with the angry hum of bees, and remnants of honeycomb lay broken at the base of the trees.

"Here?" Omwony asked, stopping.

"No," Ricky said, not slowing his pace.

Omwony hurried to catch up. "Where are we going?" he asked.

Ricky grabbed his arm and broke into a run. "Home."

# 49

# SAMUEL

A flash of headlights and crunch of dirt and rocks under tires drew the man's attention from the porch. Samuel did not look up. He knew the soldier had returned, and he knew what it meant. Panic burned in his stomach, and doubt seeped through the widening cracks in his resolve to carry out his plan.

As the man walked across the porch to meet the soldier, Samuel stared out at the boys on the field and thought of the villagers who'd stood behind him on the porch an hour before. He could still hear their clapping hands and voices joined in song with the children, and he could see them praising the performance with hugs, smiles, and tears. But regardless of how much they said they understood and how they pledged to welcome the former child soldiers back into their villages, Samuel knew they could not welcome them back into their hearts. No one could.

"Is he here for me?" he asked when the man returned.

The man put a hand on his shoulder. "Yes."

Samuel tensed, but did not pull away.

"But he needs to see to a couple of things here before you leave," the man said, removing his hand. He sat down next to Samuel and stared out at the children playing.

"Did the LRA find Ricky again?" Samuel asked.

"No. Komakech was furious when he learned Ricky had escaped again, so he sent rebels back to Ricky's village to look for him. They searched every hut, but never found him. The villagers swore they didn't know where Ricky was hiding, but agreed to hand him over when the LRA returned."

"Did they?"

"The night before they returned, Okot found Ricky hiding in the bush near his family's land. He gave him some clothes and what little money he had and told Ricky to leave northern Uganda and head south to the city of Jinja, where the war and rebels could not reach him."

Samuel struggled to imagine any place untouched by Kony's holy war and safe from his bloodthirsty rebels. His gaze traveled the road leading from the compound to the mouth of the jungle, where it ended in shadow. During their conversation, the sun had dipped behind the trees of the bush, outlining the jungle's silhouette in fiery oranges and reds. Dusk had driven inside everyone except the boys playing on the field and Samuel and the man on the porch.

"With the money Okot gave him," the man said, "Ricky took a truck to Jinja, but found the city too busy and noisy, so he walked to the slums on the outskirts of the city, where he met a group of Acholi refugees. One of them, an old woman named

Doreen, hired Ricky as night-shift security for her gin-making operation. For a year he worked for Doreen, and then one day she asked him what he most wanted to do with his life. He told her he wished to go back to school. The old woman offered to sponsor him if he kept working for her, so Ricky worked nights at the factory, and during the day he attended school with children half his age, studying under a teacher who took delight in mocking him in front of the class."

"Why didn't he drop out?" Samuel asked. "He had a job."

"Ricky had seen how men like Kony preyed on the fear and ignorance of children to further their plans and quench their desires, and he never wanted to be a victim of ignorance again. He knew an education was the only way to protect himself, to rise above ignorance and fear, just as his father had, and just as his father had hoped for his village and children. So every day, after working all night in the factory, Ricky walked to school, and walked to his future."

Samuel watched the soccer ball arc into the darkening sky and then drop back into the fading light of dusk.

"He studied hard and was accepted into Kyambogo University in Kampala. After he graduated, he took a job with the Ministry of Education and Sports. He had a good job and he was living in a peaceful city, far from the war, but still, there was something missing in his heart."

Samuel stared just above the silhouetted trees of the jungle, where a sliver of curved light softened the darkening sky. He squinted, trying to make out the mother in the moon, but if she was there, she was hidden in the shadows. "His obeno."

The man nodded. "As Ricky went about his new life in Kampala, news of the LRA's continued attacks haunted his days and nights. Not only had Kony's army destroyed his obeno, they'd also destroyed the obeno of every man, woman, and child in northern Uganda. Ricky's people and land were dying, and he felt powerless to stop it." He leaned back, and the wooden chair groaned under his weight. "Kony and the LRA polluted Ricky's every waking moment and poisoned his every sleepless night. Years after his abduction, he was weary from running. He'd run from the LRA to save his life. He'd run from Pader to escape his past, and he'd run from Jinja in search of his future. But no matter how far he ran, he could not escape the damage the LRA had inflicted on his life. So one evening as he sat in his office in Kampala, Ricky decided it was time he stopped running."

Samuel's head dipped forward, and his voice grew quiet. "Did he let go . . . like the girl at the river? Like Patrick?"

"No. He returned to northern Uganda."

Stunned, Samuel looked up. "He came back?"

"Yes. He quit his job and returned to his village."

"But the villagers wanted to hand him over to the LRA. Wasn't he afraid?"

"Of course. He had fear in his heart, but he also had forgiveness."

"Forgiveness? For the villagers?"

"Yes . . . and for the rebels."

Eyes wide with disbelief, Samuel stared at the man sitting beside him.

"A few years after he returned to northern Uganda," the man said, "Ricky saw Otim while traveling through Jinja. The wild man had lost his leg in a battle and was begging on the streets. When he noticed Ricky, he tried to crawl away. He cried and begged for mercy."

"Did Ricky kill him?" Samuel asked. He lifted his chin in unapologetic defiance of the disappointment he expected to see in the man's eyes, but he found only sadness.

"No. Ricky told him his judgment day would come. But it was not that day. And Ricky was not the one to deliver it. And then he forgave him."

Samuel pressed his fists to his eyes, no longer able to contain his anger. His voice rose in outrage. "He deserved to die. They all do! They're evil monsters! They deserve punishment, not forgiveness!"

The man's voice remained calm. "Ricky had to forgive them."

Samuel's leg burned with pain, but he could no longer remain seated. He pushed up from his chair. "No. He didn't. What the rebels did . . . what they forced Ricky and his brother to do *killed* Patrick." Rage swelled in Samuel's chest as he stood before the man, his hands trembling. "They took *everything* from him!"

"Yes. They did."

A look of betrayal creased Samuel's forehead, and tears welled in his eyes. His body and voice quivered with indignation.

"Then how could he? How could he forgive the men who destroyed his obeno, who destroyed *all* our obenos?"

The man looked up at him and in a gentle voice replied, "If Ricky had not forgiven the men who had enslaved him, he would still be their slave."

The words settled on Samuel with the weight of three years of grief, anger, pain, and guilt. They pressed him back into his chair and bowed his head. "So he came back to forgive them all," he whispered.

The man looked around at the buildings and huts that made up the Friends of Orphans compound. "No. He came back for the children. He returned to northern Uganda to help former abductees and child soldiers find their obeno."

Samuel followed his gaze to the field, where a small boy, Samuel's would-be hostage from the sidelines, broke free from the group of children. With his head held high, the boy dribbled the worn ball with his bare feet and sprinted toward a makeshift goal between two jambula trees. Samuel leaned forward in his chair as an ache crept through his legs, yearning to follow the boy, to run free.

The mob of laughing children pursued the boy, but he quickened his pace. Nearing the trees, he drew back his leg, and Samuel gripped his armrests. The boy put his full weight behind the kick. The force knocked him to the ground and sent the ball soaring through the invisible goal. Before the boy could scramble to his feet, two older boys lifted him onto their shoulders while the other children cheered. A wide smile spread across the young boy's face as he threw his arms in the air and shook them in victory.

Samuel looked at the man next to him. The boy's joyous smile was reflected on the man's face. "And by helping them find their obeno," the man said, "Ricky found his."

Desperation swelled in Samuel's chest and eyes. "How?" he asked. "How did Ricky help them find their obeno?"

Tears glistening on his cheeks, the man turned to Samuel. "He told them a story."

Samuel's breath caught as he stared into the man's knowing eyes. "Ricky?" he whispered.

The man nodded. "I share my story, so the children are free to share theirs."

Before Samuel could respond, the door creaked behind them, and the woman with all the questions stepped onto the porch. The doctor and soldier joined her. Dizzy with the revelation of the man's identity and what it meant, Samuel glanced back at them.

"It's time," the woman said, handing him another small bag of food.

"Do you want me to change your bandage before you go?" the doctor asked.

Uncertainty numbed Samuel's mind like anesthesia. He shook his head.

When the soldier extended his hand to help him from his chair, his gun, still secure in its holster, passed within Samuel's reach. Glancing at the weapon, Samuel reached up and took hold of the soldier's hand. He turned to Ricky. "Thank you for telling me your story."

Ricky smiled as he handed Samuel his crutches. "You are welcome. I hope someday, Samuel, you, too, find your obeno."

Samuel leaned on the crutches and without another word followed the soldier past the tree where the children had drawn pictures, and across the soccer field. When they reached the vehicle, the soldier opened the door to place Samuel's crutches inside, and Samuel looked back to the porch. The woman and doctor had left, but Ricky remained. Raising his hand to wave good-bye, Ricky nodded once.

As the soldier bent down to lift Samuel into the truck, Samuel cried out.

The soldier eased him to the ground, and the woman and doctor rushed out from the building and over to the vehicle. Ricky followed.

"What's wrong?" asked the soldier.

"Are you in pain?" the doctor asked.

"Yes," Samuel cried.

"What is it?" the woman asked. "What can we do to help?"

Samuel looked up at Ricky, and with tears streaming down his cheeks, asked one question.

"May I tell you a story?"

# Afterword

## By Ricky Richard Anywar

This book is based on the true story about the journey of my life as a child soldier in the Lord's Resistance Army (LRA). I hope it will help many people learn about the war in northern Uganda and the untold suffering of children being used to fight adults' wars in Africa and around the world.

I dedicate this book to those who suffered as a result of the Ugandan civil war, to all the former child soldiers, and to children affected by wars around the world. I also dedicate my story to my family members and others who did not survive to tell their stories in the twenty-three years of conflict in northern Uganda.

Child soldiering in Africa and around the world must end, but this will not happen until the world learns about the danger of using children in wars. Today's wars are different from the wars of previous generations, when armies targeted armies, and civilian populations were mainly left as witnesses. An all-too-common strategy in today's wars is to target and terrorize civilian populations.

The day in 1989 I was abducted as a child soldier to fight for the LRA, I felt like a tree split from top to bottom by lightning. I fought battles. I passed through sprays of bullets and attacks from helicopter gunships, which sent up dense smoke that could be seen for many kilometers. I have heard many stories, and people have told me many stories, but no story has ever moved me like the stories of former child soldiers who are suffering in northern Uganda. These children have wounds in their hearts and minds that need to be washed, cleaned, and treated through rehabilitation. This is the goal of Friends of Orphans, which I founded in 1999, an organization born of hope in a war zone. We know former abductees can work themselves out of poverty with dignity if we do not treat them as objects, but rather as subjects. Therefore, we use a multiplicity of strategies to combat unemployment by addressing the challenges and reality of life faced by former child soldiers because we know they did not choose their situations, they were born into them.

The LRA left these children bitter, but Friends of Orphans is helping them recover from their pasts by shaping their futures through rehabilitation, reintegration, and empowerment programs. We are helping them dry their tears, which have been rolling down their cheeks for so long. Thanks to those who help support humanitarian organizations such as Friends of Orphans, the future has never looked brighter for former child soldiers growing up in my country.

Don't miss Keely Hutton's next book,
the incredible story—inspired by true events—of four
British boys fighting a hidden war in the tunnels
underneath the Western Front during the First World War.

# Secret
# Soldiers

## Coming soon

Farrar Straus Giroux

mackids.com